A WHOLE NEW CHRISSY

CATHERINE KELAHER

To David,
Thank you for providing endless giggles.

THANK YOU READER

Hello, Reader,

I truly hope you find as much joy in reading A Whole New Chrissy as I did in writing it.

As you reach the end of Chrissy's story, don't miss the special treat I've got for you — a bonus epilogue! It's a little peek into what happens with Chrissy and her friends a month down the line. But hey, no sneaking a look until you get there!

If this book brings a smile to your face, I would be over the moon if you could share your thoughts with a review on Amazon or your favourite book platform. Your support helps keep the stories flowing.

Happy reading and lots of love,

Catherine x

1

'I'm just saying you should include a body shot, otherwise you're basically catfishing,' says my date in his posh-boy accent.

I keep my eyes down, focusing on tearing up my bread roll. Gareth is the third date I've been on since I downloaded the dating app, Zingles.

'I mean, why fake being someone you're not?' Gareth continues. 'There are men who are into bigger women. My mate Simon, he's dating a cyber fatty.'

I snap my eyes up to see Gareth holding his hands up in surrender.

'His words, not mine. From her pics, this girl looked like a model. I guess they must have been old photos because when Simon got there, she was huge.' He laughs. 'But fair play to her, she had a decent face and substantial...' Gareth cups his hands under his chest. He glugs some more of his wine.

I narrow my green eyes at him as he stretches his mouth into a grimace, exposing his perfect white teeth.

'Sorry,' he says. 'Must be first date nerves. Ignore me, you're fine. Your make-up is very... um... well done.'

'Thanks,' I say, immediately wanting to slap myself for accepting what is probably the most pathetic compliment I've ever heard. I mean, I guess I did spend the best part of an hour following a 'Baddie on a Budget' make-up tutorial on YouTube. It was one of the ten items on my Get Ready for Date with Future Husband checklist, along with giving myself a manicure, shaving every unwanted hair off my body and jotting down potential questions in case the conversation stalled. I'm gonna need one of them now.

'So, what do you do in your spare time, Gareth?' I ask, desperate to move the conversation away from my physical appearance. 'I saw a photo of a dog in your profile.'

'Ah yes, Dad's dog. He's a good old boy.'

I soften and lean in. This is more my conversation territory.

'How old is he?'

'He's been around for a while but hasn't let the team down yet. Sired a litter of pups every single year. You'd love them.'

'Your dad is a breeder?' I ask, thinking of all the dogs in shelters, who are desperate for homes.

Gareth snorts. 'Of course. Surely you know a pedigree chocolate lab goes for a few grand? Especially from a championship bloodline. Well, you must know the value of a noble bloodline, you're dating me, aren't you?' He winks and I feel a little bit sick.

I push a red curl behind my ear as I look into his face. I'd thought his blue eyes were mischievous, but now they seem cold and glinting. I try to remember the nice things he said when we chatted online. He said I reminded him of Christina Hendricks. Mind you, that was before he saw my serious lack of boobs. Even though I checked off 'put on good push-up bra' from my to-do list, it clearly hasn't fooled him.

'And what about you, Chrissy? What do you get up to when you're not out on a date with the man of your dreams?'

'Well, as you know from my profile, I'm a primary school teacher at Little Elm, and then in my spare time I walk dogs at the shelter. There's this one dog, Jonah, who's been waiting for a home for ages. I walk him up on the South Downs. He could trot along for miles and—'

'You'd think with all that running around after dogs and children, you'd be pretty fit.'

I bristle. 'Yeah, they don't do my fitness any harm, but that's not why I do it, I—'

'With that base fitness, I don't think it would take you long to get into shape if you invested in a personal trainer and counted calories for a bit. You're not "morbidly" obese.' Gareth uses finger quotations around the word *morbidly*. He leans back and looks around the table to assess my body. 'Hmm.' He twists his hand in a maybe-you-are, maybe-you-aren't gesture.

One of the many things I wish I could change about myself is my tendency to cry, whether frustrated, angry or sad. I'd say I'm feeling a pretty intense mix of all three right now, so it's no surprise to me that the sharp heat of tears is pressing against the back of my eyeballs.

Gareth reaches across the table and pulls my hands into his. I want to snatch them back.

He stares into my eyes.

'This isn't about you,' he says. 'Body weight is just something I'm passionate about. It's important to have things we're passionate about in life, isn't it? Like you and your animals.'

I crease my face up a little at his comparison between my dog walking at the local shelter and his crusade against 'cyber fatties'.

'Tell me more about you,' I say, desperate to change the topic. 'How's your work going?'

'I already told you it's amazing,' says Gareth, dropping my hands and leaning back in his chair. 'There's never been a better time to be in crypto. I'm dealing with some pretty big accounts right now.'

'I've always found crypto a bit baffling. A friend did try and explain blockchain to me, but I think I'm more of an online banking girl. Point, click and hope I don't overspend on books.'

Gareth makes a zip-it motion with his hand.

'The Dalai Lama said, "When you talk, you are only repeating what you already know. But when you listen you may learn something new."'

'I was listening.' I sigh. 'The Dalai Lama has some good quotes, but—'

Gareth snorts. 'Go to his lecture at the University of Westminster two years in a row and then perhaps you can tell me about his "good quotes".'

There are those finger quotations again. Would it be rude to lunge over the table and snap those fingers clean off?

'You've met the Dalai Lama?' I feign interest.

'Try three times.'

'I think the most famous person I've ever met is the actor who plays Toadie from *Neighbours*,' I say. 'Well, I didn't really meet him, but he was on the same bus as me.'

Gareth's face remains straight. 'You don't watch that soap drivel, do you?'

'I've watched it since I was a little girl. I love it. To be honest, I love anything Australian. *Kath and Kim, Bondi Rescue*, I even watched the Aussie version of *Love Island*.'

'TV blunts thinking. I can share some academic research with you that shows people who watch TV just aren't that smart.'

'I don't think that's true. It's a bit of escapism for the day. You seriously don't watch TV?'

'I don't even own a TV,' he says and looks around the

restaurant. It's a cosy Italian that smells of ripe tomatoes and baking bread. I chose it because there are so many vegan options.

'So do you read a lot?' I continue.

'Of course, and I can watch pretty much anything on my laptop.'

'But that's just TV on a different screen,' I mutter, but he isn't listening. He lifts his hand and clicks to summon a waiter.

Yikes, do people still do that? Surely everyone knows how pretentious that is. I must have cringe written all over my face.

'Lighten up,' he says. 'They're used to it... and look, it works.'

The waiter walks over to our table. I mouth 'sorry' to her. I'm a bit taken aback by how pretty she is with her shiny black hair tied up in a bun and a slim figure I would kill for.

She's wearing a long-sleeved white shirt. I squint at her wrists, trying to catch the details of the tattoos that peep out.

'Hi, I'm Chloe. What can I get you?' she asks.

'Oh, you're Australian,' I say, as I hear the twang in her voice.

'Yeah, from Sydney,' she says with a grin.

'Don't get this one started on Australia, unless you want an earful about *Neighbours*,' says Gareth. 'I'm starving. Do you do veal scallopini piccata?' he asks in an affected Italian accent.

'Nope, just what's on the menu or the specials board,' says Chloe.

'It's just... it's not a real Italian restaurant if they don't do that dish, you know?' he says to me.

I grimace. Of course, he wants to eat a baby cow. Totally what I'd expect from him.

'I'll get the Garden Godmother pizza, please,' I say. 'I read a review that said it's amazing.'

'It is,' says Chloe. 'Maybe you should give that a try, sir. It gets rave reviews.'

'I wouldn't be caught dead eating vegan food, but nice try with your animal rights agenda.' He looks over at the specials board. 'I'll get the parmigiana di melanzane,' he says in the same ridiculous attempt at an Italian accent. 'And make it snappy. I'm famished.'

The waiter looks at me and I detect the smallest eyeroll. We both know he's just chosen a vegan option without realising it.

'Sorry,' I say to Chloe. 'We know you don't control how long it takes to make the food.'

'It won't be too long,' she says, turning to walk away.

'Um... our drinks?' Gareth shouts after her.

'We already have drinks,' I say.

'We need top-ups. Looks like someone needs some basic training.'

Chloe turns around. This time her polite expression has darkened. Her deep brown eyes seem to flash black.

Gareth raises his eyebrows.

'The Dalai Lama said, "Smile at others and keep the world smiling." Plus, you might actually be pretty if you smiled. The Dalai Lama didn't say that last bit, but it is true. Don't you think, Chrissy?'

'You can't talk to someone like that,' I say in an angry whisper.

'She's right,' says Chloe in a much louder voice. 'I deserve to be treated with respect.'

A few other diners turn around to stare at us and I want to shrink away and hide under the table.

'I said you'd be pretty if you smiled. That's a compliment.'

'It's not my job to be pretty for you or anyone else,' she says.

'Calm down, a lot of men like the whole tough girl, tattoo thing. But most of us prefer a more classic, feminine look. Y'know like a proper lady.'

'Gareth, that was sexist,' I hiss, trying to keep my voice low.

Chloe purses her lips and sticks her chin up in an expression of defiance.

'Bloody hell. What's wrong with you women? Are you both on your—'

'Don't you dare, mate,' says Chloe. Keeping her exterior calm, she grabs Gareth's glass of red wine and throws it in his face.

Shocked, Gareth wipes the liquid from his eyes and

stands up, shaking his hands and spraying the wine onto me and my pale pink top.

'Get me the manager,' he booms. 'And you?' He turns to face me, his voice dripping with disbelief. 'You can't call someone sexist on a first date.'

'Surely it's worse to actually be sexist,' I say in a small voice.

Gareth's face twists into a shocked sneer. He opens his mouth as if to shout at me but is interrupted by a squat woman with a platinum blonde crop.

'I'm Zazz, the maître d' here. Is there something I can help you with?'

'That' – Gareth points at Chloe – 'needs to be sacked, or I'm gonna bring this place to the ground. I'm not far off Elite status on Yelp.'

I watch as the waiter spins around and stomps towards the kitchen. As the manager tries to placate Gareth, I grab my orange Matt and Nat bag and edge towards the front door. I want to get away from this horrible man and the staring eyes of the surrounding diners. Before I've taken more than a couple of steps, Chloe is by my side, her bag and coat slung over her arm.

'Are you okay?' I say, reaching out to touch her as she passes me. 'If someone had yelled at me like that, I'd be in tears right now.' Even as it is, my eyes are hot from trying not to cry.

'He's not worth my tears... or yours. Was it a first date?'

'Yup, another Zingles disaster.'

The maître d' turns her head towards us as Gareth points and gestures, his voice becoming louder as his face becomes redder.

'You know what? It's my last day. Wanna get out of here?' says Chloe.

'Yes please.' I let her grab my wrist and lead me towards the door. A slap of cold seaside air hits us as she pulls the door open and we break into giggles as we run down the street, swinging our hands like little girls.

2

Chloe and I are still giggling as we trot down the steps that lead to pebbly Brighton Beach. Closed souvenir shops, restaurants and nightclubs line the pavement. We push open the door to The V Bar, a cosy little place tucked away under the arches, lit by the warm glow of fairy lights.

'I think we've earned a drink,' says Chloe, dragging me towards the bar. She leans forward and catches the bartender's eye.

'Hey, mate, Bacardi and Coke and a...' She looks at me, eyebrows raised.

'Archers and lemonade, please.'

'Coming up,' says the barman and turns away.

I slide onto a bar stool and mouth, 'He's gorgeous.'

The man is tall and pale with beautiful dark eyes. Why is

it that naturally long eyelashes are always dished out to men when it's us women who are desperate for them? He's wearing a black shirt and his denim-clad bum is so peachy I could just bite it. Speaking of, I'm starving. I grab a menu to search for snacks.

'Tom's a fellow Aussie,' says Chloe, as the man places our drinks on the bar. 'It's pretty much obligatory for us lot to do a year or two in the UK.' She gestures at me. 'This is my new friend...' She pauses, realising she hasn't asked my name yet.

'Chrissy,' I fill her in.

'Yup, Chrissy.' Chloe nods as if she knew that all along.

'Hey,' says Tom. He holds eye contact with me for a second and my stomach does a full-blown somersault. I smile, but I think it comes out more like a grimace. I'm very aware of my wine-stained top and my hair frizzed from the salty wind. His eyes flick back to my new friend.

'Finish early tonight, Chlo?'

'Yeah, well, I kind of had to leave, what with this one' – she points at me – 'pulling me into her Zingles date disaster.' She takes a long gulp of her drink.

I can't help frowning. 'I must have "will only date terrible men" tattooed on my forehead or something.'

'That bad, eh?' asks Tom with a grin. 'Have you seen Chloe's tattoos?'

'I've only seen a hint of them. Can I have a look?'

'Sure,' Chloe says, unbuttoning her shirt cuffs and rolling up her sleeves, 'although the light's not great in here.'

My eyes fix on a tattoo depicting three birds flying free from a broken cage. The words 'Until every cage is empty' are written in a curve above the image.

'That's incredible!' I say.

'I designed it myself. You got any tattoos?'

'Not like yours.' I'm embarrassed, given that Chloe has these works of art and I have, well, a doodle from when I was seventeen.

'As long as it's not a tacky tramp stamp,' says Tom.

My face heats up as I glance down at my turquoise fingernails.

'Is it?' He laughs out loud, and I feel my cheeks flush.

'I didn't even know about tramp stamps when I got it. I was seventeen, I wanted to rebel a little and I thought Billy Bob was cute.'

'Billy Bob?' says Tom.

'Yeah, that's his name. I mean, the name of my tattoo. He's a lizard.'

'Let's see,' says Chloe and I pull down the top of my jeans, very aware I'm making my muffin top even more muffiny.

'Aww cute,' says Chloe. 'I reckon Billy Bob is my fave tramp stamp of all time.'

Tom catches my eye and shakes his head. 'Was the tramp stamp not quite tacky enough?' he asks. 'Is that why you gave it a tacky name?' He turns around to grab some glasses for a patron and laughs with the short, red-headed barman next to him.

I know he's joking, but this feels a bit too much like dealing with my high school bullies. I promised myself I'd never put up with that again. Just because I fancy someone, doesn't mean I'll let them treat me like shit. I wrack my brain, trying to think of a witty comeback. Bugger, I've got nothing. I bet it'll come to me as I'm walking home later. I stand up, letting my curls shield my face as I make my way to the table furthest from the bar. Chloe follows me to a corner table lit with dim, pink light.

'Hot, isn't he?' says Chloe.

'More like rude and arrogant,' I say, my cheeks still flaming. I glance back over to the bar and Tom holds out his hands in a where-did-you-go? motion. I turn away. I don't care how gorgeous he is; I can do without another rude man in my life.

'Speaking of rude and arrogant, what were you doing with that wanker back at the restaurant?' Chloe tosses the question into the air with a casual wave of her hand.

'He seemed like a nice guy on his profile,' I say before taking a big gulp of my drink. 'When we were messaging, we had all this stuff in common. But in real life, he was like a totally different person.'

'Isn't that always the way?' she says with a shake of her head. 'I don't have a problem meeting people on the apps, but holding on to them? That's not for me. Every single one has been a fun fling and then a quick exit.' She pauses to take a sip of her drink.

'I was so impressed when you chucked that drink over Gareth.' A giggle bubbles up from my chest as I remember the look of pure shock on my date's face.

'No regrets.' Chloe's dark eyes sparkle with mischief. 'I guess I can kiss that work reference goodbye, but who gives a shit? I'm going home tomorrow.'

'Home as in Australia?'

'Yup, roll on summer. I'll be hitting the beach in a couple of days.' She leans back, a faraway look in her eyes.

'I've always wanted to go to Sydney,' I say.

'Do it,' she urges. 'I miss the sunshine so much. I've had an awesome time this last year, but I'm ready to go home. I came over here to get some inspiration for my art, but I've kind of used the time to party and I need to get back and focus.'

'Back to all those fit Aussie men. Oh, unless you're bi? Or gay? Or—'

'I'm straight.' She cuts me off, a hint of laughter in her voice. 'What about you?'

'Straight. I've always wanted to meet some surfer type and live happily ever after.'

Chloe grins at this. 'Plenty of those where I'm from. Plenty of dickheads too, just like here.'

I let out a long sigh. 'Sometimes after a day of teaching, I wonder if I should just pack everything in and go to Oz. I could do with taking some time for myself.'

She leans forward. 'Ugh, I couldn't teach. You're a braver woman than me.'

'I like the kids. It's the parents that do my head in, and I'm covering someone's maternity leave, so it's not exactly secure.'

Chloe tips her glass in my direction. 'Sydney needs teachers too, right? Could be worth a shot?'

I take a deep breath. Why don't I give it a try? First, I put it off because Dad said a gap year would be a waste of time and money. Then a few years later my ex, Jeremy, said I should try to make something of myself before I swan off to Australia.

Then there's my list.

I have the list in my handbag. I take it everywhere with me. A bit eccentric, I know, but it's my motivator. Only my best friend Jess knows about my list. But after downing my drink, I pull the list out onto the table to show Chloe.

Things To Do When I'm Skinny.
1. Spend six months in Australia
2. Wear a bikini in public
3. Go to a group dance class
4. Learn to surf
5. Do something spontaneous

It started off with those five things back in January, but

since then I've been adding to it and it's now four pages
stapled together with goals like:

15. Wear a body-con dress
32. Spur of the moment booty call
55. Run a 10k
72. Get classy nude pics taken

Chloe's face is unreadable as she scans my list.

'Are you bloody serious?' she finally blurts out.

'What?'

'You're putting all this off until you're skinny?'

'Yeah, it's like a reward. You know, once I've dropped all
this.' I gesture to my body.

Chloe shakes her head. 'Why can't you do it now? Why
can't you book a flight and go to Australia now?'

'Well, there's my job, but that's not the only thing. I want
to enjoy the beach and not stress about food all the time.'

'Shit, Chrissy. You can't put off living your life until you
lose weight. Have you lost much so far?'

'I've only lost a couple of pounds,' I say. 'There's a long
way to go.'

'What about living now?'

'I don't think I deserve to. Well, not yet.'

'What kind of shit have you been through to make you
this way?'

I think back to walking along Brighton's bohemian North

Laine with my ex, Jeremy. I had made a real effort that day. Jess had helped me achieve a 'clean girl glow-up' look from YouTube and I was wearing a gorgeous pink dress that flattered my figure.

A beautiful, tall blonde sashayed by, and Jeremy visibly ogled her. He turned back to me, his lip pulled into a sneer.

'Why can't you be more like that?' he said. 'You know I could go and ask her out right now, but I choose to be with you, to give you a chance.' He shook his head and tutted.

Chloe places her long fingers on my forearm and I snap back to the present. 'Whatever happened, you deserve to live now. We all do. Why don't you promise yourself you'll book the trip to Sydney?'

'You know what? You're right. I, Chrissy Pember, hereby agree to book my trip to Australia sometime in the next year, but before that, I shall dance the night away with my new Aussie buddy.'

I mean what's the harm? I could book for twelve months' time and if I get a Flexi ticket I can cancel if I get a secure job, or if I don't lose enough weight.

A few more Archers and lemonades in and Chloe and I are making our way to the bathroom. As I walk past the bar, doing my best to avoid the barman who thinks I'm so tacky, a balled-up piece of paper hits me in the face. I look up to see Tom smirking.

'Littering your own workplace... Well, I never,' I mutter as I bend down to pick up the paper.

'Open it,' he mouths.

I open the paper and take it through to the bathroom.

Messy boy writing reads 'This is your next tattoo'. Underneath is a drawing of a monster with very dramatic black eyebrows and the words 'I'm sorry' in a speech bubble.

'Aww, that's cute. Is it from Tom?' asks Chloe, leaning over my shoulder.

I nod. 'I guess he felt bad for being a dick.'

I stuff the paper in my pocket. I'm smiling as I look up into the smudged mirror, but as I take in my reflection, my face drops.

I thought I looked okay out there on the dance floor, but my hair may as well be an actual bird's nest as it creates a red, frizzy halo around my head. My eyeshadow has dissolved on one eye and my mascara is creating an I-haven't-slept-for-a-week effect under my eyes. As I see my body in the mirror, I'm ashamed. Did I swell from all the dancing? I glance over at Chloe.

'How are you still stunning after all that dancing?' I ask as she pouts her lips, reapplying red lipstick.

'Um... firstly, thanks. Secondly... have you taken a look at yourself lately? You're like a bloody Rubenesque artwork.'

'I don't think so. Check this out.' I grab my stomach and wobble it. 'Meanwhile look at you.' I indicate her slim waistline.

'Don't talk about my new friend like that,' says Chloe.

'That guy, Gareth, reckoned I should lose weight. As if I

haven't been told that a million times. It isn't as easy as people make out.'

Chloe stops wiping mascara from under her eyes and pulls out her hairband. Her hair falls into a swishy black bob. She places her hands on my shoulders and gives me a little shake.

'Chrissy, I may have only just met you, but I know one thing for sure... you need to stop listening to absolute shits like that Gareth dickhead. You are bloody beautiful, so bloody embrace it. Look at this...' She pulls her phone out of her bag, opens Instagram and types #bodyliberation.

The first video in the grid shows a black woman with pink hair dancing in her underwear like she's having the time of her life. She doesn't seem to care that her flesh is wobbling as she dances or that her stretch marks glint in the ring light.

Chloe scrolls down. A stunning brunette walks toward the camera as if on a catwalk, although she's in her living room. The first thing I notice is her wide grin. The second is that she's dressed like a fairy with glittery wings. She's wearing a sparkling bikini top and a little denim skirt. Her belly hangs over the front of the waistband.

Chloe looks up at me. 'Aren't they awesome?'

I nod. 'They're brave. I could never do that.' I stare into the mirror again.

'Hey, Chrissy, do that thing again where you grabbed your stomach.'

I raise an eyebrow at her, but I've had enough Archers not to question her. I must feel empowered from the Insta posts because I lift my wine-stained, light pink cami and grab my flesh. I catch Chloe's eye and burst out laughing as she holds her phone up and takes a photo.

'If these men are making you feel bad about yourself, maybe you should just delete Zingles and enjoy being single for a while.'

'I don't want to delete it. I mean, Mr Right could still be out there.'

'How many dates have you been on from Zingles?'

'This was my third, but I've probably dated about twenty guys from other apps.'

'And all from around here?' Chloe draws a circle in the air.

I nod. 'From Brighton, yeah. Oh, and one disaster from Hove. It wouldn't make much sense to go wider.'

'So, who is your ideal man?'

'Okay, ideal man. Kind to animals, kind to humans, and definitely kind to waiters. Um, he should be funny, that's important.'

'Be shallower,' says Chloe, her hand on her hip.

'Australian. A surfer.'

'Well, you're making a big error then, girl. Change your Zingles location to Sydney. I'd say you have about ninety-nine per cent more chance of meeting an Aussie in Australia than Brighton, don't you reckon?'

'And how would that work, if I actually met a decent guy?'

'You'd work it out, no worries.'

I pull out my phone, open Zingles and change the location to Sydney, Australia.

'I know we've just met, but I bloody love you,' says Chloe pulling me into a drunken hug.

'I bloody love you too,' I say, and I grab her hand and drag her back out into the bar.

'Shots?' she mouths at me over the loud music.

'Shots!' I yell back at her.

3

I am deceased.

My head is pounding, and my tongue feels like a rotting animal carcass. My arms are as heavy as logs as I rub my eyes. I slowly lift my gravelly eyelids and see the black marks from mascara on my fists. Ugh, I left my make-up on, ignoring advice from every beauty podcast I've ever listened to.

I wiggle my fingers in front of my face to check I still have full function of my hands. My nails still look perfect. They are the one part of my body I can rely on. I roll towards my bedside table. As I lift my head, my bedroom tilts. I grasp my water bottle with two hands and glug the whole thing down, thanking last week me for remembering to buy more ibuprofen. I open the top drawer and take two of the little tablets before grabbing my phone.

Pressing the home button, I realise my phone battery is dead and plug it into the charger. As my head thuds back onto the pillow, I have flashbacks of last night – spinning around the dance floor with Chloe as if we were in a primary school playground, jumping up and down with our hands in the air and jostling for space at the bar.

I give myself twenty minutes for the painkillers to kick in before dragging my poor body out of bed. I shuffle to the kitchen, towards my flatmate Jess's super expensive, top-of-the-range coffee machine. My whole body is screaming out for caffeine.

'Looks like you need a coffee,' says Jess, grabbing another mug out of the cupboard. As always, Jess looks adorable. She is the kind of curvy I wish I was. She's only five foot one. She has the bum, the boobs, the little waist – okay not little, but smaller than the bum and the boobs. And she carries herself with confidence. Plus, she's just about the loveliest person on the face of the planet. Today she's wearing pink pyjamas with a ginger cat on the front.

'I take it the date went well?' she says, her curly blonde hair swishing as she does her trademark excited wiggle.

'Jess, it was a disaster. I think I need a break from the apps.'

She hands me a cup of coffee and I fill her in on the date from hell and the wild night of partying that followed.

'Chloe sounds like a laugh. What's her star sign?'

'No idea. But one of the fun ones. And she's Australian.'

'Oh... Australian,' says Jess with a nod. She knows all about my appreciation of everything from down under.

'She's heading back to Sydney soon, so not sure if you'll get a chance to meet her,' I say before taking a glug of my coffee and oat milk.

There's a pause as Jess fiddles around with the kitchen utensils in our crowded cupboard.

'Pancakes?' she asks, brandishing the frying pan.

My stomach lurches at the thought of food and I shake my head before holding it in my hands. 'Thanks, but the way I'm feeling, I reckon toast and marmite is all I can manage.'

Jess nods and pops some bread in the toaster for me. 'Hey, Chrissy?'

I grunt a response, still concentrating on keeping my head on my neck. I'm pretty sure it will clunk to the floor if I let go.

'I need to talk to you about Joe.'

'Oh yeah? How are things going with Mr Wonderful?'

'Things are going so well, like so, so well,' says Jess.

'That's great.' It's hard to be enthusiastic when I feel like poop on a plate, but I try.

'I was looking through Insta posts yesterday and the salsa class where we met was almost six months ago. Can you believe it? This time last year, I didn't even know him.'

To be honest, it seems like longer than six months of listening to Jess go on and on about how perfect Joe is.

'I got Joe to salsa with me last night; we're both still as

bad as ever.' She laughs and shimmies her hips to an imaginary salsa rhythm.

'I'm so glad, Jess. You deserve happiness and Joe is... well, he's really nice.'

'He is, isn't he?' she says, almost visibly fizzing. 'And...' Jess gulps. 'And, well, he's going to move in.' Jess braces herself for my response, screwing up her face as if I'm about to hit her.

Our flatty friendship whizzes in front of my eyes: me and Jess doing karaoke until one a.m., me and Jess dissecting my dating efforts, me and Jess trying and failing to learn Beyonce's latest dance moves.

I watch her big smile fade as she catches the unease on my face.

I drag myself off the stool and pull her into a hug whilst giving myself a mental shake. This is my best friend. Of course I want what is best for her and her relationship. Even if Joe is not exactly the exciting guy I imagined for her.

'That's amazing,' I say.

Jess squeals and jumps up and down, still holding on to me, but I don't have the energy to reciprocate.

'Now I see what the pancakes were about, you little cheek. Trying to bribe me to let Joe move in with us. You don't need to. He's lovely.'

Jess's body tenses and she gently pushes me away, holding me at arm's length.

'Sorry, Chrissy, that was unclear of me. I meant he and I

are going to live together... here, on our own, like a little love nest.'

'But... my room?'

'It's still your room for however long it takes to find some fab new place, but Joe has to work from home, so eventually it'll be his office.'

I think of my lovely bright room, my photos on the wall, my animal ornaments, my pink desk, all being turfed out on the street to be replaced by boring, grey, lifeless office supplies and boring, grey Joe.

'Oh... I'm so happy for you,' I say, but my face betrays my true feelings as my eyes fill with tears.

'Oh, come here.' Jess pulls me into one of her bear hugs. 'I don't want to stop living with you either and Joe loves you, but it's just the next step, you know?'

'I do know,' I say, as my body gives way to full-on sobs. 'This is your place. Joe is great. I just... I just... I like it the way it is.' Tears are now running down my face. Jess lets go of me, pulls a tissue from the box on the side and wipes my cheeks.

'You silly mare, you've left your make-up on.'

'I know... I'm a mess. A giant, fat mess.'

'No, you're gorgeous and you're always horrid to yourself when you're hungover. Come on, we need to get ready for the shelter. Eat your toast and try not to worry. I'll help you find the best apartment and flatmate you've ever had. You won't even remember me.'

I give her a small smile. Jess is always Mother Hen. She

won't tolerate me talking badly about myself even on the days when I want to rip off my fat in chunks.

'Maybe you could rent a place around the corner, and we could meet up for a power walk every day?' she says.

I wrinkle my nose.

'Or we could meet for tea and cake?'

'That's more like it,' I say in a small voice. 'And I am pleased things are going well for you guys. It's just sometimes it feels like everyone else's life is moving forward and I'm just stuck on a treadmill, well, a treadmill where I never get fit or lose weight.'

'You're only twenty-seven. There's plenty of time to do all kinds of things. You could travel the world or have ten kids or start a vegan chocolate factory, or all of the above. Don't be hard on yourself.'

'This coming from the girl who made me take a close-up photo of her bum last week to see what the "cellulite situation" was like.'

'Do as I say, not as I do,' says Jess. 'Anyway, you were the one who said that thighs with cellulite are more attractive than boring, smooth thighs.'

'Jess, I was speaking out of my arse.'

'Speaking of arses, we better get ours into gear if we're gonna walk the dogs today.'

I hold my head in my hands and groan. 'Damn those dogs for being so adorable or I'd go back to bed.'

'A shower and you'll be as good as new.'

I take another slurp of my coffee and drag myself back to my bedroom. As I enter the room, I feel a sharp pang of sadness. My room. I've been here since I finished uni and I can't imagine living anywhere else. I know things can't stay the same forever, but maybe just for another five years?

I sit on the side of the bed and pick up my phone. It's charged to thirteen per cent, so I turn it on. As I wait for it to load, I look at myself in the mirror. Talk about bed head. My hair is matted, and my make-up is smeared over my face. What a catch.

As the phone pings to life, I see I have hundreds of notifications.

I open my messages.

MS ROGERS - PRINCIPAL LITTLE ELM

Please come and see me before class on Monday. It is urgent.

Geez, what does my boss want on a Saturday? I open the next message.

MUM

I saw you in the Daily Mail! I'm thrilled to have a famous daughter even if I never thought I'd spawned a page 3 girl xxx

Okay, now I'm really confused. My next message is from Chloe.

CHLOE WAITER OZ

That was so much fun. You have to come out to Sydney so we can do it all again.

PS. Um, you're Insta famous.

With trepidation, I click to open Instagram and panic swells in my throat. What the bloody hell have I done?

4

Oh, bugger.

There are thousands of notifications.

Feeling sicker than last night's alcohol consumption warrants, I click on my profile. The first thing I notice is that I've changed my username. It used to be @ChrissyPember and now it's @awholenewchrissy. I do have vague memories of looking into the bathroom mirror, Chloe by my side, swearing that I would never let a man push me around again, that I would be a whole new Chrissy.

I scroll down to my feed.

Bum.

There, on the top row, are three posts that do not fit my carefully curated profile. When I say carefully curated, I mean a profile as bland as a Love Island contestant's chat. My profile is designed not to arouse suspicion that I have any opinions or ideas that may cause an argument. My posts had been pretty flowers and cute mushrooms I'd seen on my walks, photos of the dogs, me and Jess pulling silly faces whilst eating dairy-free Magnums. You know, just the usual stuff.

I click to open the first photo. I cover my eyes with my left hand and open my fingers enough to peep through. The photo shows me on the dance floor. My face looks gleeful as I'm caught mid-spin towards the camera, my red hair fanning out in a ring behind me.

My pretty pink top is pulled up into a knotted crop top like thin girls used to do in school. My belly is exposed. Pale white rolls crease down my side as I turn towards the camera, gravity causing the front of my tummy to bounce upwards.

A fresh wave of nausea hits me as I read my caption.

Meet my belly. She hasn't been out in a while and is so excited to see the world. Girls, embrace your body. #lovemybody #fatacceptance

I tap over to the next photo. Me in the bar bathroom, still with the stupid top tied up. The light is bright and unflattering and highlights every stretch mark on my belly. The fat rolls are out in full force now. My hands are squeezing my boobs together into the tiniest cleavage you've ever seen. I'm screwing my face up in laughter and I am leaning forward in a fit of giggles. This does nothing for either my belly rolls or my chins. I can see Chloe in the reflection, taking the photo. She has her top pulled up in the same way, except her tummy is flat.

The caption says:

Yay! I am a fully paid-up member of the itty bitty titty committee and I couldn't be happier. #fatandhappy.

I feel faint. I lay my head on the pillow and allow the room to swim around me as I look at the next little box on my grid. It's a reel. Bracing myself, I press play.

It shows me dancing with the biggest smile on my face. Thank baby Jesus, my top is normal in this one. Okay, maybe this is not as bad as the photos. I can cope with some dodgy dancing. As I spin, there's a transition. I've hiked my top up even further into a kind of bikini. I bounce up and down and when I say bounce, I mean, every bit of my body bounces. And then I grab my belly, hold on to it and move it up and down in time with the music, giggling wildly as the reel ends. It plays again on my phone, and I tap it to stop before I vomit.

The caption says:

bouncy, bouncy #loveyourself.

I'm too afraid to read the comments, even though I can see there are a lot of them. I flick out of the app as I can no longer ignore the pinging notification from Zingles. The noise usually fills me with excitement as I wonder whether my potential one true love could be contacting me, but today I just wonder how else I may have mortified myself.

I open the app to find dozens of messages. I look at my history to find I've only gone and right-swiped about a hundred guys. And they are all from Australia.

A message pops up.

BRAD

Was so good chatting to you last night. Can't wait to show you around Bondi.

There is a photo of a blonde guy with longish, wavy hair that has been bleached by the sun. He's tanned and woah... check out those muscles. I like to think I'm not easily swayed by physical appearances, but geez Louise. I can't decide whether he is more like a Viking or a blonde Jason Momoa. Either way, he's just my cup of tea. One thing I don't under-stand is why this god of a man would be interested in someone like me?

I open a message from another man named Luca. Oh no, I didn't? I responded to a dick pic. And that is an image my poor stomach can't handle in its current fragile state.

I throw myself out of bed and race into the bathroom.

5

I take a deep breath as I focus on the rolling green around me. Chilly air fills my lungs and I glance down at little Jonah the Shih Tzu cross. He looks up at me with his big brown eyes. He has an adorable underbite and his tail is wagging from side to side.

'See, the dogs aren't judging you,' says Jess. 'Are you, Layla?' Layla is a West Highland White terrier who seems to love everything about life. She was dumped after she had one too many accidents in the house. 'Not long now, Layla, and you'll be going home,' says Jess. We learned that Layla has a family lined up to adopt her tomorrow and we're over the moon for her.

'I just wish the same for Jonah.' I sigh. 'A little anxiety is off-putting for people, but all he needs is love.'

Jonah loves people, but he's afraid of a lot of things like

thunder, cars, cats, plastic bags and even shoes that aren't on people's feet. I hate to think what they put him through at his last home. Apparently, when he came into the shelter his coat was so matted, the knots obscured his eyes. Now he is such a handsome boy with his groomed brown-and-white patched fur.

Jess is flicking about on her phone as we walk.

'I can't believe your little Insta posts made it into the *Daily Mail*. You're a superstar.'

'I haven't looked and I'm not going to. How did they even make it into a story so fast?' I ask.

Jess glances up from her phone. 'I've seen this kind of thing before,' she says. 'They must have journalists keeping an eye on what's going viral on social media. It's lazy content for them, isn't it?'

'You're not reading it, are you?' I want to knock the phone out of her hand, but I shouldn't make sudden movements around Jonah.

'They're summing up what you posted and talking about the fat liberation movement. They say you've liberated your fat.'

'Oh god,' I groan and rake a hand through my freshly washed hair.

'And they highlight some comments people have left on your post.'

'I didn't read the comments,' I say. 'I've deactivated the account.'

'Oh no. You haven't?' Jess looks appalled. 'You can't. You're speaking for fat women everywhere. Let me read you the article, at least.'

'Argh, what do you think, Jonah?' I say to my little buddy as I crouch down and ruffle his ears. He places his paws on my knees in an attempt to lick my face. 'Go on then,' I say as I stand up and walk over to a nearby bench. Jess sits next to me. I lift Jonah onto my lap and Layla sniffs around the bench for other doggy smells.

'Okay, here we go...'

Insta wannabe flaunts gut to spite 'body shaming' critics.

Chrissy Pember from Brighton may be overweight, but she's not ashamed. The Insta up-and-comer has posted a series of photos exposing her less-than-perfect figure in an effort to liberate her fat. The viral reel features the music of oversized superstar, Cheynique, who commented on the post with the word 'Fire'.

Pember, a primary school teacher at Little Elm in Brighton, has been promoted to the role of body-positive influencer after her posts were viewed over 400,000 times in less than 12 hours.

Supporters jumped into the comments section to show her some love. One person said '100% gorg. You have made me feel so much better about myself. Love it.'

Another chimed in 'Girl, you work it. I wouldn't do this, but I bloody love that you have.'

However, not everyone was so positive, with some feeling that Pember should not be posting such revealing photos.

A disgruntled follower wrote 'Not what I want to see over my brekkie. Put it away, love.' Other users are concerned that Pember is promoting unhealthy eating habits. One commenter said 'Thanks, now we have another generation of girls who have been given the green light to stuff themselves and develop diabetes.' Another wrote 'Genuinely concerned. This stomach is not normal. Lose some kilos and get healthy (heart emoji).'

Miss Pember is yet to respond to critics, but it seems that, like Cheynique, she is embracing her curves, even if others won't.

Jess looks up from her phone and taps me on the knee. 'Did you hear that? They compared you to Cheynique.'

'Hardly,' I say, looking down at my nails.

'Are you upset?' says Jess, lifting my chin to see my face.

I sniff. 'I'm trying not to cry. I'm just angry at myself. How did I let this happen? I'm not a body acceptance influencer. I'm not some gorgeous booty-shaking goddess like Cheynique. I hate that I shared those posts.'

Jonah puts his paws up on the bench and licks my hand.

'Oh love, come here.' Jess pulls me towards her. 'I bet you're still feeling rotten from last night, too. But at least you've got me, Jonah and Cheynique. We all know you're gorgeous.'

'Oh my god,' I say as I pull away from Jess. 'Cheynique knows I exist.'

'This is what I'm saying,' says Jess with a squeal. 'Bloody Cheynique! Can we just forget what the dickheads think for a second and concentrate on an actual living legend?'

'That is pretty exciting,' I say with a half-formed smile.

'And what do you think of the pics she posts with her bum and boobs out?'

'I think she's fabulous, of course,' I say, because she *is* fabulous.

'So, how are you different?'

'Well, I'm me. I'm this big, pale blob.' I gesture down at my body.

'Well, we love you no matter what you look like, don't we, doggos?' Jess stands up from the bench and drags me up by the arm.

'Sorry, Jess. I'm ruining the best time of the week. I'll pull myself together,' I say, forcing a smile. 'Come on, dogs, let's get moving.'

Back at the shelter, a familiar sadness weighs down on me as I lead the dogs back into their kennels. It's not that the shelter isn't doing a good job. It was refurbished recently after someone left a bunch of money in their will. Each kennel has an outside area where the dogs can run and an inside area with a concrete floor, but with old armchairs for them to laze in or tear up. But it always feels like a betrayal to leave them when I'm going back to my plush flat. Or rather my soon-to-be-ex plush flat. I crouch down and pet Jonah's ears, pulling a little snack from my pocket and feeding it to him. I can hear Jess saying her happy goodbyes to Layla. She knows she's going to a great home soon.

'How long has it been now, Jonah?' I stand up and read his chart that hangs on the wall. Ten weeks. 'Oh darling, someone will come for you soon.'

My phone vibrates, and I pull it out of my pocket and glance at it.

'What is this? A blush?' says Jess, appearing behind me. 'Who text you?'

'You're gonna think I'm mad.'

'Oh, I already do. Just tell me.'

I fill her in on my Aussie dating capers.

'Show me the guy,' she says with an excited wiggle.

I click on Brad's profile and hold the phone out to her. 'He's kind of gorgeous. And he's a surfer.'

'So, what's the plan here? Are you gonna go on holiday to Australia or something?'

'I hadn't planned to. This was just a laugh, but I dunno. I don't believe in hippy-dippy stuff usually, but it's like the universe is telling me I need to make a change.'

Jess nods and widens her eyes. She loves this stuff. 'Yes. And you've always wanted to go.'

'Hang on,' I say, holding up my palm. 'This is just a Zingles chat, just a bit of fun.'

She grabs my phone from my hand. 'But he could be your one true love!' she cries. 'He could be your Joe!'

I shake my head, but of course I am imagining the perfect Australian beach wedding. I'll be whittled down to a toned size ten in a light, flowy wedding dress and he'll be in a suit with no jacket. The top buttons of his shirt will be undone, and his trouser legs will be rolled up as we frolic at the edge of the surf for our wedding photos. Of course there will be kangaroos hopping along the sand. In this fantasy, I am not even concerned that my snow-white skin is going to burn to a crisp.

'I can't decide if that's sweet or fat-shamey,' Jess says, pulling me out of my daydream.

'Oh, don't read the chat!' I grab the phone back, knowing from reading them myself that last night's texts got a bit spicy. I read the latest message:

> I love your passion for making the world a better place. I do the same with my personal training work. I help people become the best version of themselves. Maybe I could help train you?

I smile, and tap back my response.

> I've never been very good at exercise, but you could change all that for me.

He replies straight away.

> I'll make it fun. How could it not be
> when we'd be training on Bondi
> Beach? Bet you'd look hot in a
> bikini.

Hot as in sweaty, maybe. Oh shit. I forgot about that. Wearing a swimsuit in front of this gorgeous man would be mortifying. I reply with a blushing face emoji.

Jess giggles. 'Ha, look at you! You like him.'

'Of course I like him, but it's not like anything is gonna happen. It's a bit of fun.'

'Sure,' says Jess, narrowing her eyes.

'Ready for another walk?' I ask, desperate to change the subject away from my dating life, or lack thereof.

'Yeah, yeah and you can tell me even more about bodacious Brad.'

'Oh shush,' I say as I scruff Jonah's ears one more time before walking out of the kennel, but I can't hide the growing smile on my face.

6

I spent all last night looking for a new place to rent, but the prices are either out of this world or the locations are too far from work. I know Jess said I could take as long as I like, but I'm not sure how I'd go living with the loved-up couple.

Despite my difficulties, I can't get rid of the secret smile on my face. Brad and I have been texting all night. I haven't bothered chatting more with the multitude of military personnel and backpackers who contacted me on Zingles, because why would I when there's Brad?

I lay out my pretty stationery on my classroom desk and look over the lesson plan for the day, tapping my nails on the paper. The kids are gonna love my nails today. They're all different shades of blue, which is perfect since we're learning about the ocean. Ah, the ocean. I imagine swimming in it with Brad, our bodies slippery as we touch beneath the surface.

'Chrissy, are you ready for our meeting?'

'Of course,' I say, looking up to see Ms Rogers at the door. She insists all the teachers call her Ms Rogers rather than Sarah. You know Mrs Trunchbull in *Matilda*? Well, that is the image Ms Rogers projects. But I happen to know she has a soft centre. She doesn't realise I've seen her comforting little Lily when she was upset because Douglas said she wasn't a real pony.

My stomach rolls and my mouth is dry as I follow Ms Rogers to her office.

'Chrissy...' There's a long pause as Ms Rogers sits down at her desk, gesturing for me to take the seat opposite. 'You know we're really pleased with your work here at Little Elm, and the kids love you, too.'

'Thank you,' I say, still not allowing myself to relax.

'However, even though you're covering maternity leave, you are still under the same rules as the other teachers.'

'Oh yes,' I say.

'So, I was shocked to see this.' She opens the top drawer of her desk and places a copy of the *Daily Mail* in front of me, opening it on page six.

My stomach tightens into a knot as I see my bumpy, stretch-marked flesh blown up to a half-page. They have used a screenshot from the video where I grab my belly. My face is squidged down, creating at least three chins.

'Uh oh,' I say, feeling like I might be sick right here in the office à la the boy who Ms Trunchbull forced to eat the chocolate cake.

'Uh oh is an understatement. What were you thinking?'

'I wasn't,' I say. 'And I have no idea how this silly story made it into the paper. I deleted my Instagram account straight away.'

'Not soon enough, I'm afraid. I've heard from three separate parents and a member of the board of trustees over the weekend, all wanting your head on the chopping block. I shouldn't have to deal with complaints because little Freddie Wilson pointed to his grandad's paper and said, "Why is Miss Pember nakie?"'

'Nakie?' I repeat with a wobble in my voice.

'Yes.' Her tone is serious. 'Nakie.'

I bite my cheek. I will not cry. I will not cry.

Ms Rogers notices my distraught face and softens her tone.

'Look, I've done my bit in my time. For me, it was women's liberation. I took part in marches. I even did a nude streak to raise awareness about the sexualisation of women in the media. But I did it at college. There's a time and a place and this is not it.'

The mental image of this sturdy, uptight woman chanting naked in the streets halts my tears in their tracks.

'I wish I could go back in time and change my actions,' I

reply, trying to keep my voice level, 'but I can't. What can I do to make this right?'

'You're a good teacher,' she says and there's a pause that seems to go on way too long as she looks through the papers on her desk. 'We had an emergency meeting of the board this morning. I tried to stand up for you, but I have to say that most of them want to see the back of you. Goodness knows they've seen quite enough of the front. They weren't exactly pleased that you are flaunting your – what does it say here? – *juice* all over the newspaper. And there are more concerns than just the bad press.'

'Really?' I shouldn't be surprised. The board of trustees is made up of some of the stuffiest people I've ever met.

'There's been concern from some of the parents that you'll teach the children unhealthy eating habits.'

'But we haven't got to the lessons on nutrition yet.'

'No, not that, but...' She sighs again and shakes her head before looking me in the eye. 'Your attitude to your own body. The fact you flaunted your excess weight like that. I think it's admirable to be proud of your body, but the parents, well, they're worried their kids will end up overweight.'

'That's ridiculous,' I say, any feelings of remorse replaced by outrage.

'It doesn't make much sense to me either. However, because of the concerns of the parents and the board, I'm afraid you'll be stood down without pay whilst we look into this further.'

I close my eyes and take some deep breaths. This is a technique Jess taught me to stop me from bursting into tears every time things get hard. In through the nose, out through the mouth, good energy in, bad energy out.

'Are you okay?' asks Ms Rogers, and I open my eyes, realising I'm hyperventilating.

'Yes, I'm okay. I understand,' I say, pushing down my rage. 'Um... Thank you for the opportunity.' I wipe my eyes and take another deep breath. 'Should I... Do you think I should contact the union?'

'It's your right, but I'm not sure they'll help you here. For what it's worth, Chrissy, I don't think you did a bad thing, but it's hardly appropriate for a teacher. A sub is coming in today, so if you could collect your things... I'll be in touch in a few weeks once we reach a verdict on what will happen next.'

'Do I need to go now? Today?' The calming breaths are no longer working, and I feel tears rolling down my cheeks.

'That's correct. I'll be in touch.' Ms Rogers is still the picture of professionalism.

I stand up and smooth down my long skirt before nodding and turning for the door.

'Chrissy?'

I turn around, feeling a brief surge of hope.

'You'll need this.' Ms Rogers holds out a box, which I guess I'm meant to put my belongings in. I take it and rush out the door. I want to head straight to the loos and hide away, just as I did in high school when Leonard Martin said, 'Nice hair, shame about the face.' But I don't want to be in this place any longer. I want to go home.

I glance at my Fitbit. There are only ten minutes until class begins. As I reach the classroom, I see some students have arrived and are hanging up their coats and bags. Keeping my head down, I gather my things. I pick up my bag and place my stationery into the box. I add my plant, my phone charger and some other bits from the desk.

I take a look around the colourful classroom and I walk away.

'Miss?' There's a tug on my skirt. It's Sofia Wozniak. Her innocent face is staring up at me. Sofia has had a few problems picking up skills as fast as the other children. Along with the individualised education team, I've done my best to help her catch up. The extra time we've spent together has created a strong bond between us.

'Yes, Sofia?' I say, forcing a smile.

'I think you look lovely and when Daddy says you were funny-looking, I said, "Miss Chrissy is a princess and I love her."'

'Oh, thank you.' I crouch down so I am at eye level with the little girl. I try to steady my voice as I realise how many parents must be saying awful things about me. 'You're going to have a new teacher today, so be sure to make them feel welcome.'

'Sofia, wanna see my dog drawing?' As Sofia is called over to a friend, I sneak out the door.

'"Funny-looking"? I'll show you funny-looking,' I mutter. My uncertain walk turns into an angry stomp as I strut down the corridor and out of the school, expertly avoiding eye contact with everyone around me.

I parked down the road this morning, trying to add some extra steps to my day, and now I curse that decision as fat raindrops fall onto my head.

As the rain splashes down on me, all the frustration at my body, and all the stress from those horrible online comments comes roaring to the surface.

I can't pretend this is okay. This is so not okay.

Most of the time I avoid construction sites. Yes, I know things have changed over time. Yes, I know 'not all men' holler out at women, but some do and that is enough for me to cross the road or take a detour if a building site is ahead.

Today I am so consumed by my negative thoughts, I don't notice much of anything.

'Cheer up, love, it might never happen.'

I pull myself up to my full five foot nine inches and search for my heckler through tear-blurred eyes. I see him in his high-vis vest – a bulky framed middle-aged man holding a hammer behind the construction fencing.

'It. Has. Happened,' I yell, surprising myself and dropping my box. I storm across the road towards the building site.

This goes against every fibre of my being. My desire to avoid confrontation is so strong I once shoved down an enormous piece of my gran's home-baked fruit cake, even though fruit cake makes me gag.

Despite this, something is propelling me forward.

'We've got a live one boys,' shouts a younger-looking man to his colleagues.

Another worker is sitting on a wall sheltered by the roof of the house they're building. He's eating something from a bag and a newspaper is laid out on the wall next to him.

'Bloody hell, it's the fat lass from the paper.'

'You're bloody right,' says a skinny blonde guy.

'Yes, it is me,' I say, pointing at the men and not caring who hears me. 'I am more woman than any of you could handle and if I want – and I'm not saying I do – I could lose weight, whereas you lot... you lot are stuck being bullying bastards forever.' My tears have dried up and I notice the men's dumbfounded expressions. The middle-aged man holds his hands up in defence.

'Geez, I only meant a smile never hurt anyone.'

'I am not going around with a grin plastered on my face for your benefit, so leave me alone.' I swing around, fighting the urge to fist-pump the air as I check the road and stride back over. So focused am I on my regal departure that I don't look back. I hardly even look forward and that is how I find myself in what feels like a slow-motion trip over the kerb. I plonk down onto my knees. My skin stings as I hit the asphalt and I hear whoops and hollers from the men I thought I had set on the right path.

I take a deep breath and drag myself up, brushing the gravel out of my knees. The school bus trundles by, right through a puddle of dirty water. The brown liquid sprays over my hair, my face, and my body, soaking my skirt right through to my knickers.

'This sodding country!' I wave my fist at the sky before straightening myself up with as much dignity as I can manage. I pick up my sodden box and limp back to my car.

7

It's eleven a.m. and I'm sitting in my dressing gown. My freshly washed hair is wrapped in a towel and there are ouch plasters on my scraped knees. With a cup of tea in one hand and a mint chocolate biscuit in the other, I'm curled up on the sofa streaming *The Mindy Project*. But I'm not really paying attention to Mindy talking about how 'everyone knows her boobs are gigantic.' I'm trying to pretend it's a relaxed Sunday, but it's not. It's Monday, and I have lost my job.

I haven't told Brad about what happened. He'll be asleep now anyway and I don't want to give the impression I am some rampaging She Hulk who terrorises builders around the Greater Brighton area. Instead, I sent him a photo of me wrapped up after my shower and captioned it:

Wish you were here.

No, Brad is not the one to turn to right now. There is only one person who will help me feel better when everything is going wrong.

'Oh, hi, love.' Mum picks up the phone after one ring as if she has been waiting for my call. 'I was wondering when I'd hear from you. How are you doing?' Her usually confident voice is tentative, as if her words might crack me and release a flood of tears.

'Not so great,' I try to keep my voice steady. I tell her everything from the awful date with Gareth to the confrontation with the builders. The only thing I don't mention is Brad. I don't want to jinx it.

The wonderful thing about Mum is that she always takes my side, even when I'm in the wrong.

'He said what?' she says now, sounding outraged. 'In my day, builders could be relied upon to wolf-whistle and yell "Show us yer tits" and that was about it. When did they get so judgy?'

I can't help but chuckle as I imagine my mum enjoying the attention from builders. Knowing Mum, I wouldn't be surprised if she did a twirl and took a bow before strutting on with an extra wiggle in her step. I have Mum's red hair and green eyes, but that's about it. I sadly lack her confidence and, as awkward as it is to say this, her sex appeal. Firstly, she has boobs. Not huge boobs, but a decent set. Secondly, she's slim and never even has to go on a diet. She's shorter than me but has this inner confidence that makes her look like a six-foot-tall supermodel as she sashays around Brighton in a wave of fresh citrus scent.

Mum's always dragging me along to activities that Dad refuses to do with her. Last month I finally agreed to join her on her daily swim. I met her at sunrise on Brighton Beach to plunge my body into the icy sea. All I ended up with was self-hatred and skin itchy from cold, whereas Mum had a warm glow as she sat, wrapped in a towel, pouring us both a hot cup of tea from her flask.

'And how are you feeling about your little news story?' she asks now.

'Mortified,' I say. 'I can't believe I posted that video. My flesh is all over the paper. I just want to shed my skin and slither away.'

'Oh, Chris. I feel like I've failed you when you talk that way. Can I tell you what I thought when Miriam down the newsagents showed me the paper?'

'What?' I ask with trepidation.

'I thought that right there is my beautiful daughter, empowered and empowering others, and she's only gone and got bloomin' Cheynique on her side.'

'How do you know about Cheynique?' I ask her.

'Come on. I'm not that old. I've seen TikTok.' Mum hums a tune I recognise as one of Cheynique's hits.

I laugh at Mum's impression. I just know she'll be attempting to twerk whilst she sings because that's what she does every time she sings a line from any pop song.

'I was proud of you, Chris, because you showed people your body is beautiful just the way it is.'

Mum is always so kind about my body, but I know if she were this size, she'd be straight down to Weight Watchers.

'Thanks, Mum, but the board of Little Elm did not feel the same way.'

'They don't deserve you,' says Mum with an unexpected spit of venom.

'I need the money, though, and it's what I trained for. I love teaching. What am I going to do? No house, no job and being ridiculed for my body. Honestly, I wonder if I should just pack it all in and leave the country.' I realise as I say the words that I've said this phrase to Mum many times over the past few years.

'You know what? You absolutely should,' says Mum.

'You want to get rid of me?'

'Don't be daft. You're welcome to move in here with us, but you're always going on about travelling. What's holding you back? You could get a job abroad; you could experience life, you could have fun.'

As I listen, I wonder if my silly dream of booking a flight to Australia is so outlandish after all. Yes, I have been saving for a house deposit since secondary school, but I'm not even a quarter of the way there. If I did go to Australia, what would I be leaving behind? Well, all my friends, all my family and my beloved dog rescue. Hmm. But then there is Brad...

And I'm sure there are rescue dogs that need walking in Australia.

'Did I ever tell you about my overseas adventure back when I was young?' says Mum.

'Yup.' I nod, not wanting to hear my conception story again.

'I never regretted my time in Skiathos, and your dad wasn't complaining, either.'

'Yuck, Mum, I've heard all this before.'

'Grow up, Chris. It was a wonderful time – skinny dipping, dancing the night away, rolling in the sand dunes—'

'Okay, okay, that's enough.'

'All I'm saying is that I would love for you to have an adventure of your own.'

'So would I,' I say with a sigh.

'So do it. Go and experience life. Everyone will still be here when you get back. Oh, one sec.'

There's a pause and I allow my mind to wander. I don't have to think much about where I would go. My mind flashes through images of long beaches, tropical rainforests and bright parrots... Australia.

'I just got a text from Miriam,' Mum says, a concerned tone in her voice.

'Yeah?'

'She sent me another screenshot from the *Daily Mail* website, but it's nothing to worry about, really.'

'What now?' I try to keep my voice nonchalant, but anxiety is already swirling in my stomach.

'Just those horrible builders, Chris. I'm sure they come off looking worse than you. Nasty bullies, the lot of them. I've a good mind to call up their boss and get them all sacked.'

'Just leave it, Mum. Thanks, but it's okay. I'm okay.'

'Are you sure, love? What is it Cheynique sings?' Mum hums a few notes and then breaks into song. 'Haters make me stronger every damn day, so shut your mouth and listen to what I have to say.'

Despite myself, I stifle a giggle at my tone-deaf mother's attempt at a Cheynique impression.

'That's how it goes, isn't it?' she asks.

'Something like that. But honestly, this is all fine. I've gotta go, okay?'

As we say our goodbyes and I tap to hang up the phone, I know I haven't fooled Mum for even a moment. She knows how sensitive I am and how I've carried every insult with me ever since school. Why is it that I never remember compliments? I guess, I think the person doesn't really mean it and is just trying to be kind. Yet I hold on to insults tightly. I remember every detail of them and never question their truth. Honestly, I may as well get them tattooed on my forehead.

I take another biscuit from the packet and as my teeth crack the chocolate coating, I feel soothed. I feel safe. As the minty goodness fills my mouth, I lift another biscuit and bring it to my lips. For a moment, I am only focusing on the sugar, the chocolate and the smooth texture. For a moment I feel numb and that is the biggest relief.

8

'What's wrong with these people?' says Jess. 'Do they not have any actual news to write about? I mean, we're heading straight for climate disaster, but do they care about that? Noooo.'

I'm sitting on a stool at the kitchen bench, tapping my nails on the counter, whilst Jess scans through the new *Daily Mail* article on her phone.

'It's nonsense, Chrissy,' says Joe as he hovers by the kettle, making us tea. 'There's nothing wrong with enjoying your cake and biccies.'

Yup, he's moved in already. I guess there is no getting away from it; Jess's boyfriend is here to stay.

In truth, there's nothing wrong with the man. He's ever so kind to Jess. It's just with Joe's lanky build, his dull brown clothes and dull obsession with Fortnite, well, the whole effect is a bit... dull. And Jess is just so fabulous, it's hard to imagine he could be her forever.

I give myself a mental slap. Here I am judging someone just like the public are judging me, thanks to the latest ridiculous story online.

The headline of the article is 'Fat Teacher's Tanty'. A curious part of me wants to read more, but I won't do it. There's no point in torturing myself over the words of some intern who rewrites Insta posts all day. I guess a shamed teacher simply cannot have a meltdown these days without some James Cameron wannabe filming it on their phone and, of course, posting it online.

It's a short article and I know there's a photo.

Jess's words were, 'Not the most flattering, but could be worse.'

Joe's first word after glancing at the article was, 'Yikes.'

I kid you not.

Joe needs to learn that yikes is never a word to be uttered when shown a photo of a woman, no matter how atrocious she looks.

'That's it for me then,' I say as I take a cup of tea from Joe with a nod of thanks. 'What man is going to touch me with his ten-foot bargepole after seeing this article?'

'Ten foot? He's doing well,' scoffs Joe.

I roll my eyes.

'Well, we think you're lovely as you are,' says Jess. 'I mean, if you saw me in the paper like that' – she turns to Joe – 'like before we were dating, would it have put you off taking me out?'

'God no,' says Joe, grabbing Jess around the waist and pulling her into a hug. 'I would've loved you instantly.'

Jess giggles as Joe bends down and kisses her neck.

'See,' she says to me.

'Thanks, guys. I'm gonna go and search for jobs, see if I can't get this mess turned around.'

Taking my tea with me, I walk to my room feeling like the wheeliest third wheel that ever wheeled.

I'm not really going to search for jobs. I just want to be alone in the cocoon of my room, pretending the big, scary world does not exist.

My phone buzzes and as much as I'm trying not to get my hopes up, a wide grin spreads across my face as I flop onto the bed and open my messages.

BRAD

I had a dream about you last night.

I bounce my legs on the mattress, as I think of him thinking of me. I type back:

Tell me more

BRAD

> We were at the beach. I was rubbing sun cream onto your back and your skin was so soft. We were gonna do it right there on the sand.

A thrill runs through me as I read.

BRAD

> And then a giant crab shuffled up the beach and took the bottle right out of my hand, so I went off for a surf and he did the sun cream.

I type back with a great big smile on my face.

> The romance is too much for me to handle.

BRAD

> That pic you sent me was so hot. No wonder you were stalking my dreams.

I'm relieved. The torment of which photo to send had kept me up the night before as I flicked through my gallery, desperate to find an image that didn't portray me as a dishevelled lump. I had settled on a photo Jess had taken on the beach last summer. I still remember laughing as I tried to pull a seductive face whilst lying prone on the warm pebbles.

I was wearing a fifties-style one-piece and sarong that hid some of my wobbly bits.

I send him some blushing emojis and type:

> I've been thinking about you, too.
> Kind of wishing I was in Sydney
> right now.

BRAD

Do it! I'd take you on the best date.

I type back:

> It's weird, but I'm considering it. I
> need to move out of my place here. I
> need a new job. This could be the
> time to get some travelling in.

It seems Brad isn't a *Daily Mail* reader, as he hasn't mentioned my newly found notoriety. I have no intention of telling him.

BRAD

Want to video chat? I'm free now.

My chest tightens as excitement and fear creep up within me. We haven't spoken on the phone yet. What if he sees me and feels so nauseous, he has to excuse himself? What if his voice is so high and squeaky like Minnie Mouse that I can't stop giggling? What if we don't click?

But the phone is chiming its video-call ring and I don't have any more time to think about it, so I pick up.

'Hey, you,' he says in his Aussie accent.

As he looks at me, it appears he is not holding back vomit. He is just as gorgeous as in his photos. His arms are tanned and bulging with muscles. If any man could pick me up and throw me around the bedroom, it would be him.

'Hey,' I say, lying on my back and holding the phone above my face.

'So, tell me what's been going on?' Something about his laid-back tone just unplugs me, and I tell him everything, well, everything except the *Daily Mail* article. I don't want him Googling it and seeing me looking like Shrek on a bad day.

He's a good listener, his twinkly blue eyes intent on me as he takes it all in.

'Chrissy, that sucks,' he says. 'You deserve so much better than all this shit.'

'Thanks,' I say with a shrug. 'It's been the weirdest couple of days.'

'Maybe it's the universe,,' he says, 'telling you it's time for a big life change.'

I want to giggle, but I see his face is serious. 'Maybe,' I say.

'Look, if you came out to Sydney, I could treat you the

way you deserve,' he says. 'And if you want to lose weight, we can do that too. I run a bootcamp and if you wanted to get that Bondi butt and teeny tiny waist then it's all possible.' He gestures to his tie-dye sleeveless shirt, where a logo for Brad's Bootcamp is embroidered over his broad chest.

For a moment, I'm offended he thinks I need to change, but then I glance at his wide smile and know he is just trying to cheer me up. My mind flicks to me on Bondi Beach, laughing as Brad splashes me at the ocean's edge. I will be flaunting a perky bum in a skimpy bikini. My red hair will blow in the breeze with not a bit of frizz in sight. I imagine running my hand over my flat, hard tummy and somehow, in this fantasy, my boobs have grown a couple of sizes. I mean, when the rest of my body is smaller, surely, they will look bigger in comparison?

'... a clean diet obviously, lots of protein, chicken breasts, all that and I can show you heaps of interval training stuff. I know it sounds a bit out there, but could you... I mean, would you come out here?'

For now, I don't mention my veganism. It's not like he's going to force-feed me chicken flesh. Instead, I feel breathless with excitement. He's seen me. He's spoken to me, and he still seems to like me.

'I dunno. I guess... I mean, if I want to travel, it could be the right time,' I say. 'I do have some savings and there's not much holding me here anymore.'

'So, it's time for an adventure.' His smile gets even wider.

'With you?' I ask.

'With me,' he says, and, for a moment, we hold eye contact and say nothing.

'Would it not be too much pressure on... us?' I ask.

'Yeah, nah.' He shakes his head. 'We'd take it slow. Friends first and see where it goes from there. If it doesn't work out, that's okay. We get to hang out and get you in shape. If it does work out, well, who knows?' He gives me a cheeky wink.

For the first time in a long time, I'm excited.

We stay on the phone for another hour. Brad tells me about his life; his beach house just a few minutes' walk from Coogee Beach, his fitness routine, and his friends. I listen as if in a dream. Every time he speaks, I get more excited about my new life. The Bondi me. The me that gets up and works out at six a.m. every morning.

I have enough savings to live without working for the length of a holiday visa, and by then I might get my teaching job back. I mean, the union has already got back to me to hear my side of the story. I wonder if Brad would move to Brighton? Or perhaps, by then, I'll be in such good shape, I'll be a fitness model and will get gifted a visa as Australia will be so desperate to keep my world-class beauty in the country.

Brad has to meet a client at the beach, so we hang up and I am left lying there on my bed in a glowing pink love bubble. I'm going to do it. I am going on an adventure to Australia. And not only that, I am going to become the

Chrissy I was always meant to be. The whole new Chrissy that my Instagram handle promised.

My phone buzzes. It's a text from Chloe. I sit up straight.

> Hey, Cheynique, I mean, Chrissy (so hard to tell you two apart). I'm in Singapore on my stopover and there's a bar here that has the best cocktails. Wish you were here!

I text her back straight away.

> Me too! But I have great news. I'm coming on holiday to Australia.

> You're shitting me? You better not be messing me around. When?

> Not booked yet. But asap. I have a whole new life to dive into.

> OMG, that is AMAZING. You have to stay with me. Book now.

I jump up to get my laptop, wiggling my hips to a happy song in my head. Over the next fifteen minutes Chloe sends me multiple cheerleading texts.

> Go on.

> Do it.

Have you done it yet?

As I hold my debit card in my hand and stare at the laptop screen, I can hardly believe it. I've booked my flights to Australia... finally.

I reach over to my handbag and unfold my Things to Do When I'm Skinny list. Well, I'm the opposite of skinny, yet I can certainly check off number five: Do something spontaneous. And soon I'll be able to check off number one: Spend six months in Australia. If I start ticking things off the list, perhaps the skinniness will follow?

I leap up from my desk chair and skip out of the room.

'I'm doing it. I'm going to Australia,' I announce to... well, myself, as the room is empty. I hear moaning from Jess's room and a deep grunting from Joe, and I grimace. But I find myself laughing. I'll be out of here soon.

I walk back into my room, a reliably sex-free zone, with a little hop in my step, keen to Google anything and everything about Australia.

9

I used to read celeb magazines on the bus to work. They were absolute trash, but I loved the escapism.

I would pore over an article on Why Single Women Are Happier and then flick over to the next page which suggested 12 Standing Ab Exercises to Nab Your Perfect Man.

I'd get lost in deciding which celebrity wore it best and plan out how to copy the latest celeb diet craze.

After one fad diet disaster too many, I decided the mags were doing my self-esteem no good at all and I stopped buying them. But knowing I have a twenty-two-hour flight ahead of me fills me with a desperate need to stock up on trashy mags. At least if the plane crashes I can use them to create a handy parachute out of Celebs – They're Just Like Us articles.

I've never been on a long-haul flight, but I'm well prepared. All the items on my Things to Get Ready for Australia checklist have satisfying ticks next to them. My floral carry-on is filled with all my essential items: my Kindle, my phone loaded with podcasts and a variety of snacks to help sustain me through the flight because, let's be honest, food is thy friend on a long-arse trip.

I arrived at Heathrow Airport super early out of fear I'd miss my flight, so now I have some time to kill. I unwrap my little airport treat, a dairy free Magnum. The diet can wait until I get to Australia. A whole new Chrissy starts in twenty-four hours.

My phone buzzes with an incoming WhatsApp video call.

'Hey, Jess.'

Jess's face, complete with bold brows and metallic blue eyelids, fills my phone screen.

'Did you make it there alright? I'm so sorry I couldn't come with you,' she says.

'Don't be silly, it's not your fault I had to leave at ridiculous o'clock. Anyway, you had your shelter shift.'

'Well, that's what I wanted to call you about.' Jess pans the camera down to show little Jonah at her feet. 'He says he misses you already.'

Jonah looks like he wishes Jess would get off the phone and get on with walkies.

'I miss him too. Have you looked to see if he's had any

adoption interest over the last week?'

'I did, and no, he hasn't,' Jess lowers her voice as if Jonah may get upset by hearing this. 'I don't understand people at all. I've clipped a little moonstone crystal to his collar to help calm him and to attract good vibes into his life. He'll find his perfect family in no time.'

I raise my eyebrows but choose not to say anything negative. I hope Jess is right and the crystal really will help Jonah find his perfect home.

'But what about you?' she asks. 'Are you ready to jet off into the sunshine to meet your one true love?'

'I am so ready for the sunshine,' I say. 'But remember, no pressure. This is just me travelling to Australia for six months. The fact I'll see Brad is a happy coincidence.'

'Sure,' says Jess, narrowing her eyes. I hear a little whine. 'I think Jonah wants me to get on with the walk.'

'Go on, off you go,' I say, anxious not to keep Jonah waiting and also to get back to my ice cream. 'Give Jonah a kiss and a cuddle from me.' I wave as Jess signs off.

I flick through the first few pages of my magazine whilst nibbling the chocolate off my Magnum.

'No,' I say in a voice far louder than I had intended. There, in the corner of a double-page spread, is a photo of me. The most non-celeb, non-influential person there ever was. They've used the least offensive of my Insta posts, but that's me alright, in all my glory.

I place my hand over the magazine and glance from left

to right to check no one has seen the photo. I do realise this is a futile exercise, given that any one of these people could have already bought the magazine. I fold my arm to cover the top of the page and lean in to read, looking a lot like a student trying to stop her classmate from copying her work.

Cheynique's Fat Crusade – Can one superstar bring about fat acceptance?

The article is well and truly focused on Cheynique, not me, but there in the top right is that little photo of me with the caption:

Cheynique shared a fat liberation post from Insta activist, @awholenewchrissy, winning the creator a lot of love from women who want to see an end to fat-shaming.

The other photos are of Cheynique proudly twerking in a hotel room and flaunting her stuff in a bikini with the caption:

Werk it, big mamas.

I should be happy that I'm sharing the limelight with a superstar, but I'm just so embarrassed. And they called me an activist. Ha, hardly. I am the person least likely to speak up even when I really want to.

My phone buzzes, and a smile spreads across my face.

BRAD

So excited you'll be here soon. Will
be at the airport to pick you up.

I send him back a selfie of me blowing a kiss to the camera.

I had planned to Uber it to Chloe's place and then arrange a date with Brad, but it looks like I'll be seeing him sooner than expected.

I place my phone back on the table and flick over another page of the magazine.

First Date Dresses to Drive Him Wild.

I look down at my outfit. I've prioritised comfort with elasticated waist, pink tracksuit pants, an oversized white hoodie and rainbow flip-flops. This is not first-date appropriate.

Scoffing down the rest of my Magnum, I pack up the magazine in my hand luggage, throw my bag over my shoulder and walk towards the clothes shops. Now this will be a challenge. Most of these places don't even carry my size. The first shop I go into is a surf shop full of clothes I adore, but there is nothing over a size fourteen. Flip-flops and sunglasses are the only things that will fit me here.

The next shop I walk past is full of pretty scraps of

lingerie. Will I need that? I mean, I don't know. Is this the kind of thing where we'll get down to it straight away? Or will we do the three-date thing? I touch the black lace of the set hanging nearest to me. It is a mix of criss-cross straps and underwires. Without trying it on, I grab the set in the biggest back size and smallest cup size I can find. Future me can worry about how to get it on without tying both the bra and myself in a knot. Surely the 'new Chrissy' arriving in Australia will be able to handle that, no problem. Let's hope somewhere over Asia, I become a powerful, altogether different kind of woman.

I try two more shops with no luck finding something in my size and now I'm getting a bit hot and bothered. I've never had much patience for shopping, and this is a high-pressure situation. This is Brad's first impression of the real-life me. This could be my future husband we're talking about.

With a huff, I walk into the next shop.

'Can I help you?' asks the model-thin assistant.

'I just want something pretty, in my size,' I wail.

She looks me up and down, holds her chin in her hand and closes her eyes, as if connecting with the spirit world to lead me to my perfect look. Then she clicks her fingers, spins around and heads into the back of the shop. I wait, somewhat awkwardly, looking around at all the gorgeous clothes I could never squeeze into.

'Voila!' she exclaims as she comes back onto the shop floor, swinging a royal blue dress from a hanger.

It's not something I would have chosen. I love the colour, but this is a bandage dress best suited for thin people. I look at the size tag. Yup, too small. And oh my Lord, the price.

'It is so you,' says the assistant. 'How gorg is that colour against your hair. Want to try it on?'

I reach out and touch the fabric. It's soft and stretchy. You know what? With this material, I reckon it will pull over my wider hips and extra tummy. Ugh, but I could do without the hassle of struggling into it in the changing rooms.

What would Cheynique do?

'I'll take it,' I say with a wave of my hand like this is the kind of purchase I make all the time.

'Yay.' The sales assistant does a little hop.

'Yay,' I say back to her.

As I leave the shop having spent way more than I intended, I add a little strut to my step.

Australia, hold onto your sunhats and get ready for this jelly.

10

One thing that is not ready for this jelly is my aeroplane seat. My knees press into the seat in front and the armrests push into my sides. I guess I should be happy with my seat choice. Most of the rows on the left-hand side of the plane have three seats, but my one at the back only has two. In fabulous news, it seems like the seat next to me is empty. I hold my breath as a sweaty man with pungent body odour stops and looks at the aisle number and I breathe a sigh of relief as he keeps walking.

I gaze out the window at the grey sky and wonder what it will be like when Brad and I are together. Will we fall into each other's arms? Will it be love at first IRL sight?

'Oh no, I thought we were sitting together,' a whining voice interrupts my thoughts as a bag whacks my elbow.

The woman pats my arm. 'Mind the Gucci.'

She's slim with a sleek blonde ponytail pulled high on her head. She turns behind her, shoving her Lululemon-attired bum in my face, and lowers her voice to a whisper.

'Can you ask her to swap seats?'

I can't hear the answer.

'Be boring then.' She huffs and turns to me. 'My partner is too unassertive to ask, but would it be a bother if he swapped seats with you? You see, he's here' – she points to the vacant window seat beside me – 'and I'm here' – she points to the seat across the aisle – 'and we really want to be together.'

With a long exhale, I nod and begin to move my things over to the aisle seat opposite.

'No,' the woman says. 'I mean, could you move here?' She points to the window seat to my left. 'It's just that I need to be by the aisle. I drink a lot of water, hence the flawless skin, but it means I have to pee a lot, and Tom gets claustrophobic when he's by the window.'

My shoulders slump. I can't stand the thought of being cramped in the window seat for twenty-two hours.

'Leave her alone,' says a deep Australian voice as he lifts his carry-on luggage into the overhead compartment and edges past the woman.

I recognise him instantly. It's Tom, the rude barman.

'Hey, it's you,' he says, his eyes widening. 'Sorry again about that tattoo thing. Do you still hate me?'

'Oh, no, no, of course not. That was fine. Yup, fine,' I say, desperate to make the flight less awkward.

'Am I missing something?' says the woman, her smiling mouth dropping into a thin line.

'We're old friends, aren't we, Chrissy?' says Tom, looking down at me with those deep brown eyes.

'Ha, well, you could say that.' As I spot the scowl on the woman's face, I feel far less compelled to move for her. I pull my shoulders back and lift my chin.

'Sorry,' I say to the woman. 'I booked this aisle seat because it's where I'm most comfortable and I want to stick to it.'

The woman furrows her brows and mutters under her breath.

I stand up to let Tom pass me, pretending not to hear his partner's complaints from across the aisle.

Sinking back into my seat, I suck in my stomach and fasten the seatbelt. It digs in like an airline issued corset. I put in my earbuds, even though I'm not listening to anything, and close my eyes. These people will not ruin my flight.

Shortly after take-off, I feel a tap on my shoulder.

Pulling out one earbud, I open my eyes and glance over at Tom.

He points towards the window. 'I may have my knees pressed into my chin thanks to you, but at least there's a nice view, hey?'

'Oh shush,' I say with a smile, but I turn to where he is pointing. There is London in all its grey glory.

'Big Ben,' cries the woman and with a click of her seatbelt she flings herself across the aisle and over my lap towards Tom. 'Can you see it?'

'Janine, we've seen it a hundred times plus the seat belt sign is on,' says Tom.

'But this is special,' she insists, maintaining her awkward position across my lap. She stares at him. He stares back. I glance around hoping to attract the attention of a flight attendant who might restore some semblance of order. My silent plea for help goes unanswered. The only flight attendant I can see appears to be engaged in a heated debate with a passenger further down the aisle about the best way to fold an in-flight blanket.

'Okay, okay, I'll sit by the window,' I say, unable to put up with much more of this couple nonsense.

Janine's hands erupt in giddy applause as she moves back into her seat.

'Hooray!' she beams, her eyes alight with triumph.

I unclip my seatbelt, stand up and begin to gather my belongings.

'Sit down,' barks a shrill voice. The sharp command freezes me in place, and I look up to face the previously blanket-obsessed flight attendant. Her complexion matches her orange neck scarf and she's frowning fiercely. 'Seat belt sign.' She thrusts a finger towards the glowing symbol overhead.

'Told you,' says Tom, looking past me.

Janine sticks her tongue out at him.

My cheeks heat up. I think of the sweaty man with longing. He would have been a far better neighbour.

Twenty minutes later, the seat belt signs ping off, and I can swap seats with Tom.

'Sorry about this,' he says, and I wave off the apology.

'If it wasn't for you checking in at the last minute, we would have been able to reserve decent seats,' Janine snaps.

'Give it a rest. It's sorted now,' says Tom.

She huffs, crosses her arms and stares toward the other side of the plane. I watch as he takes her hand across the aisle and lowers his voice to speak to her. She giggles and her body relaxes. Good, the last thing we need on this flight is more drama. I pop in my headphones, close my eyes and allow my mind to wander into a beautiful daydream about Brad taking me in his arms and giving me a great big movie-style kiss.

'Oh no, I don't think so.' Janine's voice pierces through my daydream, which must have turned into an actual dream as I am jolted awake. The unappetising smell of aeroplane food wafts through the cabin. I take out my headphones.

'Sorry, your partner's seat is down for a vegan meal. We have spare chicken or lamb or—'

'It's mine,' I interrupt. 'It's because of the seat swap. Vegan meal right here, please.' I pull down my tray.

'Yours?' says Tom. 'You don't look like a carrot muncher.'

'Well, I am one. Not a carrot muncher... a vegan, even if you don't think I fit the skinny stereotype.' I can't help the snappy tone in my voice as I take the meal from the air steward. The last thing I need is this idiot having a go at me about my weight.

I catch Janine's smirk.

'No, no, I don't mean...' Tom flounders. 'I just mean, I thought vegans were unhealthy. You don't look unhealthy.'

I clench my jaw. I've lost count of how often I've been told that I 'look well' by friends who can't think of anything else nice to say.

'One thing about being vegan is you get your meal before everyone else on the plane,' I say. 'The aeroplane food is a lot nicer than—'

'I know you,' says Janine, cutting off my sentence and leaning across the aisle. Oh no, not another person who has seen my belly in all her glory.

'I don't think so.' I keep my tone even and lean over my tray to unwrap my food, allowing my hair to fall over my face.

'I do,' she says, 'but I don't know where from. It'll come to me.' She sits back in her seat, lightly stroking her throat, gazing into the distance.

I busy myself with my meal, put on the in-flight headphones and pretend to be engrossed in the romcom on my screen.

Twenty minutes later, I really am engrossed in the

romcom, but the wild gesturing at my right catches my eye. I take off my headphones.

'Who does this?' Tom points to the seat in front. 'I mean, how do they have the nerve?' I notice the person in front has their seat reclined. 'You don't do this on a plane. It's too cramped. It's a joke.'

'Calm down, Tom. We'll just get the flight attendant to ask him to move his seat forward.' Janine presses the button to call for help. Tom shoves the seat in front like a little boy throwing toys out of his pram.

I can't help but giggle.

'It's not funny, carrot muncher.' He turns to me, his face distraught. 'See this?' He gestures to the seat in front of him.

I turn away. I mean, yes, he's cramped with the tray jutting into him at an awkward angle and his big, long legs pressing into the seat in front, but this is what happens on planes. They are a bit of a nightmare, but then you get off and you are somewhere new and quite possibly wonderful.

The flight attendant arrives, listens to Tom's frantic pleas and taps the person in front on the shoulder, who moves their seat into the upright position. Drama averted. Tom is still clenching his jaw as his meal arrives. Ugh, I hate the smell of the meaty aeroplane food. I wish I could shut my nostrils like I can my eyes. Instead, I allow myself to be drawn into Jennifer Aniston and Adam Sandler's on-screen chemistry and imagine it is me and Brad.

Just as Jen and Adam share their first kiss, there is another wail.

'Are you kidding me?'

I see that now everyone has finished their meals, the person in front of Tom has reclined their seat again. Tom blows his breath out in an exaggerated huff.

I take off my headphones and tap him on the knee.

'Hey, if you recline your seat too, you'll have a bit more room.'

'And give in to the system?' he snaps. 'You know this is the problem with the world. This' – he points towards the chair and then to me – 'is why everything has gone to hell.' The man in front of Tom is doing an award-winning job of ignoring his fellow passenger, eye mask on, ear plugs in.

'Because of people reclining their seats?'

'It's not just the seat; it's what it represents,' says Tom in a raised voice as he wobbles the seat in front again. 'People like *him* not respecting others and people like *you* just going along with the system, never standing up for anything important. And before you say it, yes, we know you're vegan,' he says.

'Yeah, we know,' says Janine with an eyeroll from across the aisle.

'I didn't even say anything about that.'

I take a deep breath, ask Tom if I can squeeze by, and head to the back of the plane for a fizzy drink. My legs could do with a stretch and my brain could do with a break from the drama.

I share a grimace with the poor flight attendant who squeezes past me in the aisle. He now has to deal with Tom's tantrum.

The back of the plane is an oasis of calm in comparison. I stand out of the way of those queuing for the toilets and lean down to stretch out my hamstrings. I wrap my arms around my calves and enjoy the stretch along the back of my legs.

I wonder, if I do this on the way home, how my body will have changed. Will my calves be smaller? Will my thigh muscles be toned? Will I have a (drumroll please) thigh gap? As much as I want to find someone who loves me the way I am, I also want to look like Jennifer Aniston: toned and bronzed. When I was in secondary school, I used to be an expert daydreamer. I would flick through my teen magazines, choose a model and wish so hard that I would wake up looking like her.

So – spoiler alert – I never did magic into a model, but now I have a chance. Not to turn into some random hottie from the pages of a magazine, but to become a fitter, hotter version of me. With Brad being a personal trainer, now could be the perfect time to make some changes.

I stand up and stretch my arms above my head.

'Sorry about before,' Tom's voice interrupts my peace.

'Don't worry about it,' I say with a wave of my hand.

'It's just they don't give people enough room and then...'

As his voice rises, he stops himself and laughs. 'I should have coughed up the extra cash for premium economy.'

'It's no picnic for me either. In case you haven't noticed, I'm not the tiniest woman. If I was the hulking out type, I might have had a tantrum too.'

'I was hardly hulking out,' says Tom.

'I thought you were about to bust right out of your shirt and I'm pretty sure you were turning green.'

Tom tuts. 'Can I make it up to you?' he says.

'How?'

'Um... I could buy you a drink.'

'Nice try. The drinks are free on here.' I take a lemonade from the fridge. 'So allow me to buy you one.' I pass him a can.

'When we get to Sydney, then?' he asks. I feel a flutter in my stomach and want to give myself a kick. I mean, no doubt Tom's hot, but he's rude, and he's taken.

'Maybe,' I say. If he means a drink with him and Janine, I can't think of anything worse.

'Where do you live?' I ask.

'Bondi.'

'That's where I'm staying. Oh, you know Chloe, don't you? I'm staying with her.'

'In that case, I'll know where to find you,' he says, placing the lemonade back in the fridge and getting a bottle of water. 'Healthier,' he says.

Feeling like a rebel, I crack open my lemonade. 'I like

lemonade,' I say, and take a swig before raising my eyebrows. As I stare into his eyes, a spark shoots through me. Does he feel it too?

Never mind the fact that I said something as mundane as 'I like lemonade,' Tom is looking at me as if I am the most interesting person in the world.

11

Of course, at the exact moment I take a swig of lemonade the plane hits turbulence. The abrupt jolt sends my drink fizzing out of the can and up my nose.

I try to maintain my cool demeanour, but nope, that's a snort. Yup, I snorted and, oh heck, lemonade is coming out of my nose and onto my top. I splutter and gasp. Tom has grabbed a napkin and is dabbing at my chest and as I look into those chocolate eyes, an unexpected chortle bubbles up from within me.

'Sorry,' he says, a flush creeping up his neck, 'I was just trying to clean you up, so you're not too wet... I mean sticky.' The weirdness of hearing those words from a near stranger causes another snicker to escape my lips and Tom seems to catch my laughter, responding with a hearty guffaw that ripples through the cabin.

There's another turbulence bump and a ping as the seat-belt signs lights up.

'Come on,' he says, placing a hand on my arm to lead me back to the seats.

I glance up. Janine is standing in the aisle, staring at us.

'Seatbelts,' she says with a click of her fingers, and Tom not only lets go of my arm but throws it down.

'I just... He was just... The lemonade,' I say, as my laughter shrivels to nothing. What am I doing? Flirting with someone else's boyfriend. This is not me at all. I hope the Australian version of Chrissy won't be a massive slag.

'Want one?' I say to Janine, pointing to the drinks fridge.

'I choose not to drink my calories,' she says and snaps her fingers again. 'Seatbelts.'

Like naughty children, we follow Janine back to the seats and buckle up. As I flick through my trashy mag and listen to – you guessed it – 'Lemonade', I can't help smiling to myself as I think of laughing with Tom.

I must have fallen asleep as when I open my eyes, the cabin is in darkness. I stretch my legs out under the seat and wriggle my toes. The seat next to me is empty. Unclipping my seatbelt, I stand up and take a slow walk down the aisle.

There is a flutter of excitement in my chest as I pick my way along the cabin. I look at all the sleeping people, wondering what plans they have.

As I reach the other end of the plane, a toned backside greets me. Tom is bent over touching his toes and his bum is pointing right in my direction. I think about giving it a honk, but there's a time and a place and this is not it.

'Stretching?' I say because I guess I am Miss State-the-bleeding-obvious.

He opens his eyes and smiles at me through his legs.

As he stands up, the fizzing in my stomach gets more intense.

'How are you finding the flight?' I ask.

'Yeah, fine. Janine's a bit restless. She gets antsy on long-hauls.'

I resist the urge to roll my eyes. Janine sounds like an irritable toddler.

'It's pretty uncomfortable,' I say. 'My legs were sore, so I'm giving them a stretch.'

'Speaking of stretching and of Janine, she does yoga,' says Tom.

I sigh inwardly. Of course she does.

'I've picked up a couple of yoga poses over the years. They can be useful on a long flight. Want to do some?'

'Go on then,' I say.

'Okay, so simple one first, the downward dog.'

'Ah, yup.' I've been to at least two Body Balance classes with Jess, so I feel like I can easily tackle this one. I fold over and point my bum in the air.

Tom lets out a laugh.

'What are you giggling at?' I stick my butt further into the air, in case it's my posture that's the joke here.

'Just getting a great view of Billy Bob.'

'Leave poor Billy Bob alone.'

Tom pretends to zip his lip and bends over into his own downward dog. 'So, what's bringing you to Sydney, Chrissy?'

I lift slightly from my forward bend to answer. 'I need a change, something big. And I've always wanted to visit Australia, so it seemed like the perfect opportunity.'

I glance over at Tom, who nods in understanding as he rocks back to stretch his calves.

'It was perfect timing when I met Chloe, and she offered me a place to stay,' I continue. 'What about you? Why are you heading back?'

'We've been in the UK for six months. We were planning to run a bar in Sydney and wanted to learn from someone who had already done it. The bar we met at—'

'The V Bar?'

'Right. Janine's sister owns it.'

'That's a really great bar,' I say evenly. My stomach lurches. Here, at the back of the plane, it's fun to pretend that Janine isn't just up there in her seat. It's not like I would ever try to break up a couple (and not that I could), but this little make-believe world back here is making the flight so much more enjoyable. And okay, I may not have mentioned Brad, but where's the harm in that? Brad is not the only reason I'm travelling to Sydney.

'So, where will you be setting your bar up?' I ask as I walk my hands back to softly rise out of downward dog.

'We're looking at places around the Eastern Suburbs,' Tom replies, unfolding his body to stand tall. He gives his legs a shake relieving the tension from the pose. 'Well, we were. We broke up a couple of months ago. Janine still wants to go ahead with the bar together, but considering she cheated on me, it's not the easiest situation. We're still friends, but it's hard to move past that.'

'I thought Janine said you were partners.'

'Business partners.'

I feel giddy with relief. He is single. I am not some home-wrecking tart.

Tom lifts his right foot and presses the sole against his left inner thigh. 'Ever tried tree pose?'

Thank god, another Body Balance classic. Emboldened by my familiarity with the pose, I lift my foot to mimic his stance. My confidence, however, is short lived as I wobble precariously.

Tom chuckles. 'Let me help.'

He drops to one knee triggering a flurry of my secret wedding proposal fantasies and reaches out to support my ankle, adjusting my foot placement.

The warmth of his palm against my ankle makes my skin sparkle. Thank god I shaved my legs.

'Maybe we should do a more advanced pose,' Tom suggests, retracting his hand abruptly.

I notice his cheeks are faintly flushed and I wonder if he felt the spark too.

'How about the Crane?' he asks, his eyes not quite meeting mine.

We both crouch down. I've attempted this one before, following a YouTube guru who made it look like the easiest thing in the world. But I enjoy Tom showing me what to do, so I let him demonstrate as he sits like a frog with his palms on the ground and then leans forward to take his feet off the floor. I notice the ripple of muscle in his biceps.

'This is ridiculous,' I huff, struggling as I lean forward and attempt to lift my feet off the ground. I should keep my eyes focused on the carpet between my hands, but instead I creak my neck up to peep at him.

The second I turn my head, I wobble. I try to correct my balance, but I'm falling. Tom glances over and, caught off guard, he teeters and topples, landing with an 'oof'.

'Nailed it,' Tom jokes, his eyes crinkling at the corners.

'Clearly we are master yogis,' I say through a giggle.

I brush a strand of hair from my face, cheeks flushed. Our gazes lock for a moment longer than expected.

Tom clears his throat and leaps to his feet, seemingly flustered, and reaches a big hand down to help me up. He sits on the step that leads to the upper floor and taps the spot next to him, indicating I should sit there.

'So, tell me about your life in Australia,' I say as I sit, enjoying the way my leg presses against his.

'I'm a lifeguard. Well, I was a lifeguard. I'll be going back to that whilst we plan the bar stuff. I can't wait. There's nothing like spending my days on the beach and doing something that makes a real difference. And I'm looking forward to seeing Ned. We've had a house sitter in to care for him.'

'Ned?'

'Our dog.' Tom explains, his gaze softening.

'You have a dog. I love dogs,' I gush.

Tom grins at my reaction. 'You'd love Ned. He's a big softy. The hardest bit about being away has been leaving him.'

'What's gonna happen with Ned? Will he stay with you?'

Tom runs a hand through his hair, visibly conflicted. 'I'm not letting him go, but I'm not sure. Janine loves him too. It's all so messed up.'

'You're still planning to live together?'

'No, I have the original lease of the flat, so I'll stay there, but I don't want to make things hard for Janine. She's going to stay with a friend for now.'

'Bloody hell,' I say.

'Bloody hell,' he mocks my accent with a playful smirk.

'Oi,' I jab him in the ribs with my elbow.

We sit there, legs touching, chatting about our lives, our families and our friends. I don't know how much time passes. Speaking to Tom feels so comfortable.

'So, tell me why you're vegan?' he asks.

'I guess I just don't want anyone to suffer on my account. What the animals go through is heartbreaking,' I say.

'You really care, don't you?'

'Of course. Don't you?'

He frowns. 'I guess I haven't thought about it.'

'Now is the time,' I say and slap him on the thigh. My hand lingers there for a moment. He places his hand on mine and the warmth of his skin makes me bump up and down with a jolt of energy.

An announcement sounds for us to put our seat belts on. Oh, okay, so the bump was from turbulence, not some unseen love force.

'Back to your seats, you two,' says the flight attendant, raising his eyebrows as he notices Tom's hand on mine.

I nod and stand up, feeling like I am walking on air, which I guess I am, kind of. Tom is following behind me. I could turn around and kiss him right now. It's all I want to do, even with the flight attendant watching us. I want to lean into the fizzing energy between us.

I sit down and buckle up. Janine lifts her eye mask as Tom sits down.

'Hey, you,' I hear her sleepy voice as she reaches across the aisle and squeezes his hand.

'Hey, you,' he echoes and squeezes her hand back before letting it go and picking up his book to read.

That sure didn't look like an interaction between a couple who have broken up. I feel sick and not just because of the plane bumping around. Have they really split up? Did I imagine the sparks with Tom? I'm such an idiot. Of course, he has a girlfriend. Humiliation washes over me as I replay the flirtatious yoga session in my mind. Yet again I have projected my fantasies onto an unattainable man who was probably just trying to be friendly. I take a deep, steadying breath.

One thing I'm sure of is that as soon as we land in Sydney, I'm meeting Brad, a gorgeous Aussie hunk. Someone who is definitely single, who is into me and who is going to help me change my life.

As we prepare for landing at our stopover in Singapore, I close my eyes and lean into the daydream. New Chrissy, here I come.

12

I was only in Singapore for a couple of hours, but it was a welcome break from my plane neighbours. I wandered into the cactus garden where the air was hot and sticky. It felt like I was a million miles away from the UK and all my problems.

Now I'm back on the plane with another long slog ahead of me. Janine and Tom are chatting and laughing, looking every inch the loved-up couple.

I mentally slap myself for dreaming up that whole flirtation. I resolve not to think about Tom anymore. Brad is the one I can't wait to meet.

After many more TV shows and some Tom-free cabin walkthroughs, there is a buzz in the air. I check the flight path and see we are nearly there. One and a half hours to go, which after twenty hours seems like nothing. I don't want to faff around, getting changed at the airport. I want to be out of there as quickly as possible and into Brad's arms. I had better get ready now.

I pull my flight bag down from the overhead locker and head to the toilets. Locking myself in, I gaze at my face in the mirror. My hair is a bit more of a mess than usual and my skin is grey, but otherwise not a total disaster.

First up, make-up. I go for a chic cat eye with flicked eyeliner and a bold lip. I may not be a make-up expert like Jess, but I have to say, that's not a bad job. I dab some high-lighter on my cheeks and add some curl serum to my hair. After washing my hands, it's time. Time for the big outfit change.

I take off my top first and after a few false starts, get my arms through the right holes in my new bra. There are multiple straps because apparently many straps equals mucho sexy. The black criss-cross on my back looks, I guess, risqué-chic in a high-end escort kind of way. My flesh doesn't bulge out as much as I expected. There's not much to the bra itself, but perhaps this is the upside of having teeny boobs. I don't need the support.

Now for the knickers. Removing my tracksuit bottoms is easier said than done in this tiny cubicle. With a shimmy and a wriggle, I've done it. I pull on the skimpy knickers and study the effect in the mirror. Oh, dear. These are way too small. You know those stress balls you squeeze, and the gel pops out in blobs? Yeah, I look like that. These knickers have lots of straps too. I poke the flesh on my bum that oozes between the fabric. It's already reddening. I still have a pair of clean, comfy bikini briefs in my bag, but they're faded from the wash. Still, I don't know if I could move or sit down in these strappy ones without mutating my bum. I pull them off and smooth out the angry ridges they have left on my skin. Okay, bikini briefs it is.

As I stand in my obscene bra and faded knickers, I retrieve the dress from my bag and hold it against me. It's stunning. Yup, the sales lady was right. This colour looks lovely against my hair. I slide the dress over my head and stretch it over my arms so I can shimmy into it. It's a bit tighter than I was hoping for but needs must.

Wriggling my body, I manage to tug the lower part of the dress over my shoulders and my chest whilst my arms still point above my head. I squirm, trying to force the dress down further. I'm getting hot now, but it will all be worth it in the end. Except... bugger, this dress will not pull over my belly and the soft material now feels as rigid as metal. I stop my worm-like wriggling and take a deep breath. All I can see is blue. Okay, let's be honest, this is not going to work, Brad will just have to see me in my comfy clothes. At least I have stunning make-up. Time to reverse this whole operation.

My hands are still trapped over my head, so I grab the fabric from the inside and pull at the dress. It hardly budges at all. I tug at the fabric again and succeed in inching the hem of the dress above my boobs. It's now wedged in an immovable roll of fabric under my arms. Panic rises within me. Aeroplane bathrooms are tiny enough without the additional challenge of being stuck in a tube of the most restrictive fabric ever invented. I am so angry at this dress. How dare it pretend to be soft and stretchy, when all along it was hard and unforgiving?

I think I'm going to cry. This is why wearing a body-con dress is on my Things To Do When I'm Skinny list. I'm not skinny yet. I should never have defied the list.

'Everything okay in there?' I hear a knock at the door. 'There's a bit of a line out here.' I recognise that voice. It's Janine.

'Won't be long,' I answer, trying to sound like I am not being digested by a blue fabric snake.

Tears of frustration streak down my face. I have to get out of this. I thrash about. If anything, the thrashing makes things worse. I'm sweating and the sweat has made the fabric stick even more. There's now no way of moving this thing up or down.

There is another knock on the door.

'Sorry,' says Janine. 'All the toilets are in use, and I am bloody bursting. Could you hurry up?'

'I... need... help.' I hiccup and lean my body against the door.

'Chrissy, is that you?'

'Y-y-yes,' I stutter. 'I'm stuck in my *dress*.' The last word comes out as a wail.

'Can you open the door? I can help you,' she says.

'I'll try, but please don't let anyone else see.'

Unlocking the door is quite the manoeuvre as I crouch with my bum pressed against the toilet bowl and my arms outstretched. I feel immense relief as the lock moves across. The door opens away from me.

'Oh my,' says Janine. 'You have got your knickers in a knot. Don't worry, we'll get you out of it. Hold on..., Tom, Tom, can I get some help here?'

Oh no. No, no, no. I cannot have a man, especially Tom, see me like this.

'No, it's okay,' I call out. 'We can deal with this, just the two of us.'

'Jesus Christ.' I hear Tom's voice. 'What's going on here?'

'She's stuck,' says Janine, and I swear there's a smile in her voice.

I'm so ashamed. The kindest thing would be for someone to throw me off this plane right now.

'Okay, you take that side, I'll take this one and let's yank it off,' says Tom. 'But first... hang on.'

His arms are around me as he ties his hoodie around my waist to cover my modesty. I'm grateful and utterly humiliated at the same time. Any other time I may have felt a tingle as his breath landed on my stomach, but not now. Now I want to die.

'Right. Here we go, Chrissy. We'll get you out of this.' I

feel Tom's hands at my left side and Janine's smaller ones on my right side and then they pull. The dress does not shift.

'We need scissors,' says Tom in a lowered voice.

'No one is allowed to bring scissors on the flight,' says Janine. 'Unless...'

I hear footsteps retreating and Janine's loud voice.

'Excuse me, this woman is stuck in a dress, and we need to cut her out.'

I don't hear the other side of the conversation although I swear I pick up the words *fat* and *too small*.

Two sets of footsteps return.

'Hello, madam, I'm Clint, the senior flight attendant and I'm here to help you.' His voice is calm as if he sees this kind of thing every day. 'Do I have your permission to cut the dress?'

'Please,' I sob. 'I just want to get it off.'

Clint tugs at the fabric.

'It's tough stuff,' he says. 'Were you getting ready to meet someone special? Such a shame, the colour is stunning.'

I appreciate Clint's effort, but I'm not in the mood for small talk right now.

'Can I get a hand?' he calls, and I feel large hands pulling at the fabric at my side. Tom. Ugh.

I hear a beep and a crackle. 'Come in, assistance needed in toilet cubicle three. Code fuchsia. I repeat code fuchsia.' Clint says into his radio.

Code fuchsia? I briefly wonder if this is a specific code for 'woman wedged in dress'.

'No one else,' I plead.

'Sorry, madam, we've got to get you out of this for your own health and these scissors are barely making a dent in the fabric.'

'Just leave me,' I say.

'Can't do, madam. This is a health risk. We don't want you having a heart attack here on the plane. That wouldn't be a very good start to your holiday, would it? Ah Gracie, excellent. Can you take one side and I'll take the other?'

I let out a sob. I'm getting dizzy. Is it possible to die from being trapped in a dress? As the team tugs at the fabric, I stagger forward and feel arms under my elbows on each side.

'Woah,' says Clint. 'Come in, Margaret, please call a doctor for toilet cubicle three.'

The ding-dong of the PA system sounds.

'Attention please. Do we have a doctor on the plane? Please make your way to the back of the main cabin.'

So that's it. I guess my dignity is dead.

For a moment they leave me be and sit me on the toilet seat, arms still above my head.

'Concentrate on deep, slow breaths,' says Clint. 'Oh, are you a doctor?'

'Yup mate,' says an older man's voice.

'Me too,' says an Irish woman.

'Me three,' says an American man.

'I think she's having a panic attack, but because of her size I'm concerned about a potential heart attack,' says Clint.

They're talking about me like I'm not here.

'Please get the dress off me,' I wail as someone takes my wrist to check my pulse.

'In my professional opinion, you shouldn't proceed,' says the American doctor. 'Wait until we're in Sydney and get the tools you need to remove the item.'

'I'd have to agree,' says the female doctor. 'Due to the size of the patient, heart issues are a risk.'

'Um... excuse me. Sorry to be a bother. I've been watching and wondered if this may be any use,' says a woman with an Essex accent.

'Oh, that's not a bad idea,' says the flight attendant.

'Hi love,' says the Essex voice. 'I'm Tina, I'm a beautician, so don't worry, I've seen it all before. What I've got here, love, is some lube. Strawberry lube. It's good for sensitive skin, which yours is, judging by the welts. So, can I lube you up to see if we can get this dress sliding right off?'

'Go ahead,' I say in a small voice.

'Lovely. Now I have some gloves on from that sweetie of a flight attendant. I only have 100ml of lube. You know, flight rules and all that, but thanks to my hubby getting stage fright we didn't use any at all, so that's a boon for you.'

'No, I bloody well didn't,' a male voice calls out from further up the cabin.

I stay quiet.

'Okay, here we go.' The rubber-coated hands apply sweet-smelling gel under the dress. As the team attempt to remove the dress again, it is clear that the lube has done nothing more than make everything sticky.

'Excuse me,' an elderly voice sounds from nearby, 'I'm a priest and would like to offer my spiritual help to the patient.'

'Oh, isn't that lovely?' says the flight attendant.

'If the patient is a Catholic, I wonder, should I read her last rites?'

I let out a frustrated groan and yell, 'I just need to get out of this bloody dress!'

'Heavenly Father,' says the priest. 'This may be beyond my abilities.' He chants a prayer in Latin.

My breathing is getting faster and faster.

'Oh, for god's sake,' says Tom.

He grabs the dress on both sides and strains, like a man possessed, putting all his might into freeing me. I wriggle to help the process. After what seems like hours, but is probably thirty seconds, Tom lets out a groan and yanks even harder. The dress finally succumbs. Now past my shoulders, it slides easily over my head and off my arms. The momentum of the tug sends Tom tumbling backwards out of the cubicle. I try to steady myself, but I have been pulled forward too. As I fall, I glimpse myself in the cubicle mirror. My perfect make-up has run in black streaks down my face, my skin is bright red and the bra... oh god the bra. It looks worse than I ever imagined. Flesh bulges out of the 'sexy' holes in angry welts. Sweat is streaming down my body and sticky lube covers my top half.

I fall out the toilet doorway and into the cabin, knocking over the flight attendant, and landing straight on top of Tom.

I roll off to his side. He looks winded and his shirt is wet with lube and sweat, but I can't think of anything but being free from the dress.

'I'm sorry,' I say through fast breaths.

The flight attendant rights himself and the doctors rush over. The older doctor places both me and Tom in the recovery position and a sheet is placed over me, much like I'm a dead body. It's only then that I see how many people have crowded around me, even children and the elderly are enjoying the spectacle.

'My baby, my darling. You're a hero! It's okay; you're safe now,' says Janine, stroking Tom's hair.

'I'm fine,' says Tom.

'You've been squashed,' she says, her eyes flicking to me.

'I didn't squash him. I... I'm not an elephant,' I protest, my cheeks burning.

Janine's eyes narrow as she stares at me. 'Now I know where I recognise you from.' She points a finger at me. 'Instagram. She's the one we laughed at. Remember? Remember, Tom?' Her tone is triumphant.

As Clint the flight attendant mops my brow with a damp cloth, I close my eyes and tune out the noise.

13

One benefit of making an absolute tit of myself on a long-haul flight is that I got spirited off to a secret flight-attendant area. They let me lie down and a kind woman lent me her make-up remover so now my face is clean and fresh.

The flight attendant team turned out to be lovely and let me leave the plane last to avoid having to deal with everyone who had seen my little display. Now, as I roll my luggage over the moving walkway in Sydney airport, I wonder if I imagined the whole palaver. I am in my comfy tracksuit again. No ridiculous underwear, just my reliable knickers and no bra. I stopped in the loos to freshen up and whilst I may not be making the glam entrance I had planned, I feel so much better.

I can't believe how I acted on that flight; flirting with a

man who has a partner, believing his lies and making a total prat of myself. Go me. I resolve to put it all behind me and pretend it never happened.

Excitement bubbles in my stomach as I near the arrivals hall. I'm actually here in Sydney, Australia. And I'm about to wrap my arms around the potential man of my dreams and give him an enormous hug.

I take a deep breath as I walk through the doors. There are so many people here waiting for loved ones, but there, on the other side of the barrier, is a man holding a sign with my name on it in pink graffiti-style writing with love hearts all around it. He has a welcome balloon tied to one wrist and a koala balloon tied to the other.

'Brad,' I gasp. I rush over to his side of the gates, and he walks towards me, dropping his sign. I let go of my bag and throw my arms around him like he's a long-lost love rather than a Zingles date. As we hug, his hard body presses against my much softer one. He lifts me off my feet and squeezes me.

'You're here,' he says, and his Australian accent is even more gorgeous in real life.

'I'm here.' I push a lock of dark blonde hair off his face and gaze into his blue eyes. He looks exactly like his profile pics. Well, apart from one small thing. It's not a big deal at all, but he is a lot shorter than he said. He reckons he's five foot eleven, but he's shorter than me. I'd say he's five foot seven, but who cares? He's even more muscular than he looked in his photos, and his lazy smile makes my insides all fizzy. He smells of coconut sun cream, of holidays. He's wearing jeans and a Brad's Bootcamp tie-dye sleeveless T-shirt.

'You're even hotter in real life,' Brad says. He holds both sides of my face and gently kisses me. I close my eyes and all the horror of the flight melts away. As we part, he looks me up and down, shaking his head slowly, as if not believing his luck. And then he picks up my bag in one hand and grabs my hand in the other.

'Time to introduce you to Australia, I guess,' he says.

I bop one of the balloons. 'Thanks for these.'

'Want a coffee or anything before we go back to the car?'

'I'd just love to get into the fresh air,' I say.

'Then, Chrissy, your wish is my command.'

As we walk towards the bright sunny day, I glance around and spot Tom and Janine by the coffee stand. Tom is staring at me, looking like an abandoned puppy. I guess I didn't mention Brad to him on the aeroplane. But he wasn't honest about his relationship either. As he holds up a hand in a wave, I turn away, back to gorgeous Brad with his gorgeous face and his gorgeous hair.

As we walk out of the doors, the balmy warmth envelops me. It's hard to believe I'm here. Whilst my body is so tired I could collapse in a heap, my mind is busy trying to take everything in.

'This is me,' Brad says as we approach a bright yellow hatchback.

He opens the boot and puts my suitcase in, before running around and opening the passenger door for me.

'What a gent!' I say.

Brad tips a pretend hat towards me. 'Okay, m'lady, where to? Should we head to the beach? Do you need to rest? Are you hungry?'

'I want to explore, but that flight wrung out every bit of energy I have. Do you reckon I could have a rest first?'

'No worries,' he says, and I laugh at the use of a stereotypical Aussie phrase. 'Do you want me to drop you at your friend's now or back to mine first?'

'Chloe is at work until later, so maybe I could come back to yours? But I'd like to get to know each other before we... you know?'

'Of course. You're gonna love Coogee. It's a nice pad too. Not far from the beach.'

I pull out my phone and send Chloe a text, letting her know what I'm up to.

Brad drives and I stare out the window. As we leave the big, bland buildings of the airport, palm trees and gum trees are dotted everywhere. And, oh my gosh, cockatoos in the trees. I've only ever seen these beautiful white parrots in a dismal pet shop in Brighton when I was a kid. And then there is the water. There are glimpses of it all around. Sparkling, inviting.

Brad squeezes my thigh, and I place my hand on top of his.

'I can't believe you're here,' he says.

'Me neither, but I'm so glad I am.'

After twenty minutes, we reach Coogee. As we drive down a steep hill, I see the ocean and can't wipe the grin off my face. We turn onto a street that runs parallel to the beach. The waves are gentle today and I can see people splashing in them.

The light is so bright that the colours are more intense here, the blue of the sky, the aqua of the ocean, the golden sand.

We make our way up the headland on the other side of the beach and pull into a driveway of a very grand house. It's huge with white painted timbers and light blue walls. I love blue houses, especially when they are by the sea.

'Wow,' I say.

'Not bad, eh?' says Brad, as he parks the car beneath a double car port. So, he's a personal trainer, who just happens to be rich? Maybe he trains the rich and famous? Maybe Rebel Wilson and Chris Hemsworth go to Brad's Bootcamp.

'Do you rent this place?' I ask.

'Yeah, nah.'

'It's amazing.'

'Not a bad spot. Let me show you.' He hops out of the car and runs around to open my door. As I get out of the car, he takes my hand, spins me around and stands behind me, his arms wrapped around me as if we are newlyweds on our honeymoon.

'This is incredible,' I say as I take in the view. We're higher up here and I can see the whole curve of the beach.

'You think you'll like it here?' he asks, spinning me back around to face him.

'Very much,' I say with a smile.

Inside, the house is even grander, with giant windows overlooking the ocean and a spiral staircase. It's all immaculate. I wonder if Brad has a housekeeper, or is he just one of those rare, tidy men I've heard about?

The floor is tiled and as he leads me into the lounge I see a luxurious teal rug, a huge TV and the comfiest-looking light grey sofa with white and teal cushions. It's all so stylish. I look at this man in his jeans, black flip-flops and tie-dye top and he's gorgeous, but I wouldn't have picked him as being into interior design.

'Could I get a drink?' I ask.

'Sure,' he says. I follow him through to the open-plan kitchen, which is separated from the garden by glass sliding doors. I notice Brad's wetsuit thrown over the outdoor furniture and a surfboard propped up against the table. And there behind a gate is a pool and a jacuzzi.

'What the...? You live right by the beach, and you have a pool?'

Brad shrugs. 'You don't like it?'

'I love it,' I say. 'It's so pretty.' The outdoor area looks like a mini resort with two palm trees and an assortment of other rainforest-type plants.

'Got your swimmers?' he asks, his face brightening.

'Yup,' I say.

'Unless you just want to go in naked?' He winks.

'Haha, maybe another time. I'll grab my swimsuit.'

Brad shows me to the bathroom so I can get changed.

In my usual dating life, I do pretty much anything to avoid a guy seeing me naked. I'm a lights-out-only kind of girl and in the morning I make sure to cover up before I get out of bed. I know it makes me sound like a total prude, but I have this immense fear of a guy bursting out laughing, holding his head in his hands and saying, 'I must have had the beer goggles on last night.'

I've never been one to rip my clothes off on a first date and I don't intend to start now. Well, apart from showing my body to most of the people on the plane and readers of the tabloids, of course.

Safely in my black one-piece with its ever-so-flattering padded bra and control waist, I wrap a blue sarong around me and walk back to the pool.

'You're beautiful,' says Brad as he sees me. He's waiting by the pool and passes me a glass of water. 'Thought this would be better than a soft drink,' he says. 'I haven't forgotten my promise to help you get in shape.'

I feel a twinge of embarrassment. If you tell someone they are beautiful but then comment on their need to lose weight, does that nullify the compliment? But I remind myself that I'm the one who told him I want to change.

Taking a gulp of the icy drink, I follow Brad to the jacuzzi. I place my glass and my phone down, let my sarong fall and climb into the warm bubbles before he has even turned around. He slides in next to me and his leg slips against mine.

Squeezing my thigh under the water, he looks at me with a giddy smile. 'I can't believe you're here,' he says. 'This is incredible.'

'I know. I'm in Australia, with a gorgeous man. Who would've thought? Look at these muscles.' I run my hand over his bicep. Any excuse to touch that tanned skin.

'And I am here with this beautiful British redhead,' he says. He brushes a curl away from my face and moves closer. His blue eyes gaze into mine and he kisses me. It's deep and tender. Brad knows what he's doing. I lean into it and run my fingers through his hair and down his back. I had planned not to let things go further than a kiss, but as we kiss harder and with more intensity, it's hard to resist when he pulls me closer. He kisses my neck, and his hands are at the top of my swimsuit, slowly pulling the straps off my shoulders. Briefly, my mind wanders to the padded bra. Oh no, he's going to be disappointed when he sees my boobs are a full cup size smaller in real life, but there is no shocked gasp as he pulls the straps down.

I close my eyes and throw my head back, enjoying the sensation of the bubbles against my back and his tongue against my skin.

And then I hear the shocked gasp I have been dreading, but it's not from Brad.

'Bradley!'

My eyes ping open. There at the back door is a slim woman with a brunette lob, dressed from head to toe in white linen.

'Mum.' Brad throws me off him and I land with a splash on the other side of the jacuzzi.

14

I hold both hands over my breasts and sink beneath the bubbles, struggling to pull my swimsuit straps back on without giving more of a show.

Behind the woman, a man appears in board shorts and a white vest. He looks just like Brad, but older. The man winks at Brad, and I cringe internally.

'You must be Chrissy,' says the woman with a smile that doesn't reach her eyes.

'Gosh, I'm so sorry! I didn't know Brad was expecting company,' I blunder.

'We've been looking forward to meeting you. How about you towel off and we can show you our home?'

'Um... okay, that's so kind. Do you live nearby?'

The woman narrows her eyes and fiddles with her pearl necklace.

'Bradley, did you pretend this was your house again?' says his mum with a mean-spirited laugh. 'If only you were successful enough to afford a house like this.' She turns to me. 'Personal trainers barely earn enough to rent a place in the Eastern Suburbs, let alone buy. Now if Brad had studied law as we wanted, he wouldn't have to pretend.'

'I didn't pretend at all,' protests Brad. 'I thought it was obvious. I mean, we have family photos everywhere. And I already told you, Chrissy is helping me to become a successful personal trainer. She's my project. She's gonna be my best before-and-after yet.' He sounds like a child bragging about a new toy. 'Aren't you?' He turns to me.

'I guess,' I say, although I hadn't realised this is what he meant by helping me. I just thought we might burn some calories with a few walks on the beach and some... um... rolling around.

'Good work, son,' says Brad's dad.

He walks over to me and holds out his hand. 'I'm Doug.'

'Dad, leave her alone,' whines Brad.

I poke my hand out of the bubbles and shake Doug's hand.

'Nice to meet you,' I say. 'Again, I'm so sorry about this.'

'We're just happy to see Brad happy.'

I nod, very keen to end the awkward meet-the-parents moment.

'Don't hold back on our account.' Doug stares at me.

'We've raised Brad to be sex-positive, just like Teresa and me, haven't we, love?'

'Within reason,' says Teresa. 'I'll put some tea on. Come on, Dougie, leave them to it.' Teresa raises her eyebrows and turns away, followed by her partner.

I am so embarrassed. My face must be bright red by now. Brad takes hold of my arm and pulls me back towards him and onto his lap, wrapping his arms around me. I wriggle away and sit next to him on the jacuzzi seat.

'Not now,' I hiss. 'Could you get me a towel? I don't want to get out where they can see me.'

'You don't have to get out, just pretend they're not there,' he says.

I turn and look through the glass doors into the kitchen. Doug catches my eye and waves. I wave back and turn back to Brad.

'No, Brad, this will have to wait. Why didn't you tell me you lived with your parents?'

'Oh, I see. Now you know I'm not some rich celebrity trainer, you're not interested?'

'Don't be silly,' I say. 'I just would have liked some warning, so my first impression to your parents wasn't a naked one.'

Brad's cheeks flush red. 'I'm sorry,' he says, and my anger at him melts away.

Why did I assume Brad owned this place? There's no shame in staying with your parents to save up. God knows I wouldn't have been able to afford rent in Brighton if it wasn't for sharing with Jess. And she wouldn't be able to afford it if her parents hadn't bought the flat.

'I've been so excited about you coming here,' Brad says. 'I didn't think to mention it. My parents are cool, I promise.'

'They seem lovely, but you know, I'm staying with my friend Chloe in Bondi. I wonder if it would be a good idea to head over there soon?'

'And we'll meet up for your training tomorrow?'

'Um... yup.'

'Well, I wish you'd stay, but I guess if you're more comfortable at your friend's, I get it. Hang on, I'll get you a towel. Let me show you my room at least, and you can get changed.'

'Thanks,' I say, and peck him on the cheek. He smiles that sweet smile and hops out of the tub. I feel bad for disappointing him.

I'm sitting on the balcony, a glass of rosé in hand. Chloe's apartment isn't half as posh as Brad's parent's place. It's in a back street of North Bondi, so there are no ocean views, but it's only a ten-minute walk to the beach and there's a bustling holiday vibe.

Chloe has two bedrooms. My one is pretty small with ocean-themed art by Chloe on the walls. She's way more talented than she let on. The whole place is cute, cosy and messy with doodles everywhere, nail varnishes dotting the surfaces and piles of sketchbooks on the floor. I feel at home already.

'I still can't believe it,' says Chloe, taking a swig of her wine. 'Imagine not telling you it was his parents' place.'

'I hope I haven't hurt Brad's feelings by leaving early. It's not like we had planned to spend all our time together, but I think maybe he expected that. He took me to his room to get changed, and he has a massive bed and an ocean view. I was like, considering he has an ensuite, would I even have to see much of his parents? But then his dad knocked on the door for a little chat and I was like, get me to Chloe's.'

Chloe snorts into her glass. 'I don't blame you. It's too soon to meet the parents, let alone live with them.'

'Brad was a sweetie when he drove me here, though. When we kissed goodbye, I got a definite tingle. Like there's a genuine spark. I just feel bad for him, and I don't know if that's the sexiest thing.'

Chloe waves her hand dismissively. 'Don't even worry about it for tonight. Look around. You're in bloody Australia.'

I gaze down at the palm trees across the road. There's a sweet jasmine smell which reminds me of all good holidays.

'When are you seeing him again?' she asks.

I grimace. 'That would be tomorrow morning at six a.m.'

'Are you kidding me?'

I shake my head. 'Nope. New country, new me, remember? Brad's running his beach bootcamp and I'm going to take part.'

Chloe looks horrified, her eyes wide. 'Rather you than me. You won't be seeing me out of bed until at least ten. Six a.m. is obscene.'

I reach over and pat her knee, giving her a pleading look. 'I was hoping you would come along.'

'Sorry, Chrissy, but if exercise is part of the terms of this friendship, I'm calling it off. That's a deal-breaker.'

I shrug, grinning as I finish my drink. 'No pain, no gain though, right?'

here am I? Who am I? And why is my alarm going off in the middle of the night? Still half asleep, I grab my phone from the side table. It's five a.m.

I desperately want to crawl back under my sheets, but then I think of gorgeous Brad who will be waiting for me at the beach. I also think of the old me, who I've left behind in the UK. She may not want to get up at five a.m., but I do.

Do I?

Yes, yes, I do.

I am now the kind of person who bounces out of bed into the day and enjoys a swift jog on the beach, a few burpees and a dip in the ocean.

I swing my legs out of bed and, in a bleary daze, pull on the workout gear I had laid out the night before. Well, when I say workout gear, I mean the nearest thing I had in my suitcase. I'm not exactly known for my extensive fitness wardrobe. I've gone for black leggings, a sports bra and my softest, stretchiest top. The bright pink top is 'my colour' or so Chloe said when I modelled it for her last night.

I pull on my trainers and take a swig of water before walking through to the bathroom. As I study my face in the mirror, I notice some extra freckles have already come out since exposure to the Australian sun. I long to cover my skin with make-up and add mascara to my fair lashes, but I also realise I will most likely sweat the lot of it off.

I wash my face and add a healthy layer of factor 50. My hair looks kind of under control for once. Last night Chloe revealed a secret talent for hair and did me a Katniss Everdeen style plait which still looks pretty good. Maybe it will help me release my inner Katniss during bootcamp.

I grab my water bottle and throw my swimsuit, board shorts and a towel in my bag before creeping out of the door so as not to wake Chloe.

As I make my way down the stairs and open the main door out of the apartment block, I can't help but smile. The air is warm, the sun is rising, and rainbow lorikeets are making a racket in the gum trees. I may not have lost any weight or made much of a change in myself yet, but I am happier than I've been in a long time.

As I reach the seafront, I see there are already plenty of surfers out, little black figures bobbing on the waves. There are attractive people all around me. Joggers in tiny shorts, who somehow have no cellulite. And how do these women have huge boobs and no body fat? Unfair.

I've arranged to arrive fifteen minutes early to meet Brad. I wave as I see him at the end of the beach, laying out equipment on the sand. He runs over to me, throws his arms around my waist and lifts me up. How strong is this man?

'You're here,' he says with excitement in his eyes. 'Love your gear.'

I give a little twirl. 'Thanks.'

'This is where we'll be training. Pretty special, eh?' he sweeps his hand indicating the expansive beach around us.

'It's beautiful,' I say, before a hint of worry creeps into my voice. 'Do you reckon I'll be able to keep up with the others, though? I haven't trained since school.'

Brad chuckles lightly. 'I always give easier options for newbies. Oh, by the way, I made you something.'

He takes my hand and leads me back to his stuff. He reaches into his sports bag and pulls out a drink bottle with brown liquid inside it.

'Chocolate milkshake?' I ask.

'Kale and celery protein smoothie.'

'Oh.'

'And don't worry, I used pea protein instead of egg whites in yours. If you have that for brekkie every day, you'll be off to a great start.'

I open the lid and a strong, earthy scent wafts into my

nostrils. As I take a swig, I do my best not to screw up my face in disgust. I've had protein shakes before, but they were chocolate flavoured and tasted delicious. This is most certainly not chocolate.

I'm relieved when Brad takes the drink from me and puts it back in the bag.

'You can finish that in a moment, but before the others get here, let's take the pics.'

'The pics?'

'Yeah, the before pics.' He looks around me and assesses the beach for a suitable location.

'You're not gonna publish them online, are you?'

'Well, eventually, yes, but by then you'll be so hot you'll want your photos everywhere.'

A brief stab of hurt hits me in the chest. Does he not think I'm hot now?

'Come on,' he says, holding out his hand.

I take it and he leads me to the top of the steps and up to the walkway where all the perfect joggers are doing their thing. Along the beach wall are a series of graffiti artworks. He stands me in front of one that depicts the ocean in a mesmerising swirl of blues and greens. I notice the artist's Instagram handle in the corner. Oh my gosh.

'Brad, this is Chloe's work. You know the friend I'm staying with? She said she was an artist, but this is incredible. I had no idea. Can you take a photo of me here?'

'Sure, stand there.'

He steps back and holds up his phone. I give my biggest smile, pick one foot up off the floor like a fifty's actress and hold my hands beneath my chin in what I consider to be an adorable fashion.

'Let me see,' I say. 'Oh, she's so talented.' I send the photo over to Chloe.

'Could you change it up a bit for me?' asks Brad.

'I thought that one was pretty good.'

'We just need a few more,' he says. 'Okay, so stand facing the camera, arms by your sides. That's it.' He crouches down to take the photo.

Now, I may not be a professional model, but I do know that taking a photo from down there is the least flattering angle in the history of the world.

'Could you look down at the camera?'

I do as he says.

'Yup, that's good. And squeeze your legs closer together. Perfect. The only problem is we can't see your cellulite as it is. You don't have any shorts, do you?'

'No, I don't,' I snap. 'Just this and my swimming costume.'

'Yes, your cozzie. Can you put that on? It would be so much better for the before shots.'

'I'm not comfortable with that, Brad,' I say, unable to resist a miserable pout on my face.

'Fine, well, we can do that later. Now stand to your side, chin down, and don't suck your tummy in. That's it... great facial expression, and the other side... And finally, the back.

I'm just gonna come closer, see how you have these rolls of fat here.' He grabs my back. 'We want to see this. Oh hey, Marcel.'

I turn around to see a tower of a man in front of me.

'Bradley,' he says, taking off his dark blue hoodie to reveal a bright pink vest top which pops against his black skin. 'What are you doing to this poor woman? Hi,' he says, holding out his hand.

I shake it, so big, so strong.

'Before photos,' says Brad. 'Can you give us a hand?'

'No problem.' The man turns to me. 'I'm Marcel, by the way. Love the nails, pink is your colour.'

'Thanks,' I say. 'I'm Chrissy, I just arrived in Bondi yesterday and right back at you. Love the nails. Turquoise is your colour.'

'Well, I've gotta do something to make myself seem more gay. The ladies just throw themselves at me otherwise.' As he says this, a beautiful jogger ogles Marcel and almost trips over her own feet. 'What can I say? It's a curse to be this attractive. You know how it is, surely?'

'I wish.' I giggle, loving this man instantly.

'She will after I've finished with her,' says Brad. 'Okay, Chrissy, can you just turn back to the wall and then, Marcel, you stand at the side and just squeeze that fat right there.'

'Oh darling, no. I'm not squeezing this fabulous woman. It'll only get her hopes up. Look, the others are here. Don't you have enough of your terrible before shots? Isn't it time you started the physical torture portion of the morning?'

Brad sighs. 'Fine, these will do.'

'Can I see?' I say, walking over to him. He points his phone towards me and scrolls through.

'Oh no. These are awful.'

'That's the point,' he says with a straight face. 'These are your before photos.'

'But I don't have a triple chin like that, do I? It's a terrible angle. My face is miserable.'

'Of course it is. We haven't started the self-improvement. You haven't got anything to be happy about yet. Just wait until your after photos. You will be begging for me to post them.'

He turns around to the group, waves and jogs over the beach.

'Don't fret, dahl,' says Marcel, giving my shoulder a squeeze. His hands are large and warm. 'Sometimes I think these personal trainers are just out to hurt us, but we keep coming back. Maybe it's the eye candy?' He winks at me.

'Did he take photos like that of you?'

'Did he ever? Brad is an old school friend of mine, so he got me all the way back when I was a spotty teenager. I know, looking at this flawless skin, you'd never believe the acne, but it was there, and it was not pretty.'

'Well, you're perfect now.'

'No such thing, but you're a doll for saying so. Come on, let's go. I've got your back.'

As we walk over to the group, I see a huddle of women around Brad. There are six people in total. Why couldn't Chloe have come with me? I'm totally out of my depth. Every one of these gods and goddesses looks like they have just stepped out of a trending workout reel on TikTok.

'Most of you know how this works, but for the benefit of our newcomer, we treat this as a holistic healing experience, not just a physical bootcamp,' says Brad as we stand in a circle. 'We start the session by sharing one thing we are struggling with and one thing about our day that we are grateful for. We'll start with you, Marcel, and then work our way around.'

'Hi, I'm Marcel. So, today I'm struggling with saying no to a caramel macchiato, but I'm grateful for meeting someone new and fabulous.' He gestures towards me.

As we hear from the rest of the group, part of me is fascinated as these stunning humans talk about being grateful for 'using their inner power to say no to the chocolate brownie', and part of me is horrified.

'Hi.' I wave to the group and get a few small waves back. 'I'm Chrissy.' I glance at Brad, and he nods.

'Hi, Chrissy,' the group says in unison.

'Today I'm grateful to be here on this stunning beach surrounded by some of the most gorgeous people I've ever seen. I'm struggling with the thought of doing a bootcamp for the first time, but I appreciate the opportunity.'

When I finish, the group claps. I feel weirdly happy and accepted.

Brad is the last to go.

'Hi, I'm Brad.'

'Hi, Brad.'

'Today I am grateful for our newest group member, Chrissy. And in the spirit of honesty, I need to tell you all that Chrissy and I are an item. In fact, this woman came all the way from the UK just to be here with me.'

My cheeks heat up and I stare down at my feet.

'And I guess I'm struggling with the fact she chose not to stay with me, but I also admire her independence.'

Everyone claps.

'Okay.' He smacks his hands together. 'Let's get to it. To warm up, jog from here to the bollard and back. Then we'll get into partner boxing. Go, go, go.'

Everyone, including Brad, shoots off down the beach. I follow, going the fastest I can, which, to be honest, is not that fast.

I do my best to catch up with the others. It sure is hard to run on sand. I keep picturing the viral video of me holding my flab and it helps me to push through the discomfort. As the others turn around, I consider just turning around with them, but I keep going and make it to the bollard. The whole group makes a big fuss as I rejoin them.

Marcel hands me a pair of boxing gloves.

'You're with me,' he says as he picks up a pair of pads. 'Go for your life.'

I punch the pads as hard as I can, determined to show my strength in front of the group. As Brad yells instructions, I lean into my Katniss fantasy and punch harder.

Brad walks over to me. 'You need to change your stance up a bit. See how Mel's doing it? The power comes from your lower body.' He gestures towards one of the women, whose figure-hugging gear highlights a posterior that seems to have been sculpted by Michelangelo himself.

I adjust my footing to mirror hers.

'That's better. You've got it now,' says Brad. My skin tingles as he stands behind me and holds my arm out, going through the motions of a punch, guiding my fist to the pad.

'Okay, now try it again,' he says.

I do as I'm told and sure enough there's more power behind my punch.

'Now uppercut,' says Brad.

Marcel switches the positions of the pads. I bend down to punch them and must get it all wrong, as again Brad has to show me the correct form. Once he has shown me the upper-cut, the jab and the hook, I feel more confident. He stands at the side, yelling instructions.

'Jab, jab, jab, left hook, left hook, uppercut, uppercut, jab, jab, keep jabbing, harder, harder. That's it. Now higher, higher, lower, lower.'

As I try to follow Brad's instructions, I'm also trying to imagine myself beating up every single person that has ever said anything mean to me.

Take that, Cara Delling who said no one wants to be friends with a fatty, in year nine. Take that, Janine, with her stupid judgy face on the plane. Take that, Gareth, with his fat-shaming comments.

This is actually really satisfying.

'Jab, jab, lower, lower, higher, higher, keep jabbing.'

I go for it. I mean, I really go for it. My arms are aching, sweat is pouring off me and I let out a growl as I throw my hardest punch yet. The problem is the growl also covers up Brad's voice, so I don't hear him say *lower*.

As Marcel lowers his pads, I put all my power behind my fist and punch him square in the face.

16

Marcel falls straight back onto the sand, dropping the pads. His hands fly to his face, but there is no covering up the blood pouring from his nose. Everyone in the group has stopped what they're doing to crowd around him.

'I'm so sorry. Shall I call an ambulance?' I say.

'I think you've done enough,' Brad snaps and shoos me away like I'm an irritating mosquito.

Having recovered a little from the shock, Marcel sits up on his elbows and murmurs through a bloody face.

'It's okay, dahl, no ambulance necessary. I fancied a new nose. This is the perfect excuse.' He attempts a smile.

'Okay, everyone,' says Brad, addressing the group, 'this isn't an excuse for slacking off. Do as many push-ups as you can whilst I get Marcel sorted.'

As Brad takes one of Marcel's arms, I go to take the other one to help him up from the sand.

'That includes you, Chrissy. Push-ups.' Brad jerks his chin towards the group.

I turn back around, feeling like a naughty schoolgirl whose teacher punished the entire class instead of just her. Everyone is doing full push-ups, even the woman whose arms seem too skinny to hold a shopping bag, let alone her whole body.

I give it a go. I do okay lowering myself to the ground, but as I try to push up, my arms won't stop shaking. With all my effort, I manage to do one push-up. I lower myself again before feeling a hand on my bum.

'Keep your booty down,' says Brad, adjusting my position. This makes it much harder and as I get to the bottom of the push-up, I drop face-first into the sand.

Brad sighs.

The rest of the class is torture. I'm so much worse at every exercise than every other person. They are all friendly enough. I guess it's easy to be friendly when you look like a supermodel. Perfect bum lady Mel tries to make conversation as we hold either end of a thick rope and fling it back and forth to one another. But with salty sweat running in my eyes and my lungs bursting, I can't respond to her questions.

At the end of the longest forty-five minutes of my life, I collapse onto the sand, red-faced and covered in sweat.

'Okay, team, well done. Now let's cool off,' says Brad to

the group of shimmering supermodels. He high-fives everyone in turn as they strip off to their swimsuits.

The chiselled brigade are jogging towards the ocean like a Baywatch intro, whilst I try not to fall over as I wobble on one leg, attempting to remove my leggings. At least no one is watching me whilst I get changed. Like a contortionist, I hold a towel around myself and wriggle into my costume. I pull on my bright pink board shorts over the top, which cover up the worst of the cellulite at the top of my legs.

I gaze out at the ocean. It looks inviting and as I watch the gentle waves, the exhaustion leaves me and I am overcome with the fact that I am here, standing on Bondi bloody Beach. I start my own slow-motion jog to the ocean. I splash into the edge of the water as members of the bootcamp wave at me. The cold is an unexpected shock, but I dive straight in under a wave, allowing the water to pull back my hair.

I swim the short distance to the others and laugh as Brad swims over and holds me around the waist.

'You did amazing,' he says.

'Apart from assaulting your boot camp members?'

'Yeah, apart from that.'

I love the slippery feeling of his skin beneath the water. We duck under as another wave splashes over our heads.

'You know, you're a pretty great fitness mentor,' I say, and I peck him on the lips, tasting the salty water.

'And you are a pretty great fitness manatee,' he says, kissing me back.

'Mentee?' I say as I picture a manatee in eighties fitness gear.

'It's pronounced manatee. I'm gonna do a little swimming, okay?'

'Go for it,' I say. I float on my back, feeling like the aforementioned manatee and gaze at the sky, which is now bright blue. I take a moment to enjoy the sound of the ocean.

I could do this every day. I could come here to this beautiful beach and swim and be at one with nature. Turning onto my front, I propel forward into a breaststroke before diving under another wave.

As I pop up, I notice a blue piece of plastic floating in front of me. It doesn't matter where you are in the world, people just cannot stop themselves from littering. I reach out to grab the plastic to take it over to the bins. As I clutch the bag and turn to head to shore, an intense pain shoots up my arm and my thigh.

'Fuuuuuuuuuuuck!' I yell as the sting of a hundred bees hits me.

I throw myself towards the shore with a few wild strokes and then stagger up the sand like a sea monster.

17

'Aaaaah!'

The blue tentacles of a jellyfish are wrapped around my right arm, my swimming costume and my right thigh. I pull the creature off me from the body, the tentacles determined to remain stuck to my skin. There are angry red welts rising on my arm and thigh. I drop the jellyfish into the ocean before falling onto the sand and writhing around in pain. Hot tears roll down my cheeks as the pain intensifies. Through blurry eyes, I see a pair of powerful calf muscles standing next to me.

'You've been stung by a bluebottle.'

'Am I dying?' I sob, closing my eyes.

'Nope. I know it feels like it, but you'll be right. You've had a nasty sting, but the pain will fade. Come on, let's get you sorted.'

I'm pulled to my feet, dizzy from the shock and pain. The man puts my arm around his neck and takes most of my weight. He walks me past the lifeguard tower towards the Bondi Surf Club.

I look up at his face. It's him. It's Tom from the plane. Am I delirious? As we stand outside the surf club, I think back to every sitcom with a jellyfish sting that I've ever seen.

'Please don't pee on me.' I sob. 'No pee... No pee.'

Tom walks me into the shower room. The pain is so intense. Every gland in my body is on fire.

'Okay, pee on me,' I say, closing my eyes and turning my head so he can do his thing with some modesty.

Tom laughs. 'No need for that, this water will do the trick.' He turns on the shower and stands me under, allowing the warm water to run over my stings.

'Nice slow breaths, that's it. In and out, in and out,' he says, standing in front of me, holding my shoulders.

I focus on my breath as the hot water takes the edge off the throbbing pain.

'I'd say you have some of the best welts of the season there,' he says. 'Not the greatest introduction to Bondi, hey?'

'I dunno.' I try to smile. 'I g... g... guess I'm a real Aussie now.'

'Happens to the best of us.' He presses his radio and updates the tower on my condition, then dips his head to catch my eye. 'I have to say, I'm impressed by your commitment to an early morning swim.' He glances at his watch. It isn't even seven a.m.

'Bootcamp,' I say. 'It was h... h... hard.' I'm trying to suppress tears, which results in some very attractive hiccupping.

'Are you kidding? Day one in Oz and you're training? Are you mad?'

'I think so,' I say through another hiccup.

As the pain subsides, I notice Tom is wearing his blue lifeguard jersey. He may not have the bulging physique of Brad, but there's no denying how fit he is.

'You didn't give yourself much of a break, before getting back to work,' I say.

'I'm back on a casual basis whilst we try and sort business stuff out, but honestly, I'm pretty jet-lagged today.' I notice the 'we'. So much for him and Janine not being a couple. 'Where's your man, anyway?' he continues. 'Do you want me to give him a call?'

'My man? Oh, Brad. Um, no, it's okay. I'll go and find him later.'

'Look, Chrissy, about the plane, you know, the dress and—'

I hold up a palm. 'Let's not talk about it.'

'I just want to apologise. Some of the stuff Janine said wasn't cool.' He pauses. 'You must be sick of hearing that rubbish.'

'Yeah, I am,' I say, nodding slowly.

'Janine filled me in on the social media stuff, but you've got to understand, she's coming from a good place. She just—'

'Thanks, but I think I'll be okay now,' I say in a hurry to get rid of him. The last thing I need is to relive the humiliation of the flight.

'Are you sure? Just come to the tower if you need me. I'm on until two.'

'I'm gonna go back to Chloe's, but, yeah, I appreciate this.' I wave my hand in a vague gesture at the shower.

'Maybe pop into Woollies and get some Stingose for it on the way home.'

I nod and he turns away from me. I double over and concentrate on slow breaths.

'Chrissy?' he says, and I look up. 'It's good to see you again.'

I smile and a warm glow that isn't entirely from raging pain runs through my body.

18

'Did you pash him in the shower?' asks Chloe, glancing up from her sketchbook where she is drawing a seagull in charcoal.

'Well, I was in agony, so kissing Tom was the last thing on my mind.' I take a sip of tea. 'And he's got a partner, remember?'

'They've broken up,' says Chloe, a smirk playing at the corner of her mouth.

'Hmm, I'm not sure I believe that and I'm also dating someone, kind of.'

'You haven't even slept with Brad yet.'

'Only because his parents barged in on us.' I protest, placing my tea on the table a bit too forcefully.

A mischievous glint appears in Chloe's eyes. 'You should ask Tom on a date.'

'That is the worst idea you've had all day.'

'It's an awesome idea.'

'Even if he is single, he's not right for me. I'm... well, I'm me.' I gesture down across my body.

'Oh, get stuffed. Listen to you! "Woe is me. I'm a voluptuous beauty, boohoo."'

Chloe's high-pitched impression of me makes me giggle.

'You sound like Jess. When I filled her in on the plane debacle, she said the crowd was lucky to get a glimpse of me in my saucy underwear.'

'And she's right. Bondi bootcamps are all well and good, but don't beat up on how you look now. Show me this sting then. How bad are we talking?'

I pull the side of my dressing gown open to show her the welt on my thigh.

'Holy shit,' she says, her eyes widening. 'I guess you won't feel up to exploring with that?'

I shrug, pulling the dressing gown back over my leg. 'As much as I'd love to explore, I think I need to rest.'

'Fair enough. But if you're up to it later, there's a dog walking beach at Rose Bay. We could Uber over, watch the sunset and pat some dogs. We can take a few drinks and a little picnic.'

'That sounds like my perfect evening.'

Do I want to watch a sunset? Yes. Do I want to pet lots of gorgeous dogs? Definitely yes.

Chloe stands up, brushing her hands over her cut off

shorts to remove the charcoal dust, but only succeeds in spreading the black smudges. She grimaces at the black smears on her once clean clothes. 'I'm gonna head out for a shift in a bit, but it's just a couple of hours over the lunch rush so I'll be back soon. I'd better get cleaned up.' she says heading towards the bathroom.

'Bring me back a pie!' I call after her.

Chloe works at a vegan pie shop in Bondi. I'm not usually a pie lover, but when she gave me one to try last night, it was just about the yummiest thing I had ever tasted. According to Brad, as long as I track the calories, I can still eat that stuff, so yay for me. As much as I was hoping the Aussie Chrissy would love raw salads and celery juice, it turns out I'm still a sucker for comfort food.

I head into my bedroom and fall into bed. With the window open, I can hear people enjoying their Bondi day and a fan cools my aching body. I close my eyes, take a deep breath and relax.

What feels like only moments later, I hear the front door buzzer. I pull the sheet up over my head and ignore it.

'Chrissy, Chrissy,' Brad's voice calls from the street.

Rolling out of bed, I glance at the clock and see I have been sleeping for three hours.

I plod to the window and look down. Brad is pacing beneath.

'Hey, I'll buzz you up.' A little fizz bubbles within me at seeing him again.

I open the front door and am met with Brad's face, his brow wrinkled in worry. He pulls me into a hug.

'Ouch, careful,' I say as his body presses against my sting.

'What happened?' he asks, holding me at arm's length. 'I've been trying to call and haven't been able to get through.'

'I'm sorry,' I reply. 'My phone is still in my bag on silent. I should have messaged you.'

'Was the bootcamp too much? I thought you did well.'

'The bootcamp wasn't the problem.' I shake my head. 'I got stung by a bluebottle when we were swimming.' I lead him through to the kitchen and as I make us tea, I fill him in on my introduction to Australian wildlife, not going into detail about the lifeguard who helped me.

'No way. I didn't think there were bluebottles today. Oh man, that's quite the sting.' He takes my arm and holds it out. The angry red swirl stands out against my pale skin. 'What an introduction to Bondi, eh?' He smiles.

Tom said the same thing. A stab of guilt hits me in the gut, even though I've done nothing wrong.

'I've been resting and I'm a lot better now. It kind of took it out of me, though.'

'I got stung as a kid. If I get sick now, it still rises in this angry scar,' he says. 'I screamed the lifeguard tower down back then. So bloody painful.'

'Aww, poor little Brad. I bet you were a super cute kid.'

'If you think fat kids are cute.'

I laugh. 'Even cuter in my opinion.'

Brad presses his lips together. He gazes into my eyes, his face so close to mine I want to lean in and kiss him.

'Chrissy?'

'Yes?'

'Childhood obesity is no joke.'

And then he holds my face in his hands and kisses me as if he has just said the most romantic words ever. I blink in confusion before surrendering to the kiss. As our kisses become more urgent, he pulls back.

'Would you like me to take a better look at those stings?' he asks.

I nod and lead him through to the bedroom.

I wish I could turn off the lights, but the bright Bondi daylight is streaming into the bedroom, so there is no hiding my flab. I sit on the edge of the bed and Brad stands before me, taking off his shirt to reveal that perfectly sculpted body. He points to a very faint pink line on his abs.

'This is where I was stung.'

I trace my finger along the line. There's another more pronounced scar on his lower abdomen.

'What about this one? Does it hurt?'

'No. What about yours?' He pushes me back onto the bed and kneels over me. He holds out my arm and plants the tiniest little butterfly kisses along the scar. There is still some pain, but his touch is so light all it does is make me tingle.

His kisses move down my body and as his lips brush over my lower stomach a shiver runs through me. He pulls off my shorts. I gasp in pain as the shorts move over the sting on my thigh.

'Shall I kiss it better?' he says, looking up at me with twinkly eyes.

I nod.

Brad gently kisses around the scar, working his way slowly up my thigh.

I close my eyes and give in to the pleasure.

'You're so hot,' he says, looking up at me. 'Once you've lost all the weight, all the men will be after you. I'm gonna have some serious competition.'

I wince and it's not from the stings. My body tenses up. *Once I've lost all the weight.* He makes me sound like an obese hippo. I mustn't overreact, though. I mean, this is what he does. He's a personal trainer. I try to relax into his kisses.

He moves up my body, kissing my neck.

I run my hands down his back, lightly scratching with my fingernails.

'I want you,' he breathes.

'I want you too.'

'You are going to be so fit. You are going to be so beautiful,' he whispers urgently in my ear. 'All of this will be gone. Say goodbye, ugly fat.' He holds my stomach much as a doctor would if measuring my body fat percentage.

'Wait... what?' I pull myself away from him.

'You tease.' He smiles and pulls my hips back towards him.

'No, I mean it, Brad. Stop a minute.'

He looks mystified as I wriggle out from under him.

'I don't want to be your project. I want you to find me attractive now, not just in the future,' I say, pulling the sheet up to cover myself.

'I didn't mean that.' Brad sighs, lying down next to me. 'You are attractive now. It's just this is nothing compared to what you will be.'

'I don't want to be controlled,' I say and there is a tremble in my voice. 'I've been in that kind of relationship before. I don't want that again.'

'You mean in the bedroom? You can be on top if you like. Reverse cowgirl?'

'I don't mean in the bedroom,' I say, because let's be honest, I love the thought of being controlled in the bedroom. 'I mean, in life.'

'Don't you want to lose weight, though?'

'I do. I just want to do it on my own terms. And I need to enjoy the process, not be made to feel I'm not good enough.'

'I didn't mean that.'

'I know.' Now I look into those sincere blue eyes, I feel stupid. Brad didn't mean to offend me. I've totally ruined the moment. I think I'm going to cry.

'Come here.' Rather than being angry, he pulls me into a hug and holds me. He plants a kiss in my hair, and we lie together. 'I've been where you are,' he says softly. 'I've hated myself and thought there was no way anyone could find me attractive. I promise it gets better.'

I tilt my face up to him. He kisses my tears away and then kisses me on the mouth before pulling me into a hug again.

'Brad?' I ask.

'Yes.'

'Is it okay if we take things a bit slower? Could we spend some more time getting to know each other?'

'Oh... yeah, sure,' he says, not doing so well at covering up his disappointment. He kisses my forehead much like someone would kiss farewell to an elderly aunt.

'I'm sorry,' I say again, which I know is stupid. I mean, I'm not the one in the wrong here. I pull the sheet over myself and close my eyes. I wish I could press rewind and cover my body a whole lot better. Maybe invest in some blackout curtains. 'It's the sting. It really took it out of me.'

'Why don't you rest?' he says gently. 'I'll make you some tea.'

'Thanks.' I have now made the full transition to Brad's elderly aunt.

I'm not sure what the time is when I open my eyes. Chloe is whispering at me, 'Babe, are you okay?'

'I fell asleep. Is Brad still here?'

'He's watching sport,' she says, screwing up her face in disgust, 'but you know what else is here? Pies.' She holds up a paper bag and does a little happy dance in my doorway.

I smile. 'I'll be out in a sec.' My body aches as I slide out of bed, pull on my dressing gown and pad through into the living room.

'Hey, sleepyhead.' Brad flicks off the TV and walks over to me. 'Feeling better?'

'Yeah, thanks, I didn't realise how exhausted I was. You must have been bored out of your mind.'

'Yeah, nah, I was having a bit of a chill-out sesh here watching the cricket. Then each ad break I do push-ups or crunches.'

I nod. 'Thanks for waiting for me.'

'I wanted to make sure you were okay,' he says.

I catch Chloe's face as she makes an 'aww' expression.

'Okay, pie time,' says Chloe. 'Do you want one, Brad? I got extra. They're the ones that weren't perfect enough to sell, but they're good, just a bit misshapen, that's all.'

'I can relate,' I say as I sit on the sofa and draw my knees up to my chest.

Chloe swats at the air as if swatting away my remark. 'Shush you.'

Brad moves to the kitchen to inspect the pies. He lifts one and his brows knit together in scrutiny. 'Thanks. What are the macros?'

'At least fifty per cent protein,' says Chloe with a wink at me.

'It's not a joke,' says Brad. 'Chrissy is trying to get into shape. You don't want to derail her progress.'

I frown at him. 'I thought if I logged it in the app, I could eat whatever?'

'You have a lot to learn.' He lets out a weary sigh and shakes his head. 'Eat the pie this time if you want, but it can't be a regular thing.'

'Lighten up, man. You'll love it if you try it,' says Chloe.

Brad narrows his eye at the pie. 'Is there a real one? Like real chicken, not fake?'

Chloe crosses her arms across her chest. 'It is real. It's just made from plants.'

'Cute, but I'm being serious. I need my protein. I'm not being vain but keeping my body in shape is my business.'

'Dude, you're a health guy and you don't know there's as much protein in plants? Come on.'

Brad pulls his hand through his golden hair in frustration.

'I'll try it... for Chrissy.'

'Noble,' says Chloe and dishes out the rest of the pies onto plates before bringing one over to me. She also has a tub of mashed potatoes and peas leftover from the shop and as she drizzles onion gravy over our plates, I realise just how hungry I am.

'Okay, it's good,' Brad says through a mouthful of pie. 'Probably a week's worth of carbs but good.'

I don't know what to say. It is delicious, but if I make too much of a big deal about that I'll seem like a big fatty, so I settle for, 'Thanks, Chloe. Hey, are we still heading to Rose Bay for the sunset?'

'For sure. If we grab an Uber at about seven thirty, we'll have time to have a glass of wine on the beach, get some serious dog patting in and watch the sunset.'

'Uber?' says Brad, almost choking on his pie. 'It's not a hard walk. If we power walk it, we can burn off some of this.' He gestures to my plate.

'A walk could be nice,' I say, wanting to show Brad my desire to burn off some calories.

Chloe lets out a theatrical groan. 'It's so far.'

'You don't have to come.' Brad's gaze hardens.

Chloe huffs. 'You're not getting rid of me that easily.'

'It'll be fun if we all go,' I say.

'Whatever you say,' says Chloe, with an eyeroll.

n hour later, I am wishing with all my heart that I'd worn leggings. My shorts keep riding up and I have serious thigh chaffage.

'Come on, ladies, let's pick up the pace,' calls Brad from further up the path.

'Take some time off,' Chloe yells back at him. 'We're not your personal training clients.'

'I kind of am,' I say quietly to her.

'Right now, your focus is dog patting, so get to it.'

A scruffy brown dog runs up to me and wiggles into my legs for attention.

'Hey, there,' I say, bending over and showering her in pats and kisses.

Brad jogs on the spot, up ahead.

'Come on, Chrissy,' he calls. 'Jog to the next lamp post. You can do it.'

I take a deep breath, give the dog one more scruff of the ears and set off. I count to ten in my head as I push forward. Surely, I can do anything for ten seconds? Even something as hideous as jogging. Brad lets out a whoop of encouragement. My flesh is bouncing in all directions. I know people are watching me, especially with Chloe yelling, 'Go, Chrissy,' from behind me, but I block them out as I throw myself into Brad's arms. He lifts me a little off the ground.

'Great effort,' he says as he guides me into a playful twirl under his outstretched arm as if we were on a dancefloor, not a pavement. 'Okay, let's walk to the next lamp post and then jog to the one after that. How does that sound?'

'I reckon I can do it,' I say with a big smile. It feels good to be pushing my body.

'I reckon I need a drink,' puffs Chloe as she arrives at my side.

Brad folds his arms across his broad chest. 'Come on,' he says. 'This is all part of Chrissy's recovery.'

The walk/running seems to work well for me. It helps to have a gorgeous man to chase. Plus, it gives me and Chloe time to pet dogs in between runs.

An hour later, I am not so enthusiastic. We've been walking for ages and my energy is waning. After the boot-camp this morning and my jellyfish sting, my body is crying out for a rest.

Much of the walk is residential, but in between, there are ocean views, rugged cliff tops and crashing waves.

As we walk over the boardwalk towards Diamond Bay Reserve, I lean forward and hold onto my thighs, taking deep breaths.

'Are you okay?' asks Chloe at my side.

'This walk is a whole lot further than I expected.'

She glances at her phone. 'Yup, and there's still, like, five kilometres to go.'

'Ugh, can we sit for a minute?' I plonk myself down on the boardwalk, my legs hanging over the side. 'I can't go any further. My legs have turned to jelly.'

As I sit, I enjoy the cool shade from the cliff and take a deep breath. Brad jogs back to us.

'I've overdone it,' I tell him.

'It's just your mindset.' He crouches down next to me. 'If you think you've overdone it, then you have. If you think you're just getting started, then you are.'

'Well, I think I've overdone it.' I feel like a toddler on the verge of a tantrum.

'Come on, just along this boardwalk. Not long to go now,' he says, clapping his hands together.

'You said that half an hour ago,' says Chloe, her voice laced with irritation. 'I thought we were gonna cut through the streets, not do the whole cliff walk.'

Brad ignores her.

I remember when my parents used to watch that show

The Biggest Loser, where fat people were over-trained to the point of vomiting on their first day. Inevitably, there was always one contestant who would have a meltdown and refuse to do any more training. I can so relate.

'Brad, I've gone from hardly any exercise to doing a forty-five-minute bootcamp and an hour jog. Isn't that enough for today?'

'You've been walking nearly the whole time and you're not even carrying the backpack,' he replies. He points to his back where he is carrying our snacks and drinks.

He looks dejected, like a little boy, and I can almost imagine chubby little Brad at five years old.

'I'm sorry,' I say. 'I just need a break.'

'Come on,' he says again as if calling a stubborn terrier to heel.

'No.' I slam my hand onto the boardwalk, tears of frustration welling up in my eyes. No matter how much I would like to avoid an argument, I will not allow a man to push me around again. 'I am not walking any further today and that is that. No way, I'm not doing it.' Lowering my body onto the boardwalk, I lie in a most unattractive foetal position. It's bliss to be lying down. Chloe tries to stifle a giggle at my side.

'So, what are you going to do?' says Brad with a sigh.

'I live here now.' I gesture above me with my arm.

'You're acting like a child.' Brad takes a deep breath and lowers himself to sit on the edge of the boardwalk. He places a hand on my jellyfish-sting-free thigh.

'I know it's hard,' he says. 'Look, I'll finish jogging to Rose Bay. Why don't you two grab an Uber from up there?' He points to a path that leads to a residential street. 'I'll meet you on the beach.'

'That, my friend, is a brilliant idea,' says Chloe.

'I'm sorry,' I say, and a frustrated tear rolls down my cheek and plops onto the boardwalk.

Brad stands up and offers me a reassuring smile. 'It's okay.' His footsteps pound away.

'Why am I such a loser?' I screw my eyes up tight against the world.

'A better question is,' says Chloe in my ear, 'why the hell do you keep apologising? I must have heard you say sorry about fifty times since you got here, and it's bullshit.'

'I don't want to start a fight.'

'Well, it might be time to woman up and start some fights. Let people react to you however they want. Don't apologise for being you.'

I jump as I feel a wet nose snuffling my cheek and hear Chloe say, 'Oh hello, gorgeous.'

I open my eyes and laugh as a handsome, if slightly overweight, red cattle dog leans his wiggly body into me. As I stroke his fur, he pants with what looks like a big smile on his face.

Looking up, I'm surprised to find Tom staring down at me. The fact Tom must have witnessed my tantrum makes me want to jump off the boardwalk and land with a plop in the creek below. From past experience, I would guess my face is as red as my hair from exertion and stress and there are likely tear stains down my cheeks.

I decide to distract from the state of myself by focusing all my attention on the dog.

'Tom, your dog is so handsome. Aren't you, boy? Yes, you are.'

'Hey, neighbour,' says Chloe as she pats the wiggly, waggly body of the red dog. She looks up to Tom. 'Great to see you on this side of the world.'

'Neighbour? Seriously?' A jolt sparks through me.

'Yeah, Tom and Janine live upstairs from us,' says Chloe. 'Well, just Tom now, I guess. Did I not tell you that?'

'No, you didn't, Chloe,' I say with a glare.

'How's the sting? I'm surprised you're out and about,' Tom asks, crouching down and – to my delight – sitting next to me.

'It still hurts, but it's loads better than it was.' I lift the edge of my shorts to reveal the lower part of the scar on my thigh. The sweat and rubbing of the fabric have irritated it and the sting is angry and inflamed.

He winces. 'Ouch.'

'Told you exercise is bad for your health,' says Chloe as Ned covers her in licks.

'How far are you walking?' I ask Tom.

'We're going to the dog beach at Rose Bay. Ned's on a health kick, aren't you, Neddy? He was underweight when we adopted him from the shelter. We've been so keen on getting him back to health, we may have gone too far in the other direction. The house-sitter reckons she couldn't say no when he begged for treats.'

'Are you walking there and back?' says Chloe, aghast. 'That's, like, a million kilometres.'

'We're getting a lift back. Janine's checking out a bar over there, so...'

'To buy?' asks Chloe.

'Maybe.' Tom shrugs. 'It's between this one or a place in Bondi.'

A surge of jealousy spreads through me, that I am definitely not entitled to.

'Okay, well, we better head off,' he says as he gets up. He meets my eyes and there it is. That buzz between us.

'We'll come too,' I say, without thinking it through. I push myself up, ignoring the ache in my legs and the sting of my chafing thighs.

'No, we bloody won't,' says Chloe. 'We're getting an Uber, remember?'

'Now I've had a rest, I feel, I dunno, like I can do it. I mean, it's not the worst thing being here.' I gesture to the ocean view to my side.

We take a shortcut through residential streets and the remaining two kilometres pass in a flash. Ned leads the way, keen to greet everyone he sees and to pee on all enticing lamp posts. Tom and I walk side by side and, some five metres behind, Chloe lags. When I glance back at her, she huffs and pretends to stagger.

'I used to walk dogs at the shelter back home,' I say. 'I'd like to do some volunteering whilst I'm here, too.'

'You should,' says Tom. 'I do sometimes, although I always want to adopt someone new when I'm there. That's the hard bit.'

'Oh god yes. I want to adopt everyone.' I pull out my phone to show Tom photos of Jonah at the rescue centre.

'Brad will be impressed with all this exercise,' calls Chloe after us. 'Did you tell him we'd be longer than we said?'

'Um, not exactly,' I call back, feeling awful. Brad will probably be waiting for us at the beach.

As we walk down the path from Rose Bay shops to the sandy beach, I take a moment to take in the view. There in front of me, across the water, is Sydney Harbour Bridge, below a fading sun. I can't believe I'm here.

Tom unclips Ned's lead and the red dog bounds down the beach, splashing into the calm water. A black Labrador zooms in after him, tail wagging. There are dogs everywhere; a little terrier playing fetch with his person, a pair of greyhounds with their shelter bandanas, snoozing on the sand; a kelpie zooming into the surf.

I glance back to see Chloe drop onto the sand in an exhausted heap, only for a wet Ned to bound towards her and cover her in water. I giggle and Tom catches my eye and smiles. We walk to the edge of the water and stand side by side, our hands so close they could almost touch.

Tom gives me a quick once over, a playful smile tugging at his lips. 'You've put in a hell of a workout today; you must be about ready to pass out.'

I flash him a grin, brushing the sweat dampened hair away from my forehead. 'Now we're here, I've got a bit of a second wind,' I say. 'I keep fit at home with the dog walking and there are some epic hills to trek up in Brighton.'

'Shame I didn't meet you earlier. We could have walked the dogs together.' Tom holds eye contact with me. His dark brown irises are like melted chocolate. Either I'm delirious from exhaustion or we are having a moment.

'Brighton was a cool place. I loved it. Did you grow up there?' he asks.

'I grew up not too far away, in Lewes. But after uni, my friend Jess and I moved to Brighton straight away. It's just such an open-minded kind of place. And I love the seaside.'

'"The seaside." So British,' says Tom, copying my accent. 'Cute.'

'Neddy.' Janine's shrill voice cuts through our moment.

20

Ned looks up from the water and lifts his nose in the air, trying to catch the scent of his human. Then, tail wagging furiously, he hurls himself across the sand and up the beach. Janine looks elegant in a bold print dress, her olive skin glowing and her long blonde hair falling in waves as she releases it from a bun. She was holding her sandals but drops them to the sand and slaps her thighs. Ned bounds up to her and even though he's soaking wet, she doesn't flinch. He presses his furry, wet body against her and then rolls onto his back for a tummy rub.

Janine flops down onto the sand, next to Chloe's prone body and covers her dog friend in pats. Tom walks towards her. My stomach lurches. Why am I even thinking about Tom when he has this glamazon in his life? I can't look away and as Janine gestures to her dress, Tom unzips it. It's so intimate, I may as well be watching them in the bedroom. She wriggles out of the dress and folds it into her bag. Beneath the dress is a black bikini that shows off her taut tummy and long thighs. Goddammit, she even has a thigh gap.

I can't hear what they are saying, but Janine is still laughing to herself as she glides past me in an elegant jog. Ned bounds after her, that doggy smile on his face. The water isn't deep, and Janine runs until she elegantly slides beneath it. She's still in the shallows and she rolls onto her back, floating, her hair fanning out around her.

I look down at my own body, my pink shorts, my red thighs, my belly. I glance back up the beach to see Tom sitting next to Chloe, chatting. He's just a friendly guy – the kind of guy who will chat to anyone.

This is a bit of a pattern of mine, the whole 'falling for a man because they're a little bit kind to me' thing. Like that time at school when a group of girls were throwing my pencil case to each other. An older boy, Jason Perez, strode over and grabbed the pencil case. He gave it back to me and told the girls to leave me alone. That was it. I was in love. That gangly boy with badly bleached blonde tips was my destiny. As it turned out, a couple of months later, I saw him get off with Stacey Vella at the school disco. I was heartbroken. To me, a boy being kind was as good as a marriage proposal.

I guess that was what happened with Jeremy, the only real boyfriend I have ever had. I remember how he complimented me, gazed into my eyes and told me I was the most beautiful woman in the bar. We had walked along Brighton pier and played on the penny machines. He won me a teddy bear keyring. I was smitten. For all I knew, he could have been a total monster. Well, as I found out a few months later... he kind of was.

A cold splash of water against my leg makes me jump and I'm pulled out of the memory.

'You were ages,' says Brad as I turn to face him. He should be annoyed, but he has a smile on his face. 'Did you walk the rest of it?'

I nod. 'I even ran a little bit.'

His smile broadens to reveal those perfect white teeth. I glow under his approval. He puts his arm around me, as we both gaze out towards the city.

'I'm impressed,' he says. 'You're amazing.'

The cold memories of Jeremy drown under the praise from Brad.

'I feel amazing,' I say. 'Exhausted though.'

'Not as exhausted as Chloe.' Brad gestures to Chloe, who is still sprawled on the sand. 'Come on, let's have a stretch and then enjoy this sunset.'

'THAT'S IT,' says Brad with a groan. He's leaning his weight into my groin as he holds my right leg up above my head.

'Get a room!' Chloe takes her flask out of her backpack and takes a sip.

'It's important to stretch,' says Brad. He moves my leg further back, pressing more of his weight into me.

'Is that what you call it?' Chloe asks. 'Looks pornographic from where I'm sitting.'

I wriggle out from Brad's hold. 'She's not wrong,' I say, sitting up on the sand.

'Don't come whingeing to me when your glutes are on fire tomorrow.' Brad frowns and shakes his head. But he doesn't push it. He sits next to me on the sand and places a hand on my knee.

'Wine?' says Chloe, with a mischievous twinkle in her eye.

'You cheeky thing.' I hold a hand to my chest in mock horror. 'I thought that was water.'

'We need a reward,' she says as I accept the flask with a chuckle. I take a sip, enjoying the warmth in my throat.

Brad watches this exchange with furrowed brows and shakes his head in mild exasperation. 'Chloe, do you want to help Chrissy on her wellness journey, or do you want to be an enabler?'

Chloe glances over at him. 'Can I choose both?'

I hold up my hand to interject. 'Just a sip, I promise. I've already had, like, three litres of water today.'

'How can I say no to that face?' Brad squidges my cheeks together before planting a kiss on my lips.

A voice sounds from behind us. 'Oh my gosh, Bootcamp Brad with the girl from the plane. What a small world.' I turn to see Janine approaching, a look of wide-eyed surprise on her face.

'I thought you could do with a proper introduction,' says Tom, walking behind her as Ned bounds towards me and plops onto the sand.

'Chrissy, you remember Janine. Janine, this is Chrissy, and you already know Chloe.'

'Hi,' I give a little wave. 'You have a great dog.'

'He is pretty special. All the men in my life are pretty special.' She bats her eyelashes at Tom. 'And how good to see you again, Brad.'

Brad gets up and gives Janine a hug before holding her at arm's length.

'Missing bootcamp doesn't seem to have set you back at all,' he says. 'Looking good!'

'He's a real task master this one, isn't he?' says Janine as she kneels down on the sand next to Chloe. 'I got into CrossFit in the UK, but I'm ready to get back to bootcamp soon.' She looks at me. 'When I met you on the plane, I never in a million years imagined you'd be with someone like Brad. Go you. Keep punching up, girlfriend.' She holds her hand up in a high five, and I reluctantly return the gesture. 'I saw you on Insta,' she continues. 'I'd say there's been an improvement already.'

'I don't have an Insta account anymore. I had to delete it because of work. It must have been someone else.'

'No, on Brad's Bondi Bootcamp page. Brave, if you ask me. You wouldn't see me flaunting my wobbly bits up there.'

It takes all my willpower not to yell, 'What wobbly bits? You deluded old bint!'

Janine stretches out her tanned limbs on the sand, and Tom sits next to Brad. All of us face out towards the water as the sun begins to redden and dip.

'Brad, did you have Chrissy's permission to post this?' asks Chloe, who has already pulled up the Instagram page on her phone.

'What is it?' I ask, panic rising in my stomach.

Chloe hands me the phone and I hold it, feeling nauseous. There are my before photos in all their ugly, jiggly horror.

There are four photos, all from different angles, all seemingly worse than the last.

In one, my belly is peeping out from between my shirt and leggings in a mottled bulge.

'You said you'd only post these once I had a stunning after photo,' I say, rubbing my brow.

The caption reads:

We all have to start somewhere. Epic transformation loading.

I notice the hashtags match those from my notorious viral Instagram posts.

I turn to Chloe and whisper, 'Please tell me it's just a bad angle.' I keep my face turned to her. I don't want to let the others see that I am about to burst into tears.

'Shocking angle,' she says in a quiet voice and places a hand on my shoulder. 'Chrissy, they are just bad photos, I promise you. You don't look like that.'

But I know in my heart that I do. My belly is pressed against my thighs as I sit here on the sand with my knees up. I look out at the ocean and kind of wish I could run into it and let the sharks have at my excess flesh.

The sun is melting into a swirl of red and pink. I press my chin onto my knees, trying to hide. Brad places his hand on my back and I pull away. I want to tell him to take down the photos, but I don't want to draw any extra attention to myself.

Ned must sense that I need cheering up as he pushes his body weight against me and flops down for a belly pat. Okay, even in my sulky state, I can't resist Ned. I unfurl myself to rub his belly. He's a little overweight, or let's say well-fed, but he is just gorgeous. I wish I could think the same about myself.

'Don't worry, Chrissy,' says Janine. 'The worse the before photo, the more people will be amazed at the after photo. You are going to stun them.'

'How about this sunset?' says Tom in a clear attempt to change the subject. 'I mean...'

I look up to see him gesture to the sky in general. Gold star for effort.

Brad pokes my arm lightly. I turn my face towards him.

'Sorry,' he mouths at me, and I nod. Maybe I need this motivation. Maybe the after photo really will be even more stunning for the hideous before photo.

'You know what I feel like?' says Janine. 'Fish and chips.'

'Oh yum, me too, well, hot chips at least,' says Chloe.

'Tom, will you run up and get some?' Janine asks.

'How about chips and veggie burgers since we have our vego friends here?' He points to me and Chloe.

I think of the salty, vinegary goodness featuring a major food group of mine: fried potato.

God knows I've burnt enough calories to eat a few.

'Let me guess,' says Tom, standing up and dusting sand off his legs. 'I should get vinegar on yours. I know what you Brits are like.'

Usually, he'd have it one hundred per cent right. I adore vinegar on chips. Well, on pretty much any savoury food. But that photo has served as just about the best appetite suppressant I have ever tried (and let me tell you, I've tried more than my fair share.)

'None for me, thanks. Brad brought us smoothies in his bag.'

Tom shrugs. He's even more handsome in the dying reddish light. 'Maybe just get over that photo stuff. How you look is how you look. Who cares?'

I feel a bit sick. Tom must think I look as bad as those photos all the time. And now he also thinks I'm shallow. Maybe I am? But it's hard not to be when the whole world seems so focused on my appearance.

Brad pulls a smoothie out of his bag and hands it to me.

'Ignore him,' he says. 'This is all part of it. People get jealous and try to block your progress.'

Tom mutters something under his breath and heads up the beach towards the shops.

'We're just trying to help Chrissy realise there is so much more to her than how she looks,' says Chloe with a slight glare, crossing her arms across her chest.

'I know, I know,' I say, waving off her comment. 'But honestly, I'm not even hungry. I'm exhausted after today and could just fall asleep right here on the sand. I might just get an Uber back if that's okay?'

With an understanding nod, Chloe glances at Janine. 'I'll get a lift back with you then?' she asks her.

Janine responds with a thumbs up.

My legs are so heavy and sore I'm not even sure how I manage to drag myself up the beach to the street where Brad and I book an Uber.

Once inside the comfortable, air-conditioned car, the drive back to Chloe's apartment is a blur. The hum of the car's engine is a lullaby to my tired ears.

We pull up outside the building and Brad turns to me,

concern etched on his handsome features. 'Do you want me to come in?' he asks.

'I need to sleep,' I say, my eyelids heavy. 'I'm sorry.'

'It's okay. You've done so well today and ignore that stuff at the beach. I promise the before photos are the key to your motivation.'

I nod, and he kisses me briefly on the lips. As I walk up to Chloe's apartment, I feel worlds away from my old life.

After a much-needed shower, I flop onto the bed. There's just one person I want to speak to.

'Hi, Jess,' I say as she picks up.

It's early morning there and Jess is halfway through doing her make-up.

'Chrissy!' she exclaims with the enthusiasm only Jess can put into that one word. She props her phone up. 'I already miss you more than life itself. How has your first full day been? Has Brad swept you off your feet?'

I take a deep breath and fill her in, feeling like I'm home.

21

I slam my hand down on the bedside table as the alarm sounds. It feels like I only went to sleep about thirty minutes ago. But as I glance at my phone, I see it is indeed time to haul myself out of bed. How can it only be day two of my new training regime? My muscles ache as if they've been putting up with this slog for years.

I tap to open a WhatsApp message from Jess and laugh. She has sent me a series of photos showing off her double chins. Now Jess may be voluptuous, but I swear I've never noticed a double chin on her before. Yet in one photo she manages to create about three of them.

The text says:

> You're not the only one who can rock a double chin. Any more whining about your weight and I'll post these on Insta, and it will be all your fault!

I throw my legs over the side of the bed.

Within minutes I have dressed and grabbed my backpack, ready for another day in the Australian sun. As I push the front door of the apartments open, I hear footsteps behind me.

'We missed you last night.' Tom's deep voice makes me jump and I turn around to see him in his blue lifeguard shorts and jersey.

'Yeah, sorry about that. I can't believe I turned down chips.'

'Are you walking to the beach?' he asks, raising his dark eyebrows.

'Sure am, ready to kick arse at bootcamp.'

Why did I say that? I don't say things like 'kick arse'.

I turn back to the path and Tom falls in line next to me. 'I didn't mean to be offensive last night,' he says. 'I just meant there's heaps you can enjoy about life now. You don't have to wait until you're a certain size.'

'I get it. Maybe I've been a bit shallow since I got here. In the UK, I was always worrying about the kids at school, worrying about the dogs at the shelter, worrying about the whole world. For the first time, I'm in between jobs and I don't have to worry about others. I just want to do something for me, for my health.'

'Makes sense,' he says, 'but I hope you give yourself time to enjoy the journey, not just the destination.'

I snort. 'Did I just walk into a Tony Robbins seminar?'

'I don't know what you mean,' he says in a deep American accent, and I giggle.

'I intend to enjoy every moment that I'm here. I mean, how can I not?' I wave my hand at the street in front of me. Palm trees line the path. A cockatoo sits on a bench and there's a glimpse of the ocean down the hill. I can already spot the little black dots of surfers gliding down the waves.

'Do you surf?' I ask.

Tom chuckles lightly and runs a hand through his hair. 'Kind of. I give it a crack, but I prefer bodyboarding.'

'You mean like the little kids do?' I ask, casting him a teasing look.

Unfazed he counters with a nod. 'I guess, but it's a pro sport too and there's nothing like riding a wave on a bodyboard. You're closer to the water, closer to the wave. I love it. What about you? Have you ever surfed?'

'Absolutely not, but I've always wanted to give it a go. It's on my list.'

'Like a list of stuff to do here?'

I hesitate, chewing my lip. 'Um, kind of. A list of things to do when I'm ready.'

I don't think Tom will be impressed if I tell him about my Things To Do When I'm Skinny list.

He nods in understanding, an encouraging smile on his face. 'You should have a go. Janine has a surfboard in the garage that you could borrow.'

'It's not like clothes, is it? Would I need a bigger size than her?'

'There are different sizes, but it's more on height, and you and Janine are about the same. I don't think the weight difference is anything to worry about.'

I cringe inside, partly at yet another mention of Janine and partly because I can hear myself bringing everything back to my weight. I swear I didn't always focus on my size this much, but since the *Daily Mail* article, it seems like every conversation I have comes back to my flab.

'You're here for six months, aren't you?' he asks.

'Yup and I love it.'

He grins at my answer. 'So any big plans whilst you're here?'

'I want to explore.' My words come tumbling out as excitement bubbles within me. 'I want to visit the local animal sanctuaries. I'm already missing walking the dogs at the shelter. I want to go on a bushwalk. I want to go snorkelling, see kangaroos in the wild and, oh, I'd love to do the Sydney bridge climb.'

Tom chuckles. 'You're gonna be busy.'

'Well, first up, I'm focusing on my fitness. I kind of need to earn the right to do that stuff.'

'Bullshit,' says Tom with a force I wasn't expecting.

I blink in astonishment. 'Excuse me?'

'Bullshit. Training will take up an hour of your day, tops. Why put off the other stuff? Go snorkelling today, call a rescue centre and ask them if you can visit this week, book the bridge climb.'

'But I've got to be careful not to lose focus.'

He sighs dramatically. 'You and me, Chrissy, this afternoon, Clovelly, gropers. It's happening.'

'Gropers?' I ask, sounding shocked.

Tom laughs. 'Calm down, they're a fish. An enormous, friendly fish and you're gonna hang out with them today.'

'But I don't have a—'

'I'll bring the snorkel. We'll leave at three when I'm back from work. Deal?'

'But don't you think I should lose—'

'Don't you dare say it,' he snaps. 'You said you're not shallow, so don't act like it. Now shut up and tell me more about those rescue dogs.'

'How can I shut up and tell you?' I say and a small chuckle escapes my lips.

Tom rolls his eyes. 'See, this is your fault. I've lost the ability to make sense.'

It's a ten-minute walk to the beach, but it feels like thirty seconds. Time seems to whizz by when I'm with Tom.

By the time I reach the beach, I can hardly keep the smile off my face. I drop Tom off at the lifeguard tower and take off my trainers so I can splash my feet through the water. As I walk towards the other end of the beach, I fix my eyes on the white bubbles of water in front of me. I'm keeping a close eye out for anything blue. I do not want to get stung again. My skin is still covered in red, raised welts as it is.

'You made it,' says Brad, lolloping over to me. He squeezes my shoulder and kisses me on the cheek.

'Of course,' I say. 'I have that awful before photo seared onto my retinas. I need to get to the after picture asap.'

'You should see mine,' says Marcel, giving me a welcome hug.

'But you were pleased when I posted the after photo?' says Brad.

'Well, it would be cruel not to share this with the world.' Marcel does a little twirl. 'Fabulous, despite the bruises.' He gestures to his face where, sure enough, purple and blue bruises pool out from his eyes across the top of his nose.

'I'm so sorry,' I say.

'Come along to my dance class and all will be forgiven,' says Marcel.

'You teach dance?' I ask with an excited hop, immediately thinking of the item on my Things To Do When I'm Skinny list – take a group dance class.

'Yup and it would be perfect for you. We have people of all shapes and sizes, including fabulous ones like yours,' says Marcel, throwing his hands towards me for emphasis.

'You know,' Brad begins as he flicks some sand from his arm. 'That would be a good reward once you achieve your first weight loss goal. Non-food rewards are great motivators.'

Brad's words sting. Shouldn't he be encouraging me to have fun?

'You could do it once you've lost five kilos.' He continues, seemingly oblivious to the irritation that is no doubt written across my face. 'That will be something to look forward to.'

'Seriously, Chrissy, come along this week. It's so much fun.' Marcel holds his hands together as if praying for me to come and shake my booty.

I pull out my phone to add Marcel's details. 'It sounds great—'

Brad cuts me off. 'Chrissy needs to focus on proper training first. Bootcamp, running, that kind of thing. Silly stuff like dancing can be for later.'

'Oh, you party pooper,' says Marcel with a pout. He turns to me. 'I run the classes a few times a week, so just text me if you want to come along.'

As my gaze meets Brad's a forced smile plays on my lips. 'You're right, I can't possibly dance now. I wouldn't want to squash any of the other dancers.' I know I sound bitchy.

Sadness flickers over Brad's usually sparkly eyes and I instantly regret my tone. This gorgeous man is helping me with my health. He's giving me free bootcamp classes and motivation and I'm throwing it back in his face.

'Sorry,' I say.

'I'm just trying to help you.'

'I know and I am grateful. I'm still a bit wrung out from the jet lag and everything.'

'Got it,' says Brad, but he still looks dejected.

As the others arrive and we get started, I resolve to give my absolute all to the session. I don't want to be ungrateful when Brad is being so supportive.

As the session progresses and I burpee, box and bicycle crunch my way through the early morning, I feel a glow of pride, well it could be a glow of sweat, but either way, it feels good. My muscles ache, my belly wobbles and there are two moments when I'm terrified that I may vomit, but I don't whine about it. I keep going and at the end, as I splash my way into the sea, I find I am not so worried about my thigh dimples, my silvery stretch marks or purple spider veins. I am just in the moment with the Bondi surf around me and thankfully no sign of any bluebottles.

Now, as I stand on the beach with a towel around me, I want to show Brad I am grateful for his help.

'Brad, sorry I was moody earlier. Can I make it up to you? Could we go out for a drink or something?' I shuffle my bare feet, digging my toes into the sand.

'I'm working today. Got a couple of PT sessions, but yeah, maybe later. I could do about three?'

'Um, I have plans this afternoon... with a friend, but how about this evening?'

He smiles at me and my tummy flip-flops.

'Go on then,' he says, pulling me into a hug and kissing me on the lips. Okay, so this is not how you'd kiss an elderly aunt, at least I hope not.

Should I tell him I'm going snorkelling with Tom? I mean, it's not a crime to go snorkelling with a friend, is it? Even if that friend is male and ridiculously hot.

Brad holds me out in front of him. 'You did well today. I know sometimes I can seem harsh in training sessions, but it comes from a good place. Remember, I used to be bigger. Being overweight is difficult. There are the things people say. The way I couldn't catch my breath when I was trudging up a hill. The way others acted towards me and even now when people treat me differently, I'm like, "Oh, so now I'm good enough to talk to." It's a weird world we live in.'

I see a painful memory pass over his tanned face, and I kiss him again. Brad has a little boy lost quality where I just want to protect him.

I flop down onto the sand and move my hands down to my feet, stretching my hamstrings.

'Well, I'm done,' I say. 'You've officially worn me out.'

'You have some decent fitness there already. Must be all that dog walking.'

I feel a glow of pride.

'You're making good progress with the boxing.' he continues with a playful smirk. 'Lucky you got the aim right today or poor Mel would have been knocked out cold.'

'You can thank TikTok for that,' I say as he sits down next to me and his hand smooths over my leg.

'Fitspo?' he asks.

'Not quite.' I chuckle lightly. 'Animal cruelty, actually. I watched a video on pig farming that made me so mad, I had to take my anger out on something.'

Brad's face softens, his gaze reflective. 'That's not a bad idea, picturing something that makes you angry and then taking it out on the punching bag.' He pauses, his thumb tracing circles on my leg. 'For me it would be bullies, I reckon. My little cousin has been having a hard time at school.'

'Hang on, are you picturing knocking out six-year-olds?' I ask with a smile.

'He's twelve, but yeah, kind of. Or I would knock out the concept of bullying in the first place.'

'That's awful about your cousin.' I shuffle closer to Brad as my own school memories surge back. 'What's his name?'

'Ben. He's a good kid. Sensitive though. It's like the other kids pick up that he's vulnerable.'

'That sucks.' My voice is sombre. 'I can relate, you know? You only need one thing different about you in school, whether it's being overweight, having red hair or just being the quiet kid. I had all three. What is it with Ben?' I take a swig of the smoothie Brad made me. This time it's chocolate and oat and way yummier than yesterday.

Brad's brows are furrowed in thought. 'He has a strawberry birthmark on his face. But he's this good-looking kid. He's funny and caring. Really sweet, but the kids are so cruel.'

I find my hand reaching for Brad's muscular thigh and

squeezing it lightly. 'It's nice he has an older cousin who cares so much.' His blonde leg hairs catch the sunlight and I wonder at how I've managed to find a man this gorgeous.

'I hate bullying too,' I say, my eyes fixed on Brad's. 'I've seen some of it in my past relationships and, well, now when I see what people do to animals, I get this surge of anger. I never want to contribute to their suffering.'

'I get it. They're not human though, are they? So, it's not as bad.'

'It's pretty bad.'

'Let's not talk about that right now.' He takes my hands in his and looks into my eyes. 'What happened in your relationship?'

I've been asked this a bunch of times and I always hold back. Even when telling my own mother, I gave a very brief rundown of what happened with Jeremy.

The weird thing is that I thought he would be my forever. I thought he was the one.

I take a deep breath. 'I won't go into it, apart from to say I thought I had met this incredible man. I thought we had a future and then, well, everything changed. It ended badly.'

I pause and a silence hangs between us as we watch a flock of seagulls splashing in a pool of water.

'If you want to open up to me about anything, you can,' says Brad.

'Thanks.' I turn towards him and reach up, running my fingers through his shag of hair.

'And you can talk to me too... about anything.'

He leans in and kisses me lightly on the lips. 'I've gotta go. I've got a very demanding D list client to whip into shape, but I can't wait to see you later.' He kisses my nose.

As I watch him walk away, a surge of affection runs through me. This man seems so dedicated to my improvement, to helping me live my best life. Should I cancel snorkelling with Tom and go with Brad, instead? A wave of guilt hits my stomach.

I lean back on the sand and close my eyes, enjoying the warm morning sun on my skin as I breathe in the fresh ocean air.

Jeremy's face flashes into my head. His icy blue eyes narrowed. I sit up with a gasp, as if waking from a nightmare.

I stand up and grab my bag. Walking back along the beach towards home, I think about how I will never change my plans for a man. I will never change who I am for a man. So even if Brad does seem like a nice guy, if I want to go snorkelling with Tom, then that is what I will do.

I walk with a determined pace and enjoy the burn in my thighs as I trudge through the heavy sand.

22

I open the apartment door to find Tom holding out a pink snorkel and fins.

'Here you go,' he says. 'You're one step away from the gropers.'

'Thanks.' I bounce on my toes, unable to contain my excitement. Okay so I wasn't planning to go snorkelling until I lost weight, but after searching Google for info on gropers, I can't wait.

I take the snorkel and fins and put them in my backpack.

'It's about a 3k walk, or we could drive?' he asks.

Honestly, the way my body aches from bootcamp, it probably would be a good idea to drive, but the more time with Tom the better.

'Let's walk,' I say.

As I fall into step beside him, Tom tells me about how he

had to pull a man from the surf today. The poor guy was having a panic attack. Turns out he just had seaweed wrapped around his leg.

I chuckle and use my hand to shield my eyes from the bright sun. 'You never know. This is Australia. It could be killer seaweed.'

'True,' he says. 'Ned says hi by the way.'

Pretending to be formal, I tip an imaginary hat. 'And of course, my kindest regards to Ned.'

'I can give you a heads up the next time I go to the rescue centre if you fancy it. Just some dog walking and cleaning. There are other animals there too, so there could be some cat cuddles on offer.'

A grin spreads across my face at the thought. 'Sounds amazing. I'd love to.'

Thinking of spending more time with Tom makes me want to skip along this coastal path. I may not look like the busty blonde joggers with their snatched waists, but I feel great. As I gaze out at the ocean below, I can hardly believe how my life has changed.

Tom's phone buzzes in his pocket. He pulls it out and glances at the screen. My stomach lurches. It's a text from Janine. He still has a loved-up photo of the pair of them as his lock screen.

'Have you done much exploring of Sydney yet?' he asks, ignoring the message and putting the phone back in his pocket.

'Not really, what with getting over the jet lag, but I think Chloe is taking me on the tourist trail on Friday. I'm excited to do all the things – Centrepoint Tower, the Botanical Gardens, the Opera House. We're going to get the ferry.'

'You sound like an excited kid.'

'I feel like one. There's something about this country.' I want to add, *there's something about you.*

He contemplates my statement for a moment before shifting gears. 'How are you finding the bootcamp stuff?'

I laugh and shake my head. 'I'm in a love-hate relationship with it. I hate it whilst I'm doing it, but I'm so happy when I've done it.'

'Janine is into all that,' he says, and my chest seems to constrict at the mention of her name.

I force a casual smile, trying to brush off the discomfort. 'I can tell. She's gorgeous.'

Did he just roll his eyes?

'There is so much more to people than how they look though, isn't there?' he says.

'Oh yeah, for sure. They can't all be supermodels and brain surgeons like us.'

My words make him smile.

'Do your family live around here?' I ask.

'Dad lives up the Central Coast. He's a good bloke. We go fishing together... I mean... we hang out at the beach, y'know?'

I guess it's sweet he spared me the details of his recreational killing of animals.

'What about you?' he continues. 'Is it only Chloe you know here?'

'Yup, no family here. Mum and Dad call most nights. They're great. Just worried I'll get eaten by a crocodile. I keep saying there are no crocodiles in New South Wales.'

'Even the crocs in Queensland are more at risk from humans than we are from them,' says Tom.

As we walk further along the path, it feels as if we could talk forever and never run out of things to say.

We round the corner and I get my first glance of Clovelly Beach. The bay is narrow and the water flows between two concrete ridges. There are already a few people snorkelling, bums bobbing. At the side of the deep water is a path and a ladder to climb down. Along the concrete, people are lazing in the sun on towels or chatting and laughing with friends.

We walk down to the edge of the deep water and lay out our things. Tom takes off his shirt.

'Let me just fiddle with my snorkel,' he says as he adjusts his head strap.

He catches my eye, and I can't stop a snort of laughter escaping.

'Mind out of the gutter, Chrissy,' he says.

I can't help sneaking a peek at that gorgeous body. Long and lean with defined muscles.

Tom has seen me in my swimming costume before. In

fact, he saw far worse than this on the plane, when I was lubed up and crammed into the world's least flattering bra. Despite this, I still feel self-conscious as I pull off my blue sundress. Some women are lying on their fronts, their bikini straps undone. Where do they get the self-confidence? Getting my boobs out for all to see would send me into a panic.

I rush to the edge and sit on the warm concrete. My plan is to jump in straight away in an effort for my body not to be on display for too long. I let my legs hang in the water...

'Eek!' The temperature is a shock.

Tom laughs. 'Pretty cold, eh? It's more noticeable without the waves to distract you. You know there is only one way to get over it, right?' He takes an exaggerated run-up and jumps in, making a huge splash.

'Argh, nope, still cold,' he says and begins a front crawl in an effort to warm himself up. He swims back to me and places his hands on the concrete. 'Do you need a push?' He gives me a menacing little smile. 'Or a pull?'

With that, he pulls my ankles and yanks me into the water. I shriek as the cold water engulfs me. As I bob to the surface, I splash Tom and begin a swift breaststroke.

After a few minutes of swimming, my body is warming up and I take a moment to swirl around in a circle and look at my surroundings. This is like a dream with the blue sky above and the calm waters cradling me.

Something tugs at my leg, and I shriek before Tom bobs up beside me, pulling off his snorkel and laughing.

'Don't you dare. You could have been a shark,' I scold him, the relief in my voice palpable.

He laughs, his eyes sparkling. 'I think you'd know by now if I were a shark.'

'Okay, shark boy, show me these gropers then.'

Tom wiggles his dark eyebrows and I pull the pink snorkel down and lower my face under the surface.

It's beautiful down here. There are small silver fish darting around the rocks. I gesture a thumbs up to Tom as a stingray glides towards the shallower beach. I feel like I've just stepped into *Finding Nemo*.

We must have been paddling for ten minutes when Tom's slippery hand taps my leg. I turn around and see a giant fish with an upturned mouth like he's having a bit of a grumpy day. He is blue and shimmery and huge, almost the size of my torso. The child part of me wants to reach out and touch him, but I don't. Behind him is a smaller female in shades of brown. The fish are so curious. They swim around us as if we were the attraction.

After some time, I pop up to the surface and pull off the mask. 'That was amazing!'

Tom beams back at me. 'How cool are they? And they're protected, so no one can hurt them.'

The fact he told me that makes me all tingly inside. He already knows what is important to me and he seems to genuinely care. After snorkelling for another few minutes, we swim to the side and hold on to the concrete wall.

'I love how excited you get,' he says as we bob side by side.

I am so weightless here in the water. I kind of wish I could stay here forever. But my teeth are chattering. The still, deep water really is cold. I climb up the ladder onto the concrete and lay out my towel, ready to sit down and relax.

'Need some more sunscreen?' asks Tom as I pull off my snorkel and begin to pat myself dry.

'Oh yeah, I do need some more. Am I burnt?'

'Not yet, but with skin as fair as yours, it won't take long.' He flips into lifeguard mode. 'Lie down on the towel.'

I do as I'm told, a little thrill shooting through me. See, this is the kind of bossing around I can put up with. Tom kneels over me. Oh geez. His bits are right on my back with just a teeny scrap of board-short material between us. I hear a squirt and then his hands, strong and soft, rub over my skin. If anything, he's setting my skin on fire. He runs his hands under the straps of my swimming costume to make sure all my skin is covered.

His strokes are slow and firm. He's taking his time.

'Oh, hi, Billy Bob,' he says. 'Looking as trashy, I mean as dashing as ever.' As he pulled down my costume, he must have revealed my tramp stamp.

'Oi,' I say, reaching around to slap his thigh.

'You know, I reckon, now I've got used to him, he's kind of cute.'

Luckily my face is towards the ground as I'm grinning, and I don't want Tom to know how happy he makes me.

He moves off me and stands up, placing a towel next to me.

I sit up. 'Thanks for creaming me,' I say and we both snigger at my choice of words.

'So do you reckon our fish friends have names?' he asks, lying on his towel.

I give a determined nod. 'Clive and Sheila, for sure.'

'I was thinking Antonio and Serena.' He gives a little laugh. 'But obviously they led me to believe they are more exotic than they really are.'

'Yeah, you've gotta be careful with fishes. They can be tricky,' I deadpan, and as our eyes meet a bubble of laughter rises between us.

23

As we stand outside Tom's apartment, I am happy and worn out from sun and exertion. I have such a big crush on Tom I think I may explode into a cloud of glitter. He unlocks the door and Ned wiggles and wags his tail as he greets us.

The delicious smell of baking chocolate hits me and I realise how hungry I am. A piece of chocolate would really hit the spot about now.

I drop my bag on the floor and take out the snorkel, so I don't forget to wash it and return it.

Tom is still patting Ned as he looks up at me and asks, 'What is that delicious smell?'

'My natural odour,' I say, immediately wanting to kick myself for saying the word odour in the presence of this gorgeous man.

'Cookies!'

Janine's head pops up from the other side of the kitchen counter. 'For my hard-working man... oh hi, Chrissy.'

I muster a 'Hi' in response, doing my best to conceal my disappointment at her presence. 'They smell so good.'

'Where have you two been? Somewhere getting wet by the looks of you dripping all over the floor.'

My hair is almost dry, so I'm not sure what she's on about.

'We went snorkelling. It was amazing. We saw Sheila and Clive... I mean, the gropers.'

Janine raises her groomed eyebrows as she plates up the cookies. Her posture is stiff as she blinks rapidly.

Tom walks over and squeezes her shoulder. 'Look at this for service,' he says. Her whole demeanour softens at his touch, and she gives him just about the sweetest smile I've ever seen. 'What brings you here?'

'Well... Oh my god, this is exciting. So, I checked out Beaches Bar on Bondi Road and, Tom... I think it's the one. I really do. I can't wait to show you.' She clasps her oven-gloved hands in front of her chest and squeals, seemingly unable to contain her excitement. 'This is it, Tom. This is the start of our future.' She turns to me, and her mouth drops into a hard line. 'But I didn't realise you had company.'

'Oh, Chrissy doesn't mind, do you?' says Tom and I feel like a child, left to play with the dog whilst the adults talk about proper adult things. Not that I mind playing with Ned, of course.

'Hang on, is that... my snorkel?' Janine asks as she spots the pink plastic in my hand.

'Um yeah. Tom said I could borrow it. I hope that's okay. I'm gonna give it a good wash.' I hold the snorkel out to her.

She snatches it and mutters something under her breath.

'What was that?' I ask.

'I said, it's all stretched out... and I was planning on going to Shelly Beach over the weekend. Thanks a lot.'

'I haven't stretched it out, I promise. I reckon our head size is pretty much the same, but I can buy you a new one if there's a problem.'

Janine's eyes dart up and down my body. The old me would apologise, turn around and walk out the door, but I'm trying to be a different person here. I'm trying to be a confident Aussie beach babe.

'I don't want a new one; I want this one,' she says with a pout.

'Believe it or not, I do not have an obese head. My skull is probably the same size as yours.'

Janine stares at me. Seconds of silence stretch out between us.

'How dare you?' she spits, slow and deliberate. 'I have something called self-control. I don't stuff myself full of cake and chocolate, so I don't end up with a great, big, fat head... unlike some people.'

'Don't be a brat, Jan,' says Tom.

'Here's your fucking cookies, Tom. Make sure you get one

before she eats them all.' Janine shoves the baking tray across the counter and throws her oven gloves on the table before storming out of the room. A door slams.

'I thought she'd be fine with you borrowing the snorkel,' says Tom with a shrug, 'and I didn't know she'd be here. I'm sorry.'

'It's... It's okay?' I say, but it comes out as a question because let's be real, this is not okay. 'What is she doing here? She still has a key?'

'Yeah, she has a key in case she wants to see Ned. She's only just started moving out. I mean, we didn't get back long ago, did we? I don't mind her being here, but she shouldn't talk to you like that. It's not on.'

'I guess I should go then?' I feel like I've gone from walking on air to trudging through a thick pile of factory farm sludge.

I'm hoping he'll ask me to stay. Surely, he'll ask me to stay.

'Probably best,' he says. I walk towards the door. Ned is still wiggling up against me. At least someone is happy I'm here.

'Hey, Chrissy?' Tom says, and I turn to look at him, one hand on the door handle.

Maybe he wants me to stay after all?

'Your head isn't that fat.'

He smiles as if he's given me the best compliment I could

ever get. And as I give Ned one last pat and pull the door behind me, I hear his voice.

'Janny, are you okay?'

I kind of want to punch a hole in the wall.

As I open my eyes, I'm hit with the realisation that yesterday I was called a giant fat-headed freak, or something to that effect. I grab my phone from my bedside table. I have a vague memory of texting Tom last night. Did I?

Yup, yup I did.

> Tom, why didn't you stand up for me earlier? Just letting you know that even though I had a lovely time, my head is NOT fat. I just have a lot of hair!

I've also sent a photo of, yup, it's a close-up of my hair.

I did pop out for a quick drink with Brad last night. But it was the bottle of wine with Chloe, when I got home, that did the damage. It was Chloe who encouraged me to stand up for myself and now it seems I've made a big deal about nothing. After all, it was Janine who made a fuss about the snorkel, not Tom. As Tom said, Janine is still moving her stuff out, and they both share Ned. I guess they're trying to work out how to untangle their lives.

But saying that, I sent that text at nine p.m. last night. Is it just me, or should Tom have texted me back by now? Maybe with an apology or at least a *How are you*? Anything! Well, I'm not texting him again. Not unless he texts me first. No Way.

Although perhaps if I haven't heard from him by lunch, I should check in. I could make it clear that I'm not that annoyed. A chill girl like me takes these things in her stride.

Somehow, I drag my body into my workout clothes, glug my water and roll myself out the door.

I stand for a moment at the front of the unit block, looking out onto the street. I take a deep breath before taking my first steps towards Bondi Beach.

'Oh hey, Chrissy.'

I turn around to find Janine in her workout gear. She's wearing a tiny white crop top and sky-blue leggings. As suspected, she looks like an actual fitness model.

I nod but say nothing.

'I need to apologise about last night,' she says, wincing and rubbing the back of her neck.

I lift my hand to wave the apology off but stop myself. She acted like a spoilt brat, so let's hear this.

'So, after talking to Tom, I realised there's a chance I was a bit unreasonable. It's not like you were purposefully wrecking my stuff. How about we wipe the slate clean and start again?'

'Sounds good.'

'Thanks,' she replies. 'Oh, and I got your number off

Tom, so I'll send you a link to get the replacement snorkel. I'm glad we've sorted things. I'll be seeing a lot more of you if I keep staying over.' She crosses her fingers and does a little hop.

And then it hits me. Janine doesn't live here anymore. That means she stayed over with Tom, after Tom insisted they were no longer together.

A wave of nausea ripples through me.

As Janine's pert bottom bounces off down the road, I turn around and head back towards my bed.

24

'y parents are so excited to see you again,' says Brad, as he takes my hand. 'Are you sure you're up to it? Or are you still crook?'

I give a meek smile. 'I'm all good, thanks.'

Don't judge me for the little white lie. I called Brad from my cosy bed and told him I was going to miss bootcamp. After my run-in with Janine, I just wanted to hide away, but I couldn't exactly tell Brad that.

If you'd asked me this time yesterday, I would have said I was going to cancel dinner with Brad's parents. But now I see I'm onto a good thing with Brad. He's really into me. And there's no needy ex hanging around trying to ruin everything.

Brad is driving us to Coogee. I gaze out the window and

take in the sweep of Coogee Beach. I could have been living here with Brad. Well, Brad and his mum and dad. But still.

We pull up to the big beach house. I feel foolish now for thinking Brad owned this. It looks like such a parents' house with its manicured roses in the front garden.

'There she is.' Brad's dad opens the front door.

As I get out of the car, he bounds towards me, the same way Brad does, opens his arms and pulls me into a hug. 'Come on in. We've been busy in the kitchen. Well, the catering people have.' He laughs.

'Hi, Dad.' Brad gives his dad a quick hug, before guiding me into the house I had once thought would be our love nest.

'And don't worry, Chrissy,' Doug adds, 'there's vegan stuff galore. Eggplant this, tofu that.'

'That's so good of you,' I say.

Doug would make a lovely father-in-law; so happy and friendly. I bet Tom's parents aren't anywhere near as nice.

'And for me?' asks Brad.

'Big old slabs of meat. Our boy needs his protein.' Doug slaps Brad on the back.

I think back to how Tom chose to eat vegan food around me, and I feel a pang. I check my phone. He still hasn't text back. Did he come to the realisation that my head was, in fact, much larger than he thought, and no, he could not handle that level of fat-headedness in his life?

All day I've had a knot in my stomach. It's irritating me that I even care what Tom is doing or whether he gets in touch, especially since he spent the night with Little Miss Pert Bottom.

I follow the men through to the back garden.

'Christina.' Teresa looks as perfectly groomed as ever. How the heck she keeps her hair in order in this sea breeze is beyond me.

'It's Chrissy,' says Brad.

'Christina is nicer though, isn't it?' she says. 'Come and sit down and we'll get you a drink.'

'Just water for us,' says Brad, patting his six-pack abs.

As it happens, the last thing I want to do is drink alcohol, but I would like to be given the choice.

'What's it been, just a few days?' says Doug, looking me up and down as we pull out the chairs to sit down.

'Just three days. I'm still getting over the jet lag, but I'm loving it so far,' I say.

'You've already lost weight. I can see it in your face. That's the Brad magic, eh?' Doug elbows his son.

'Thanks,' I say, shuffling in my seat. It's weird that he's commenting so openly about my body. Surely, it's impossible that there's been any noticeable change in such a short time.

'Not that there is anything wrong with being a larger lass,' Doug continues. 'Gives our Brad something to hold on to, eh?' He chortles and I want to shrink into my seat and disappear. Maybe Doug isn't the ideal father-in-law I imagined.

'Dad!' says Brad, sounding like a mortified teenager.

'Don't go on, Douglas,' snaps Teresa as she places a bowl of salad in the middle of the table. 'Leave the poor girl alone.'

Doug shrugs, unperturbed. 'It's a compliment.'

I clear my throat and force a smile. 'How have your weeks been?' I ask, desperate to change the subject.

'Oh yeah, not bad, love. I've been hard at work whilst this one' – he points a thumb at Teresa – 'has been hard at shopping.'

Teresa rolls her eyes. How does she get that flick of eyeliner so perfect? Whenever I try to do it, I end up with one good eye and one wonky-looking one. I wonder if she has a glam squad like the Kardashians.

'I've been doing my charity work with the Women of Waverley,' says Teresa as she sits down at the table.

'Of course, my wife would be a part of a group called WOW. That's what everyone says when they see her,' says Doug, reaching out and squeezing her hand.

'Oh Doug, please. It's not WOW, it's Women of Waverley. Don't be uncouth. You know, you might be interested in this, Christin— Chrissy. As much as Douglas plays it down, I do a lot of fundraising for charities, usually cancer research and the like. However, just recently, we've taken on a weird little charity called Nahla's Place.'

'You mean the animal rescue?' I lean forward with interest.

'You know it?'

I nod eagerly. 'Yeah, that young girl who rescued all the hens from battery cages?'

Teresa picks at her salad thoughtfully, her forehead creasing into a frown. 'That's it, so it's a bit of an odd sell for me. I'm used to talking to people about curing illness or helping homeless children... but chickens? I was saying to you – wasn't I, Douglas? – why worry about chickens when there are starving children in the world?'

'You did say that, yes.' Doug nods as he places a big plate of animal flesh on the table next to the sweet potato salad.

'The Women of Waverley are a committee of local fundraisers and there's a woman there who is very into it all. Apparently, her life is too hectic for her to go, so she's asked me to go and visit the charity. I don't think I even own a pair of gum boots.' She gestures to her feet, which are encased in delicate sandals.

'Would you like me to go for you, Teresa? I'd love to. We could go, couldn't we Brad?' I cast a hopeful glance at him and can't help bringing my hands together in a light clap.

Brad runs a hand through his hair, a pensive expression crossing his face. 'Ugh, I guess,' he says. 'Not for a couple of weeks, though. My personal training has to come first.'

'Yes, yes. Bradley,' says Teresa, raising her wine glass. 'You could take some photos we can use for the fundraiser. Interview the chicken girl and see if we can put an interesting spin on it.'

'I can't wait,' I say, a wide grin spreading across my face.

'Odd thing to be excited about, but good for you,' says Doug as he pulls a big slab of chicken onto his plate.

25

I'm jogging along the beach. Well, okay, I'm kind of power walking with an added bounce. I've only been training for a couple of weeks and whilst my thighs are still chaffing, I'm sure I'm getting fitter. My hair is wet from the little dip I just enjoyed (jellyfish free, thank you very much) and I have enough freckles that it almost looks like I have a tan.

Jess owned up and said she guessed I would drop out of bootcamp after the first day. Well, look at me now, Jess.

So, I did get a text from Tom the day after he ditched me for Janine, but not until late that night. That's, like, twenty-four hours of me glancing at my phone, trying not to be bothered, but being one hundred per cent bothered.

The text finally came through when I was in bed that

night, my mind buzzing with thoughts of meeting one of my animal rescue heroes.

TOM

> Hey, your head is normal-sized.
> Hope to see you soon.

That was it.

Seriously? That is what I had been waiting for all day? I almost text back, so grateful was I for the kernel of communication, but I called Jess instead, who swiftly talked me out of it.

Since then, I've been keeping myself busy without Tom.

Chloe's been a brilliant tour guide. She knows all the best restaurants and cafes and we've totally leaned into the tourist vibe, having drinks at The Opera Bar one day and feeding ducks bird seed in Centennial Park the next. As for Brad, I've racked up more steps on my Fitbit than ever before, thanks to our hikes together. If he'd just leave off about my weight for a second, he could well be the perfect man.

As much as Brad was pushing his smoothies and calorie counting, I've decided not to diet. It's just not for me. I found myself obsessing over food more than ever before. Instead, I've resolved to eat more fruit and veggies and a bit less processed stuff. But let's be honest, Cheynique would never let a man boss her around, so neither will I.

As for weighing myself, it's way too triggering. If I see I've lost weight, I feel amazing, but if I gain a little, I feel awful for the rest of the day. So, to Brad's dismay, there will be no more scales in my life.

I'm not thinking about Tom at all. In fact, I wish him and Janine the best, I really do. The only reason I pick up my pace as I near the lifeguard tower is to challenge my body, not to increase my chances of running into Tom. And not to show him my increased fitness. No, not me.

Tom hasn't been at work the last few days. Well, I haven't seen him at least. I don't allow myself to feel disappointed. If he cared about me, he would have texted me since last week and he hasn't.

The lifeguard tower is just ahead of me, and I speed up even more. My calves burn as I power through the deeper sand near the tower. Brad would be so proud. I pull my phone out of my pocket as I run.

Holding the phone out in front of me, I make a video for my family WhatsApp group.

'I couldn't run this far a week ago and now I'm ploughing through this sand like nobody's business— Argh.'

My foot hits a soft mound, and I lose my balance. Gravity takes over and there is nothing I can do to right myself. With a thud, I land flat on my face in the sand. Looking up, I see a discarded backpack and towel were the culprits that caused my fall.

'Bugger.'

'Are you okay?'

I wipe the sand from my eyes.

Tom is standing above me, trying not to laugh.

'What was the plan?' he asks. 'I've seen all kinds of influencer wannabes on this beach, but this is the first time I've seen someone try to run and film themselves at the same time.'

'Well, I guess it's your lucky day,' I say, pushing myself up and dusting the sand off my phone.

'Still enjoying your get skinny stuff?' he asks, raising his dark eyebrows.

Squinting against the sun, I roll my eyes slightly. 'I'm not trying to get skinny. Well, not anymore. But if you mean get fit, then yes, I am enjoying it... mostly.'

'Careful not to get sunburnt,' he says and lifts a hand to touch my shoulder, which is now a light, freckled brown.

A spark runs through me as he touches my skin and I jerk my shoulder away.

'I am being careful,' I snap.

Unfazed by my reaction, Tom shifts his weight and shoves his hands in his pockets. 'I was gonna text you, actually, about going to the rescue centre sometime.'

I cross my arms over my chest. 'I'm going to one with Brad.' The words come out colder than I intended.

His face falls. 'Oh... right, well, if you change your mind, let me know.'

'How's Janine?' I ask. I could not care less about Janine, but I want to remind Tom that I am very aware of her, and I will not be flirting with him anytime soon.

He glances towards the waves before shrugging. 'Um, okay, I guess.'

'Good. I better get back to it. Say hi to Ned for me.' Turning away, I jog towards the edge of the water, propelled by the need to get away from Tom.

I should feel great. I got to turn him down for once. It's no longer me waiting on the end of the phone for a measly little text. But instead, I want to cry as my feet splash through the white foamy water. I was mean, and that's not the real me. Not to mention I've done myself out of spending time with rescue dogs.

'Chrissy.' I hear Tom's voice behind me, and I turn. He's holding up a piece of paper.

'You dropped this.'

I stand still for a second, wondering what I dropped, and then it dawns on me. I jog back up to Tom and snatch the paper from his hand.

'Thanks,' I mumble as my cheeks heat up.

'Things To Do When I'm Skinny?'

I sigh. Of course, he read it. Great. Another thing to make him think I'm a shallow weirdo. Chloe had told me to get rid of the list, but I like having it in my pocket. As Brad says, I need goals and rewards to work towards. When other people take a drink of water in bootcamp, I sometimes pull out my list and remind myself why I'm working so hard on my fitness.

'What's that about?' Tom asks.

'It's pretty self-explanatory,' I say, but I can't keep up the bitchy act any longer. I plonk myself on the sand and he sits next to me. I unfold the list and pass it to him.

'It's just my goals. You know, stuff I want to do once I've lost all this.' I gesture to my body.

Tom is silent whilst he reads the list.

'You've done some of this stuff already,' he says as he notices my ticked-off items.

I manage a small nod. 'Yeah, well, a few things happened which gave me a bit of a kick.'

His eyes flicker up to meet mine. 'And do you regret doing those things, like coming to Australia, before you're super skinny?'

'No, I wish I had come earlier, but the rest of it is on the list for a reason. I need to be skinnier to do that stuff.'

'You need to be skinnier to go to a group dance class?'

His question catches me off guard. 'Well, yeah, if I don't want to make a fool of myself.'

'Didn't you think that about snorkelling, though? And we had a great time.'

'Yeah,' I say. 'That's true. But it's not like anyone was watching me snorkel, apart from you.'

A corner of his mouth tilts up. 'And Clive and Sheila.'

'Well, that goes without saying.' I can't stop myself from smiling. 'But even then, Janine had a go about her stretched-out snorkel.'

Tom shakes his head dismissively. 'Oh, don't listen to her.

I reckon you should go dancing now. What have you got to lose?'

'A whole lot of kilos.'

Tom looks unimpressed. 'I'll come with you.'

'Seriously?'

His face softens. 'Yeah, it'll be fun.'

My stomach flips as I think of a dancing date with Tom.

'I know of a class, actually,' I say. 'My friend Marcel from bootcamp runs one.'

'Well, what are we waiting for?' Tom playfully flicks a little sand at my leg.

'Okay, yeah, let's do it. I'll get the details.' I pause and gaze into his kind eyes. 'And Tom... if you do end up going to the rescue centre, let me know. I'd love to come.'

A beaming grin spreads across his face and I want to lean into those delicious lips and kiss him.

'Text me when dancing is on, and you can invite Chloe if you like... and Brad.'

I'm slapped in the face by a wave of disappointment.

Ah, so not a date then.

26

'I'm so excited to be here,' I say, as Amanda, a teenage girl with wild red hair, pulls me into a hug.

'You're from the Women of Waverley?' she asks in a British accent with a slight Australian twang.

'Kind of.' I shuffle from one foot to the other, tucking a stray curl behind my ear. 'Brad's mum is involved, and she knew I'd jump at the opportunity to visit this place. Sorry it took a couple of weeks to arrange it. Brad had a load of personal training clients to reschedule.'

The drive to Nahla's Place animal sanctuary on the Central Coast was beautiful. Even though a lot of the route was on the motorway, there were views of lagoons and palm trees to keep me entertained. We drove across a bridge where boats bobbed beneath us and pelicans circled above. It's the kind of landscape I can imagine dinosaurs roaming through.

And here, only ninety minutes from Sydney, in a little beach-side town, called Woollybutt, is the animal sanctuary I have read so much about.

'It's hard to believe you've done all this at such a young age,' I say as I gesture around me.

We are standing in the middle of several acres of orange groves. There is a driveway that snakes through the property and along it are chicken enclosures. As Amanda shows us into one of the predator-proof areas, it's like walking into a tropical jungle. Within that jungle are little chickens who seem so curious, running up and cocking their heads to look at us.

'So here is the famous Nahla,' says Amanda as a brown hen comes running up and gently pecks my legs. 'She loves preening. I bet she'd love your nails.'

I crouch down and spread my fingers out for the little hen. Today I painted my nails in a clear polish with a topcoat of silver sparkles that catches the sunlight. Nahla pecks at them and I laugh.

'They've been through a rough time in the battery cages and yet they love meeting new people,' says Amanda.

Brad is still rooted to his spot, outside of the enclosure.

'Come and meet the girls,' I call, waving my hand.

His response is less than enthusiastic. 'I'll stay out here. I don't want to get pecked.'

I can't help a sigh of disappointment as I wonder if I should have come with Chloe instead. Brad is clearly not interested in this at all.

'You're gonna have to come in. You need to take the photos for your mum.' I remind him, trying to mask my frustration.

'Can you do it between the two of you? There's chicken shit in there.' His face is pulled into a grimace.

I exchange a glance with Amanda, and she raises a fair eyebrow at me.

'It's pretty clean,' she says, hands on her hips. 'Volunteers were here earlier, and we cleaned it all out. We don't let the girls stand around in poop. This isn't a battery farm anymore.'

This is the impressive thing about Nahla's Place. It used to be a caged egg farm. Amanda was only thirteen when she somehow convinced the farmer to turn it into a sanctuary. I mean... my hero much?

Brad huffs like a five-year-old forced to go to bed early and opens the gate.

Nahla runs up to him and begins preening his legs. At first, he steps back as if he's dealing with a velociraptor, not a little hen, but then I notice his jaw unclench and he smiles down at her.

'So, Nahla was in a cage?' he asks.

'Yup, stuffed in there.' Amanda nods solemnly, spreading her hands apart to demonstrate the limited space. 'She'd lost heaps of feathers and the only way she'd be getting out would be on the truck to slaughter. Somehow, she's ended up as a real people person. She comes home with me sometimes and sleeps on the bed.' Amanda looks down at Nahla with clear affection. 'Just about the coolest thing ever.' Her smile falls. 'Don't tell Dad.'

'We won't.' I hold my hands up.

As we walk around the sanctuary, Amanda tells us the stories of the residents. We take lots of photos, of the animals, of Amanda, and of the landscape, for the Women of Waverley fundraiser. Brad takes everything in. He seems fascinated as he watches recovering hens dust bathing and flicking dirt over themselves.

I sit on the ground and the more confident hens of the flock come and investigate. They preen my hair, and one girl even hops on my knee.

'Can you take a photo on my phone?' I ask Brad. He takes my phone, crouches down, and snaps a photo.

'Hmm,' he says as he looks at it. 'You might want to lift your chin a bit more. You've still got a way to go to get rid of the extra ones.'

I lift my chin, and he takes another photo. I try to ignore the twist in my gut.

As he passes back the phone, I catch Amanda's eye. She looks unimpressed.

I send the photo to Jess with the caption:

Don't be too jealous, but I'm at Nahla's Place and it's better than I even imagined.

I'm beaming in the photo. You'd never guess from looking at it that Brad had just made me feel like shit.

'Take a look behind you,' says Amanda, and I turn.

'Oh my gosh, kangaroos,' I say in an excited whisper as I see a family of them through the wire fence of the enclosure. They're so close. 'A baby. Brad, a baby,' I keep my voice low, but there's no way I can conceal my excitement. I mean, a joey is right in front of me, peeping out of his mother's pouch. Come on, people.

Amanda's own excitement shows on her face. 'It doesn't matter how many times I see them, it's still amazing.' Her eyes follow a cockatoo with a stumpy tail who flies on a bumpy path like a bumblebee and lands on the net above us.

'This is Sunny. He was my first Aussie friend.'

'Can I just move in?' I can't resist blurting. 'Like live in a spare chicken coop or something?'

Amanda giggles.

'Argh! Get off me! Argh!' Terrified screams yank us out of our moment with the wildlife. Our heads whip around to find Brad, wild-eyed with terror, being chased by a rather large duck who seems intent on attacking his legs.

Bursting into action, I scramble to my feet as Amanda dashes towards the pandemonium. 'Levi, stop that.' Her voice is firm yet soothing, but the duck is undeterred.

'Get off, get off, get off!' yells Brad as he kicks his leg out.

'Stop running,' says Amanda. 'You're making it worse. Levi's getting worked up.'

Brad runs.

Levi follows, grabbing onto his leg and twisting his beak.

Amanda swoops in and secures the large duck, his wings trapped under her firm hold. Her tone is soothing as she carries him into another area.

'Are you okay?' I ask Brad as I reach him.

'No, I don't think so.' His tone is sharp. 'We have to go.' He turns to the enclosure door and storms out like a stroppy teenager, forcing Nahla to fly out of the way of his legs.

Outside the enclosure, Sunny, the cockatoo, flies above us, and a big Rottweiler named Keith bounds over and nuzzles into my legs. The kangaroos are bounding off, scared by the commotion.

Brad's eyes widen as he spots the gentle dog.

'Get me out of here. And you' – he jerks a finger towards Amanda – 'you need to put that duck down. It's a dangerous animal.'

Oh my gosh are those...? Yup, those are tears in his eyes.

'You need to bugger off,' says Amanda. 'Levi is from an abusive background, and he needs people to be gentle with him.'

'That duck is not the only one who has been through stuff, little girl. I'll be telling Mum to ditch this place.'

And with that, he storms off towards the car, leaving me standing next to Amanda. I'm absolutely mortified.

'I... I'm so sorry,' I stutter. 'Don't worry, I won't let him say anything like that to Teresa. This place is amazing. You're amazing.' My words are tumbling over each other.

Amanda's cheeks are so red they match her hair, and her eyes are narrowed and determined. 'These animals have been through enough without being kicked at by some idiot.'

'I know. I don't know what came over him. Can I make it up to you? Can I make a donation?' I'm about to cry. This was something I was so looking forward to and now it feels awful.

Amanda stares at me, and her face softens.

'It's okay,' she says, a gentle tone entering her voice. 'You're great, but I'm guessing he's not exactly an animal person?' She tilts her head towards Brad as he stumbles over a patch of blackberries, and we hear him yell again before righting himself.

She turns to me, her gaze serious. 'Chrissy?'

'Yeah?'

'You two aren't, like, together, are you?' An edge of worry has crept into her voice.

I nod and she grimaces.

'No, it's okay. He's not usually like this.' I sigh deeply. 'Would it be okay if I came back another time? On my own?'

'Of course,' she says. 'You're always welcome here. For now though, I have a slightly frazzled duck to attend to.'

I nod again and thank her before crouching down and giving Keith the dog a goodbye hug.

As I trudge back to the car, I wonder what the heck I'm

doing. I didn't come to Australia to be a grown man's babysitter.

WOOLLYBUTT BEACH IS A VERY different beach to Bondi. It's much quieter with just a few people walking their dogs. There are a couple of swimmers and just one bodyboarder enjoying the gentle waves. There are a few small houses along the beach front which is lined by bushland. A little way out is a sand island peeping out of the water. It would be perfect except I have a moody man-child next to me.

Part of me just wants to drive home and get this day over with, but the other part of me thinks, no, I'm going to enjoy myself, no matter what anyone else says.

Brad and I are sitting side by side looking out at the ocean. The sky is grey today with dark clouds.

'Fancy a dip?' I ask.

'Sure,' says Brad without looking up from gazing at his feet.

'Maybe the salt water will help your war wound.' I reach out and brush his leg where a small bruise is appearing.

The fleeting contact causes him to wince. 'It hurts more than it looks. I don't know why the bruise isn't bigger.'

'I'm only teasing,' I say, trying to keep the mood light. 'But let's not let it ruin the day. So, you overreacted. We've all done it. God knows I have.'

Brad jerks his head up to face me.

'I didn't overreact,' he snaps. 'That arsehole duck was trying to kill me.'

'Right,' I say. I don't want a fight, but he needs to grow up. Feeling restless, I get to my feet, brushing sand off my legs.

'Chrissy.' Brad stands up next to me. His tone is softer now and as I turn to him, there is an apologetic look on his face. 'I didn't mean to ruin the day. I just, well, I don't need bruises on this.' He gestures down to his body. 'This is like the advertising for my business, you know?'

I suppress my instinct to yell, 'You're a massive douche,' in his face and instead I nod.

'And I can't tolerate violence of any kind.'

'I don't think Levi was being violent. He was defending his territory.'

'Well, it seemed violent to me.' says Brad, the muscles in his jaw clenching tightly. 'I've been through that, Chrissy. I've had my skin twisted. I've had to run before.'

'What do you mean?'

'At school. I was bullied so badly, I ended up in hospital. When I get confronted with anything that might hurt me, I panic.' He lifts his sleeveless top to show off his six-pack abs, and he runs a finger across the scar on his lower abdomen. I remember noticing it back when he showed me his jellyfish sting.

'Bullies did this,' he says, his voice barely above a whisper. 'Stabbed me with a protractor.'

'Oh my god, Brad, that's terrible.'

'It was... well, it is. Now I can never have a truly perfect body, what with the ugly scar.'

'The scar is part of what makes you who you are,' I say, placing my hand on his shoulder as he lets his top fall back down.

'Did you not hear me when I said my body is an advert for my business?' His gaze finds mine, his blue eyes filled with a desperate vulnerability. 'I know I was a bit irrational with that angry duck and I'm sorry. You mean a lot to me. I don't want us to throw this away.'

Despite myself, my heart aches for the little boy Brad who ended up in hospital because of big, mean bullies. I pull him into a hug, my arms wrapping around his waist. I press a tender kiss to his shoulder.

'It's okay,' I murmur, my words soft against his skin. 'I'm sorry you went through that. No one deserves that.'

Brad holds me away from him. 'Yup, that duck was a bastard.'

'I meant the bullies.'

'I know.' A genuine laugh bubbles out of him, a welcome break from the tense conversation. He pulls me towards him and kisses me more deeply than he ever has before. His hands are firm but gentle as they rake through my hair.

And yet as I close my eyes and lose myself in the sensation, another face intrudes on my thoughts. Here I am, with the best-looking guy in Woollybutt, perhaps even New

South Wales, but why does Tom's face keep popping into my head?

27

I 'm having another one of those surreal 'I'm really in Sydney' moments. I'm on the ferry, leaning against the railing with Tom by my side. The sun is dipping as we chug into Circular Quay.

'Say vegan cheese,' says Chloe as she snaps a photo of us with the harbour and the opera house in the background. She shows me the picture. I don't look too bad. Marcel said to wear activewear, so I'm in my standard leggings and a vest top. My hair is whipping back in the wind, but it's Tom I can't keep my eyes off. He's wearing black jeans and a shirt as if he's going out to a club rather than a fitness class. He looks gorgeous. I thought he had been posing for the camera, but he was looking at me, the biggest grin on his face.

'You make me feel like such a tourist,' he says, as he glances at the photo.

I smile back at him.

I haven't done much dancing before, well, unless you count drunken nights out. When I was in high school, I took a dance class. I was having a great time until one of the most popular girls came up to me and said, 'I love watching you dance. It's so funny.'

I've avoided dance classes ever since. I'll admit part of me still wants to wait until I'm slim, but the other part of me (and Tom) says screw the skinny list. Do the things now.

The dance studio is in Kings Cross, which Chloe informs me used to be Sydney's red-light district. It turns out street prostitution is legal in New South Wales, and you know what? I'm happy if it means these people can make a living in a safer way. Sure, the place has a bit of a seedy vibe, but it's vibrant and bustling with people excited for their night out. There's a giant Coca-Cola sign that dominates the view down the street. It kind of makes me want a Coke. Nope, must stick to water. I take a glug from my bottle.

'Looks like we're here.' Chloe points to a red door in between a sex shop and a twenty-four-hour convenience store. A hand-drawn sign hangs on the door. It reads *Marcel's Boogie Box*.

Chloe pushes open the door to reveal a staircase with a red velvet carpet and fairy lights around the banister. We walk up the stairs and arrive in a spacious, bright dance studio with mirrors everywhere. Talk about confronting. I can see my flab from angles I had never dreamed of.

Latin music is playing at a low volume and people are chatting, stretching, and bobbing to the music all around me.

'You made it.' Marcel bounds over to us. He's wearing a black mesh top and neon pink harem pants.

'This is amazing.' I spin around, my arms flung wide.

'Thanks, babe.' Marcel grins at me. 'It's been a lot of work, but things are taking off now. People are getting right into the classes and I'm loving it. If it keeps going like this, my finance job can bugger right off.'

I giggle. 'I need to warn you I'm not much good at dancing,' I confess as I tug at the hem of my shirt. 'I mean, I enjoy it, but I don't have any talent.'

Marcel shakes his head, but before he can say anything Chloe butts in.

'Shut up. Out of all the people here, which one has been endorsed by THE Cheynique?'

I can't help let out a burst of laughter. 'That wasn't based on my dancing skills.'

'Marcel, this all looks fabulous,' Chloe says as her eyes sweep across the room. 'And don't you worry, Chrissy and I will obviously be naturals. We'll do our best not to show everyone else up, but no promises.'

'Ladies, it's just about having fun. And I see you brought some eye candy for me.'

Tom laughs, lifting his hands in surrender.

As I head over to the corner of the room to stash my bag, I check out the other people in the class. There are a few who could easily fit into a Broadway adaptation of Step-Up with their toned abs on display.

But then there are larger women like me, non-binary folk, an old lady dressed as Dolly Parton, and a gaggle of women in eighties fitness gear. As they bob around together chatting, they seem to have found the place they fit in.

The volume of the music increases, and Marcel pulls down the blinds and hops up onto a little stage at the front of the room. Disco lights flash around us and Marcel steps side to side, clapping his hands above his head.

'Welcome everybody.'

Everyone falls into rhythm, copying his movements and I join in, a smile spread wide on my face. I feel hidden in the disco setting and allow my movements to loosen up. I glance to my left. Tom is having no problem joining in.

'A reminder, loves, that Mohammed will be snapping pics and videos for our socials throughout. No pressure to post them, but they can all be found on our webpage. I'd love the help to get the word out about the studio.'

I spot a tubby, bald man in a violet shell suit prancing about the room with his phone. Chloe and I jiggle extra hard for the camera. When it's pointed at Tom, he busts out some breakdancing moves that I was definitely not expecting. My shriek of appreciation causes Tom to chuckle as he brushes off imaginary dust from his jeans and takes a casual bow.

'No matter what a shitty day you've had. No matter how that bitch at work has treated you' – Marcel points at a skinny woman in the back who lets out a *woohoo* – 'no matter what you've been dealing with, you are now in Marcel's Boogie Box, and we appreciate you and know your worth. So, beautiful people, let's do this.' His voice rises at the end and the class cheers and jumps up and down.

'We're gonna start with a booty-shaking dance in celebration of one of our newcomers.'

The beat shifts and I recognise a Cheynique hit as it booms through the speakers.

'Follow along as best as you can and if you get lost, just keep moving your body.'

Marcel wiggles his waist in a circle, pushing his butt out as he goes. I copy him and as I catch Tom's eye, I know I made the right decision, not mentioning this to Brad. He would probably hate it, so why upset him?

About ten minutes in, we're told to get into pairs. Chloe's pulled off to the side by Dolly Parton, and I stare awkwardly at Tom for a moment. He holds out a hand and I take it. The new song starts, and Marcel instructs us through some basic salsa moves. Tom's hands are on my waist. His eyes are locked on mine. And our hips are moving in time, so close together. I glance at the stage to see what to do next, but it's hard to concentrate with Tom so close to me. Hidden under the disco lights, I wonder if I could reach up and pull his lips to mine.

Tom twirls me away from him. Giddy, I stumble and try to right myself and pick up the routine again. I can't stop thinking about it, our bodies so close together. The buzz that vibrates between us. I wish I could stay like this forever.

Forty-five minutes later, I am sweating buckets. The songs have been so joyful that I found myself putting in more effort than I ever have in bootcamp. My top is drenched, and I've pulled my hair up into a high pony on top of my head.

'That's it, stretch and breathe as you reach up to the sky. Now say it with me: *I am awesome!*'

Those words would usually make me cringe, but as I shout them, I kind of believe what I'm saying.

There's another cheer, and the class erupts into applause. The energy remains electric as Marcel takes a bow and hops down into the room to high-five and hug his sweaty friends.

'Incredible,' I praise him as he strides over to me.

'You get out what you put in.' His eyes flick to my sweat drenched top.

'Loved it,' says Chloe, high-fiving him. 'Although I need, like, five pizzas, to recover.'

'Killed it, man,' says Tom, clapping him on the shoulder.

'Hey, are you all headed back to Bondi?' asks Marcel. 'I'll give you a lift.'

We help Marcel tidy up and lock the studio. Then we cram into his hatchback exhausted but buzzing from the intense workout. The tinny beep of Marcel's phone fills the car.

'Photos are ready,' he coos as he passes the phone to Chloe.

Scrolling through the candid shots, Chloe's eyes widen with delight. 'These are gold. Check it out, Chrissy. Here's one of you.'

The photo shows me with the biggest smile on my face. Despite the disco lights, you can see my skin is pink from exertion. My hip juts out to the side and my arms are behind my head. That must have been the wiggly hip dance. I remember losing track of the choreography, so I just kept wiggling until it got to a bit I could follow. At first, I felt self-conscious, but then I realised no one was judging me. They were all too busy enjoying themselves.

'I love it,' I say, 'and look at you.' I flick to a photo of Chloe and me grinning at each other whilst holding hands for one of the partner dances.

'That's frame-worthy,' she declares.

'Let's have a look.' Tom takes the phone. 'Woah!' he says. 'You both look fantastic. You loved it, didn't you?'

'So much!' I say with a grin as we drive through the Sydney streets. 'I couldn't be happier right now.'

'Thank the dance endorphins,' says Marcel.

Maybe he's right, or maybe it's more to do with a certain tall, dark man sitting right next to me.

28

'Sounds fun,' says Brad, the next morning, as he lays out a variety of resistance bands on the sand.

'It was so good, Brad. You should give it a try.'

'Not really my scene.' He scrunches his face. 'Dance is decent cardio, but building muscle is the priority. That's why I thought you might like to save the class until you've made more progress.'

I decide to ignore Brad's negativity.

'We got some great photos. They have this guy, Mohammed, who bops around taking pics the whole time. He's such a vibe.'

I hold my phone out to Brad and show him the photos of me and Chloe from the night before. I'm careful not to show him any photos of Tom. Why make Brad jealous when there is no need?

Brad leans forward, peering at my phone. 'That's a good one.' He chuckles as he takes in the photo of me twirling in the hip-shaking song. 'Could you send it to me?'

'Oh, yeah?' I smile and a glow of happiness fills me.

'It'll make an even better before photo than the one I posted.'

My smile drops.

'Before photo?'

'Don't get me wrong, it's a cute pic. It's just with you jumping around, it's easy to see your fat rolls. It shows how far you have to go. Can you imagine in six months when you go to that class again and they take another photo? We could highlight how your muscle definition has improved.' He grabs my bum in a playful gesture and pulls me towards him.

I wriggle free and step back.

'You are going to be stunning,' he declares, squatting down to retrieve more equipment from his bulging sports bag.

He thinks he's complimenting me. Don't start a fight when he doesn't mean any harm by it. Do not start a fight.

'I like the photo,' I lift my chin in defiance.

'Me too,' he says with a shrug, and I figure this isn't worth it.

'I'm going for a jog.'

'Bootcamp's about to start,' he protests, his eyebrows knitted together in confusion.

'I'm gonna give it a miss today.'

'But your progress...'

He's still talking, but I don't listen. I'm running as fast as I can away from him, down the beach, my eyes filling with tears.

I'll say one thing about feeling super angry: it fills me with energy. I power along the sand with more speed than I ever have before. I can't believe that Brad still sees me as a before photo.

Stop being a brat, I think to myself. This isn't Brad's fault. He's just trying to help me. He might not see my progress, but I know it's easier for me to run along this beach than it was three weeks ago. Yes, my thighs are still rubbing together, but my muscles are stronger and more powerful as they propel me over the sand. I slow to a walk and stop to take off my trainers. Leaving them on the beach, I run barefoot to the water. I welcome the shock of cold as the water washes over my ankles and splashes as I run.

The adrenaline is wearing off and my running slows to a jog and then a walk and then a plod.

'Chrissy.'

I glance up. Tom is walking down from the lifeguard tower, waving at me.

'Hey,' I call back, my mood lifting.

As he reaches me, he quirks an eyebrow. 'Aren't you meant to be at bootcamp now?'

'I fancied a jog instead. What about you? I thought your shift wasn't until later?'

Tom nods, scratching the back of his neck. 'I'm covering for someone,' he explains. 'But I've got a little time before I start, if you fancy some company?'

Now that I've stopped running, my legs ache from the sprint. I fall in step next to him and we walk together at the edge of the surf, our hands by our sides, almost touching.

'That was so much fun last night,' he says. 'I'll go again if you will.'

'I'd love to.'

He cocks his head to the side with a teasing smile. 'You lied, though.'

Taken aback, I stop in my tracks. 'What do you mean? No, I didn't.'

Tom chuckles, bending to pick up a seashell from the sand. He examines it briefly before tossing it back into the ocean. 'You said you couldn't dance.'

I cross my arms. 'I can't.'

'Come off it. I couldn't keep my eyes off you.'

I glance up at him, but those brown eyes are so intense that I look back down at the sand.

'What about you with your surprise breakdancing moves?' I counter, trying to move the attention away from myself.

He shrugs and pulls a bashful face.

'I'm serious though, Chrissy.' His voice softens. 'You did great. Aren't you pleased we went?'

'Yeah, yeah I am.' I look up at him, enjoying the fizz

between us for just a moment. 'Gah!' A seagull swoops low over our heads and a wet splat soaks through my hair to my scalp. So much for a romantic moment.

'Oh no,' says Tom, not doing very well at containing a laugh.

'Yuck! Is it bad? It is, isn't it? It's bad.'

'It's not great,' he says through his laughter.

I pull out my phone and check my reflection.

'Ew, I'm covered. How can one little bird have that much poop inside them?' Without any thought I strip off my clothes to reveal my sports bra and knickers beneath. I leave my phone nestled in the pile of clothes on the sand and run into the ocean.

As I pop out from under a wave, I rub at my hair, trying to get the poop out.

'Come here.' Tom has taken off his top and followed me in. Even in my poo-covered state, I want to run my fingers over his chest.

'Has it come off?' I ask.

'Not exactly,' he says. 'Lie back and float, and I'll get it out for you.' I do as I'm instructed and gaze at the blue sky as Tom pulls gently at my hair, rubbing it between his fingers. 'That's better,' he says. 'You're gonna have some serious luck today.'

For a moment, before I turn over, I marvel at the fact I am not self-conscious as I float with my tummy in the air. I stand up and find myself in waist-deep water, with Tom close in front of me. I could so easily reach out, hook my fingers under the waistband of his shorts, and draw him to me.

'You got it all out?' I ask, to defuse the tension.

'I got it,' he says, before ducking under a small wave and popping up on the other side.

He stands in front of me now, his brown hair dripping over his face. His hands grasp mine under the water. I don't move away. I love the feeling of his fingers intertwined with mine.

As we gaze into each other's eyes, I notice flecks of hazel mixed within the dark chocolate.

There's that spark again. I assumed it would've buggered off since the night he spent with Janine, but nope, it's there and as strong as ever.

He leans his head closer to mine. And even though there are people all around, it's like we can't fight the attraction. We are being drawn together. Still holding my hands, his lips brush mine. I can taste the salt water. It's a brief and soft kiss yet it electrifies every nerve.

'We shouldn't be doing this,' he murmurs, stepping back and releasing my hands.

Reaching for him, I pull him towards me, kissing him more passionately this time.

Tom's hands reach around my waist. His fingers press into my wet skin. Sparks of pleasure shoot through me as I place my hands on his strong shoulders.

And the weird thing is, it feels right. I'm where I'm meant

to be, with the man I am meant to be with, and for the moment, nothing else matters. I don't want it to end and as we kiss, I run my hands up into his dark curls.

'Excuse me. There are children present,' shouts a woman with a piercing Scottish accent. Her voice cuts through our moment. As I turn my head, I find that, sure enough, the woman is holding a tiny baby and there are two young children playing in the shallow water near us. I hadn't even noticed them.

As I look back into Tom's eyes, an uncontrollable giggle rises from my chest. This is so not the situation I expected to find myself in today.

The woman tuts loudly and beckons the children to move away from us. She has fine features and a chic black crop of hair.

'What are we going to do?' Tom asks me, his face becoming serious. 'I'm not a cheater. Well, not usually. This isn't like me.'

'Will you tell Janine?' The reality of the situation is dawning and a pang of guilt punches me in the guts.

'You know me and Jan are just friends. I'm talking about your bloke.'

'But you're sleeping with her.' I frown. 'I saw her leaving the apartment a couple of weeks ago.'

He waves a hand dismissively. 'She slept in the bed. I slept on the sofa. It's over.'

'Oh... but what about the bar? That Beaches place?'

'It's all just business. We're not together. But what about Brad? You need to tell him.'

'Yup, yup, I will, when the time is right. I don't want to upset him.'

I pull my hands through my hair, wishing I could pull the stress out of the strands and send it out to sea.

Tom takes a step back. 'I'd better get back to the tower,' he says. 'Lives to save and all that. But how about ticking another thing off your list? Want to try surfing tomorrow?'

I may not have tried it before, but in my heart, I know I will be terrible at surfing. Still, there's no way I'm turning down more time with Tom.

'Yes, please.'

Tom's smile broadens. 'I'll text you,' he says as we walk out of the ocean side by side. I watch in a daze as he jogs back to the lifeguard tower. He turns back and playfully blows me a kiss. I'm so happy I could swoop up into the sky with the seagulls. I walk back up the beach and sit by my clothes, trying to process everything.

'Hey, Chrissy.' I jump as Brad calls down to me from the path above. 'I've been looking for you.'

All of a sudden, I feel very much on display. I'm sitting here in my underwear with all my wobbly bits out for the world to see. Grabbing my T-shirt, I pull it over my wet bra. I wave and as Brad bounds towards me, every cell of my body turns red with guilt.

'I just needed a moment.' I wonder whether I look as guilty as I feel. 'Why aren't you teaching bootcamp?'

'Don't worry about bootcamp. Marcel is covering for me. He loves the power trip.' Brad kneels in front of me and takes both my hands in his. 'I need to say something, Chrissy.' Has he been crying? His eyes are extra blue and his cheeks redder than their usual perfect bronze.

'I was a dick,' he says. 'You looked great in that photo, and I can see your progress. I reckon the reason I was harsh is that I know how shit it was to feel like I wasn't living up to my potential. I don't want you to go through that. You deserve to be happy, and well, I think I'm falling for you, Chrissy.'

He pauses.

I open my mouth to say something in reply. 'I... I...'

He places a finger on my lips.

'Please let me get this out. I've been going over it in my head for the past thirty minutes. You're awesome. You're beautiful. You're funny. You're kind. I just feel this is all meant to be. Please don't let my shit past ruin that.'

'Brad, I think you're wonderful too,' I say.

'You do? Oh, thank god,' he draws me into his arms and rocks me side to side in an excited hug.

I gently push him back. 'I need to tell you something.'

'First, can I tell you something?'

I nod.

'The bullying stuff has affected me more than I thought. Spending time with you, I've realised I let it mess me up. It was so bad, Chrissy. That protractor stuff was just one thing, but every day was a nightmare. I want to change. I don't want to be so focused on looks, and I know you can help me with that.'

An image of young Brad with his cute, chubby cheeks pops into my head and I want to cry.

'I mean, you don't care about looks at all, do you?' he continues.

'Well, erm—'

His voice drops lower. 'I was just ten when I was stabbed.' His finger ghosts the hidden scar. 'It hurt me physically, but even worse was the mental stuff.'

'I'm so sorry,' I whisper, and I pull him back into a hug.

'Thank you for being here with me,' he murmurs into my hair as I stare over his shoulder and out across the beach.

Well, that's it then. There's no way I can break up with Brad right now. I'm not a total monster.

As I rest my head on his shoulder, I catch the eye of the Scottish woman as she leads her children up the beach. She shakes her head at me with her mouth puckered.

'Disgusting honeypants,' she mutters under her breath.

29

'Hang on... so he, like, loves you?' Jess looks quite astonished on the other end of the Zoom call.

I roll my eyes. 'Is that so hard to believe?'

'No, don't be silly.' She pauses, biting her lip in contemplation. 'It's just I wasn't getting the love vibe from you.'

I sigh deeply. 'It's because it's not there, but he can be so sweet. When he seems nasty about my weight, it's just because he's trying to protect me from bullying.'

Mum who had been sipping her wine, puts down her glass with a clink and leans forward towards her screen. 'Well, that, my dear, is a gigantic pile of crap,' she declares.

'I agree with you, Maddie,' says Jess, who always refers to my mum by her first name.

I rub my forehead, realising that perhaps it was a bad

idea to get Mum and Jess together on a Zoom call. They always did like to gang up on me.

'You agree that my love life is a load of crap?' I throw the question at Jess, my tone defensive.

'I agree that making excuses for a controlling man is a load of crap.'

Mum is nodding vehemently. 'I've taught her better than to put up with this, Jess.'

'I know you have, and Chrissy, as your friend, I need to be honest with you. I saw what you went through with Jeremy. It's great you're ready to date again, but this controlling behaviour is just not on.'

'Oh, no, Brad is so different from... y'know. He's like a big puppy dog.' I look down at my shirt and fiddle with a loose thread. 'Yes, he's a bit much sometimes, but he's a personal trainer. This is what they do. It's not control, it's guidance. I don't want to break his heart.'

'So what? You're gonna cheat on him instead?'

'Jess!'

My mum lets out a snort of laughter.

'It's true though, isn't it?' Jess continues. 'You snogged the face off this other guy and the next minute Brad was confessing his love. I might be on the side of the bitch with the kids here.'

'I'm not cheating. We never said we'd be exclusive.'

Jess's face scrunches up in disbelief. 'Well, you're also not on Love Island, so that hardly applies.'

I huff. 'Fine, let's not talk about it anymore. Tell me what you've been up to. What about you, Mum?'

'Chrissy!' Jess cries. 'You can't change the subject every time a conversation gets difficult.'

I look at my nails. Today they are gold and shimmery, like sun-kissed sand.

'Okay. Yes, you're right, I'm wrong.' Sarcasm drips from my words.

'Chris, I'm on your side with the cheating thing,' says Mum. 'You're in Sydney to have a good time, not to get tied down. And, okay, I haven't dated in a while, but surely, it's still the done thing to have a chat about whether you're seeing other people? I mean, after her divorce, Miriam had a few gents on the go. It was only when she and Tony had a good chat that they decided to make it exclusive. Of course, later they got into swinging, but that's another story.'

I let out a groan. 'Mum! TMI.'

'Excuse us older women for having healthy sex lives,' she says with a wry smile. 'So, what about this Tom, then?'

I feel my cheeks heat up. 'Well, he's just... He's...'

'The look on your face tells us everything we need to know,' Jess cuts in.

'But he's got this complicated relationship with his ex. I wonder if I should stay with Brad because we do make a good team.'

'A good team?' Jess narrows her eyes.

'A good team is one thing, Chris, but what about the electricity? The spark? You want to chase that excitement,' says Mum.

'I'm meant to be going surfing with Tom tomorrow.'

Mum claps her hands. 'That's my girl!'

'You need to cancel.' Jess frowns.

'I thought having both of you on the call would help, but now you're confusing me even more.'

'Going on a surfing date with Tom is cheating on Brad. You can't do that,' says Jess.

'It's not cheating,' Mum interjects. 'And anyway, you said yourself he's being controlling.'

'Yes.' Jess nods slowly. 'But he still deserves a proper break-up.'

'Ugh, okay, I'll decide tomorrow. Let's talk about something else. Jess, how is it all going with Joe? Are you still loving living together?'

Jess hesitates, a slight shadow passing over her face. 'I am... yeah.'

'Trouble in paradise?' asks Mum, her eyebrows arched.

'No, no. I love Joe to pieces. And we do have that spark. Every time I see him, I'm like hubba hubba. But you know how much the shelter means to me. Like it does to you, Chrissy.'

I nod, and Mum does the same. She hears about the dogs nonstop from both of us.

'We've been having a great time living together, but he never wants to come to the rescue centre with me. He's always busy gaming or something and when I tell him about the dogs, I just want him to be excited, you know?'

'You can't expect him to have all the same interests as you,' says Mum. 'Having differences keeps a relationship interesting.'

Jess's voice becomes tense. 'I get that, but I was telling him about Jonah. The shelter is starting to get to him now. I'm noticing changes in his behaviour, like he's not coping.'

'That's awful.' I feel like I might cry, thinking about the poor little dog, trembling in his kennel.

'Yeah, and Joe was just like, "You can't take on all the world's problems."'

'Really? That doesn't sound like him. Maybe he was having a bad day?' I ask.

'Or maybe he's a wanker and you need to kick him to the kerb,' says Mum taking a swig of her wine.

'Mum!' I cry. 'It'll be okay, Jess. Could you explain how important the shelter is to you? He likes dogs, doesn't he?'

Jess seems to wilt a little. 'Yeah, I thought he loved animals, but he doesn't seem that interested. It's fine though. It's really fine.'

It's hard to imagine Joe being cold towards Jess. Mind you, that's what everyone used to think about Jeremy. Yet each time I would come back from the rescue centre, he'd be moody. I remember one time I asked him what was wrong.

'Nothing,' he'd snapped, his mouth a hard line. 'Nothing

at all. I wanted to spend time with you, but I guess I come second to cleaning up dog crap. But it's your choice.'

Other times, he would just give me the silent treatment.

After a few weeks of this, I decided to skip the shelter and stay home. He was happy at first. We were having a great time watching funny shows on Netflix together. But then I caught him staring at me.

'What is it?' I asked.

'Just wondering how we ended up here,' he said. 'I was dating a cheerleader at uni and now I'm with someone who can't even get up off the couch.'

I'd laughed it off, but it hurt.

The bang of the front door interrupts my thoughts as Chloe returns from her latest Zingles date.

'Hey Chloe, I'm on a call,' I say.

She walks by the phone and waves to the screen.

'How was the date?' I ask her.

She grins. 'He was pretty hot. Huge.'

'Tall?'

'No, I mean, huge.' She eyes down at her crotch.

'You slept with him?'

'Yeah, we don't all take weeks to get them between the sheets. What if they're a dud root? Then you've wasted a month of faffing about for nothing.'

'Um, I should say I'm chatting to Jess AND my mum.'

'Don't hold back on my account,' says Mum. 'Oh my gosh, look at your tattoos. Amazing. Can you show me, love?'

I hold my phone up towards Chloe's arm.

'Oh, Chris,' Mum coos. 'It's times like this I wish I had a tattooed daughter. Did you design those yourself, Chloe?'

'Sure did.'

'Mum, you do realise most parents try to stop their kids from getting tattoos. And I have Billy Bob, anyway.'

'That little lizard? It hardly counts. What about a full sleeve?'

'It looks great on Chloe, but it's not me.'

'Cheating isn't you either, Chrissy,' Jess butts in. 'Promise me you won't go surfing with Tom until you've broken up with Brad.'

'Oh, go on. Let her live a little.' Mum fires back.

'I won't do anything to hurt anyone,' I assure them, and I mean it. At least I think I do.

30

As I stroll along the beach, I feel something verging on confidence. Chloe and I went for a dip the other day and when she saw me in my swimsuit, her eyes widened.

'Time to chuck the boring black cossie. It's hanging off you.'

Even though I keep telling myself that I'm transforming my health, not chasing weight loss, a surge of happiness shot through me.

I guess my efforts are paying off.

I was planning on ordering the same swimsuit in a smaller size, but Chloe wasn't having it. She insisted on dragging me around the Bondi boutiques. I almost passed out when she made me try on a tiny purple bikini. The top had those upside-down triangle cups that look great on models but made me look like I got dressed in the dark. And the G-string bottoms may as well have been an actual loin cloth. The colour was gorgeous, but since I am not Cardi B, I decided to give it a miss. As a compromise, I agreed to branch out from black.

'Get something that reflects your personality,' Chloe had said, holding up a bright orange number.

The swimming costume had a low cut-out in the back and leg holes higher than I have ever worn before. As a rule, I find changing room mirrors traumatising, but as I pulled the costume on over my knickers, I was filled with something other than the usual horror. I think it was pride. I have dropped a whole dress size and feel almost... Kardashian-esque.

It's weird because I can't have lost much weight in this short time, but I can already see a change in my body shape. I think it's from wriggling around at Marcel's Boogie Box, embracing my inner tourist as I traipse the streets of Sydney, and of course, the dreaded bootcamp.

Now, as I walk along the beach, I have an extra strut in my step. Although I'm wearing a black sundress, the orange swimsuit beneath boosts my confidence. The only thing I'm worried about is that all these beachgoers are about to see more of me than they ever wanted to.

My worry falls away as I catch a glimpse of Tom waiting for me under the lifeguard tower. It's as if he is drawn into focus and everyone else fades into the background.

As I near him, I can't help thinking about that kiss.

I'm not sure of the protocol after a first kiss, especially a kiss as good as that one. Should I go for a simple peck on the cheek? A fist pump (with or without hand-explosion)? Or maybe a full-on snog?

You know what? That was the best kiss of my life, with the most gorgeous man on the planet. I'm gonna snog him. I'm gonna do it.

I speed up as I near Tom and hold my arms out to pull him towards me.

'Hey, Chriss—'

His voice muffles as my lips smoosh against his and our teeth crash in the least sexy kiss since Uncle Derek laid one on me at Christmas.

'Sorry. Are you okay?' I draw back. Bugger, I think I bit his lip.

Tom laughs and rubs his mouth. 'You and Ned should start an overenthusiastic kissers club.'

'Sorry, I guess I was nervous.'

As much as I love Ned, I was rather hoping my kiss would outshine his. I crouch down and rummage through my beach bag in an attempt to hide my flaming cheeks.

Shrugging off my sundress, I stuff it in the bag, keen to get into the ocean and away from this awkwardness.

'How are you, anyway? I'm good,' I blather. 'I've been searching for temporary teaching jobs all morning. You know, need to top up the old bank balance. I've gotta sort out the visa stuff to allow me to work. It'll be good to work with some Aussie kids. Cute accents. I'm excited about this though.' I gesture towards the ocean. 'People at home won't believe I'm a surfer chick now.'

'Chrissy.' Tom interrupts my jittering monologue, his voice slow and relaxed in comparison. I fall silent and look into those deep brown eyes. He holds his hand out to me and I take it, warmth running through my entire body as he helps me up. We stand facing each other and he takes both my reddened cheeks in his hands and pulls me into a firm and passionate kiss. My body relaxes under his touch. I lean into the kiss, pressing my fingers into his strong back.

'You don't need to be nervous around me,' he says as he steps back. 'Also, um, wow.' He takes in my bright orange costume.

I drop into a dramatic curtsy and immediately want to slap myself for my theatrics.

He smiles and shakes his head.

'Do you want to borrow a rashie?' he asks reaching into his bag and offering me some blue fabric.

'If you have a spare one? I can tell you now that Janine's won't fit me.'

'This is one of mine. Will that do?'

I nod and catch the blue rash vest as he throws it to me. As I pull it on over my orange swimming costume, my Kim K vibe takes a nosedive.

I had imagined myself looking teeny tiny in his baggy

rash vest, but in fact, it's too tight on me and clashes with my orange swimsuit. Well, that knocks my confidence down a peg or two.

He gestures to the sand. 'Here's your board. You could've borrowed Jan's, but it's easier with a beginner's board, so I hired you a nice big one from up there.' He points to the hire shop by the beach.

'Are you not surfing with me?' I ask.

The corners of his mouth crinkle into a smile. 'Nah, I want to help push you onto the waves. I prefer bodyboarding anyway. And you said you haven't surfed before?'

'Definitely not.'

His grin widens. 'I'm sure you'll be a natural. Follow me. You can practise on the sand first.'

He walks towards the flatter sand near the water's edge.

I pick up my board, imagining I'm Kate Bosworth in *Blue Crush*. But it's harder to manage than I expected. The wind is strong, and it catches my big board like a sail. I'm blown a few staggering steps down the beach.

'Okay, lie down,' says Tom.

I drop the board to the sand and do as he says. Gosh, this commanding thing is quite hot, actually.

'What are you doing?' Tom rubs his stubbled chin and frowns.

'Um... lying down on the board.'

'You're gonna surf on your back?' he asks with a chuckle.

I pull my hands to my face to cover my embarrassment. I

had thought he might be about to give me a lecture on how to surf and just wanted me to get comfy. But nope, I've made a twat of myself already.

'Like this,' he says, lying on the sand next to me and pretending to paddle his arms.

I flip over and copy Tom. Hey, this isn't too bad. Lying on my front, pushing the sand back between my fingers, is quite soothing.

'So now we're gonna practise the pop-up. Here I'll show you.' He gestures for me to move, and I roll off onto the sand.

He lowers himself onto the board, places his hands on its sides, and pushes himself up in one gliding motion. I notice his biceps ripple as he lifts his weight and lands in a perfect surfer pose. I mean, it looks easy. If this is all there is to surfing, maybe this could be my thing. Maybe I'm a naturally talented surfer and I just don't know it yet.

'Now you have a go,' he says as he hops up onto the sand.

I clamber back onto the board.

'So, my hands here?'

'Yup, on the rails.'

I try to push up. My arms are wobbling under the strain of my body weight. I'm kind of wishing I had listened to Brad and tried full-body push-ups, not just kneeling ones. As I stagger up, frustration rises within me.

'That's it, but try again and this time, use your arms and kind of pop into place.'

Tom makes it sound easy, but when I try it, my arms

tremble and my body remains defiantly on the board. In the end, we settle for a kind of half pop up, half drag up.

After ten minutes or so, Tom rather optimistically deems me ready to try my luck in the water. We walk out through small white waves until I'm up to my chest.

He holds the surfboard in place as I scramble up and paddle a few strokes.

'The surfer look suits you.' He moves my board around, placing one hand on the surfboard and one on my thigh, so I'm facing towards the beach. 'Very hot.' His brown eyes have a mischievous glint and I kind of want to jump into the water and snog his face off, but no, I'm a surfer now. My focus must remain on the waves.

'So how do I catch one of these wave thingies then?'

'You would usually wait facing out to sea and watch for a good wave, but to start, I'm going to help you catch one. Don't even worry about standing up, for now. Just paddle when I say.'

Nerves buzz within me as I sit, bobbing and waiting.

'Okay... paddle, paddle, paddle,' Tom calls from behind me.

As the wave catches the board, I am pushed forward and up.

'Woohoo!' I yell. It feels like being on a rollercoaster as I bump down the wave. I grasp onto the rails of the board until I arrive with a soft scrape on the wet sand. Sitting up, I turn towards the ocean and wave at Tom, who is cheering and splashing the water.

I get up and drag the board with me, making my way back to him.

I go through this routine a few times, feeling like a dolphin who spins and surfs the waves each day for fun.

'Now it's time to give standing up a go,' says Tom as I reach him again. 'This time when you feel that push of the wave, use all your arm strength and pop up. Then it's just a matter of balancing.'

I wrinkle my nose. 'Just a matter of balancing, huh?'

As the next wave pushes me forward, I place my hands on the rails and try to muster all my strength. I push the front of my body up as if I'm doing a cobra pose. But nope, my arms are refusing to take the rest of my weight. I attempt to drag my left leg forward and immediately fall to the right with a splash. The small wave tumbles over me and for a moment I'm caught in an ocean washing machine. I pop up, spluttering. With my hair plastered over my face, I look less like Kate Bosworth and more like a monster from the deep.

'Good try,' shouts Tom.

I never expected to stand up first go, did I? Well, okay, maybe I did.

I try to keep the frustration off my face as I yank the board by the leash and make my way back out to Tom.

After five more tries, I am more than a little familiar with the ocean floor rubbing against my face. The local council should advertise this as a facial exfoliation treatment. I'm sure Gwyneth Paltrow's followers would pay thousands.

'It takes practice. You're doing great,' says Tom as he gives me a salty ocean kiss.

'This is tiring,' I say.

'My kisses?'

I splash him as he kisses my nose.

'Okay, I'm giving it another try, but after this, I need a break.'

As he helps push me onto another wave, I don't know whether it's some magical kiss power, but I somehow scramble up to my feet. There's no way you could call it a pop. If you imagine a piece of toast popping up from the toaster, this is more like when you put in a bit of bread that's too thick. You know, when it gets all lodged down the side and you have to use a knife to dislodge it? But it doesn't matter how I got here. The fact is, I'm up. I'm only standing for a second and I wobble like mad, but I'm doing it. I'm really doing it. I fall off into the water with a splash and jump back up. Tom is beaming at me, his dark curls wet across his face.

As I stand in the shallows, I don't think anything could wipe the smile off my face. I turn to the beach and give myself a moment to take everything in. There are children at my sides jumping over and under the waves. The beach is filled with tourists and locals enjoying the sunshine. Brad is walking along the edge of the ocean. Wait, what? No, he can't see me here on my surf lesson with Tom. Not before I've had a chance to talk to him.

Turning around, I take several long strides out to sea and duck under a wave, dragging the surfboard behind me on my ankle leash.

A forceful tug on my leash yanks me back to the surface.

'What the heck do you think you're doing? You could kill someone with that thing.'

I rub the salt water out of my eyes and recognise the sharp-nosed face and crop of black hair. It's the same woman who gave me a filthy look yesterday.

'It's you,' she says in her Scottish accent, so piercing that I am sure everyone on the beach can hear.

'I'm sorry.' I grab my ankle leash and tug the board back to me.

'The honeypants.' She sneers.

I notice some young boys sniggering.

'The what?' I ask.

'You know what. First, you lure all the men to the honeypot and now you're attempting to assault me with your board.' She tuts and shakes her head.

'I said I'm sorry.'

She seems to be ramping up to yell again.

Brad still hasn't seen me. I turn around and grip the board, so it doesn't whack the woman again. Although let's be honest, the way she's acting, she deserves a good whack.

'Don't you turn away from me, you disrespectful hussy,' she shrieks.

I dive under the next wave, and I guess the urgency of the situation has upped my skill level as I kind of pull off a duck dive with just my bum sticking up out of the water.

After about thirty seconds of hiding, I feel a hand on my back and lift my head to find a puzzled Tom staring at me.

'What are you doing?' he asks.

'I was on my way out to you.' I assure him, attempting to sound casual.

'But you were just kind of floating there.'

'Enjoying the moment,' I say, glancing at the beach and thanking baby Jesus that Brad has walked past.

'And what about the fact you just stood up?' Tom beams at me.

'I can't believe it. I guess I'm pretty much a pro now?'

'You'll be up against Kelly Slater next.'

'Who?'

Tom gasps in faux horror and dives onto a wave, body surfing his way back to the beach. I jump onto the board just in time for the next wave. This time I don't even try to stand up. I keep my head down and enjoy the ride back to the sand.

As we trudge up the beach, my muscles ache and I'm exhausted, but I know I've accomplished something special.

'I'd love to do that again,' I say.

'Next time we can hire you a bodyboard. I reckon you'll love that even more.'

I nod, wondering if perhaps bodyboarding will be the thing I am naturally skilled at.

'What was with that woman? Was she having a go at you?' asks Tom.

'Oh her? I think she was just worried about the board hitting her. Fair enough,' I say with a shrug.

'You don't like to fight, do you?'

I shake my head.

Little does he know the lengths I will go to avoid an argument. A pang of guilt twists my stomach as I think of Brad. What the heck am I going to do? Can I really stay with a man out of politeness? Especially when I feel such a powerful draw towards Tom.

31

I'm sitting on Tom's sofa with Ned snuggled against me. I think I have PTSD from the cookie incident, as I still worry that Janine might spring up from behind the TV.

Tom is pouring us drinks in the kitchen.

I pick up a framed photo from the side table. 'Who's this?' A slim, pretty woman with big brown eyes sits on a bicycle, a little boy in a seat behind her.

Tom's gaze trails to the picture. 'That's Mum.'

'Is that you?'

He nods, his eyes glued to the photograph.

'You were such a cutie. And she's stunning. Does she still look like this? I'd kill for that figure.'

A shadow crosses his face. 'She's dead.'

Tom says the words with a bluntness and a lightness that

suggests he's been through this conversation many times before.

Taken aback, I stumble over my words. 'Oh no, I'm so sorry.'

Tom gives a slight shrug, his eyes distant. His expression is carefully blank, as if he has practised over the years to ensure his emotions stays hidden. 'It was ages ago,' he says. 'She died when I was thirteen.'

I gently trace the woman's outline with my finger. 'That must have been so hard. Was she a model?' I take in her long legs and her exposed midriff – taut and toned.

He nods, running his fingers through his hair. 'Yeah, she did a bit of modelling before I was born.'

'I see where you get your good looks,' I say, raising my eyebrows.

A hint of a smile plays on Tom's lips as he flicks imaginary hair over his shoulder and pouts his lips, making me giggle.

'I wonder what her fitness routine was?' I ponder aloud.

Tom's smile fades and he takes a deep breath. 'You know, I wish you would stop this fixation on people's bodies.'

My cheeks heat up. He's right. What am I becoming? Someone who focuses on how people look... even dead people.

'You're like my mum in that way,' he continues. 'She was way too focused on how she looked. If it wasn't for that, she might still be alive.'

Okay, now I feel terrible.

'Sorry,' I mumble, burying my face into Ned's fur. I bite the inside of my cheek to distract myself from feeling so bloody awkward.

'Ah, no, I'm sorry.' Tom's voice softens. 'Mum had a pretty messed up past with anorexia. You weren't to know. She tried so hard to get through it.'

'I wish I could've met her. If she's anything like you... well, we would've got on.' I manage to say, my voice barely above a whisper.

'She would've loved you. She was a real softie with animals, too. I think that's where I get it from, hey, Neddy?'

Ned cocks his head at the mention of his name.

'And as for you' – Tom gazes at me – 'there's loads to love about you, not just that you're super hot.' He lifts a corner of his mouth in a half smile. 'You're adorable, you're funny, you're smart and one of the most caring people I've ever met.'

Did he just say the L word? I mean, he didn't say he loved me, but he did say there was stuff to love about me.

'Tom, I—' I start, but the buzz of his phone against the coffee table distracts me.

The screen lights up with a message from Janine. For once, I don't care about his ex, because there is my smiling face lit up on Tom's phone. It's the dancing photo that Brad thought was so bad. Tom has made me his lock screen photo.

'Tom, you got a message,' I say, a wide grin across my face.

He picks up his phone. 'Just Janine on at me to commit to that Beaches Bar. She can wait.' He places the phone back on the table and catches me beaming at him. 'What are you smiling about?'

'I may have just caught a glimpse of the hotty on your lock screen.'

Tom always seems so confident, so it's odd to notice a hint of red appear on his cheeks.

'It's a cool photo.' He shrugs.

'Brad thought it was so bad, I should use it as a before photo.'

'Well, Brad reckons one-armed press-ups are a good time, so forgive me for not trusting his opinion.'

Tom sits on the sofa next to me, places our drinks on the table and takes my hands in his.

'You were so happy at that dance class,' he says. 'Don't listen to anyone who says you need to change.' He's running his thumb against my palm as he talks, making my stomach flip-flop with lust.

Looking into Tom's eyes is so intense that I feel like I need to fill the silence, or I may spontaneously combust.

'Marcel's done such a good job with his studio. It's like I can be myself there.'

'I wish you could feel that way everywhere,' says Tom, still holding eye contact, still stroking my palm.

'Me too.' I swallow loudly. 'I feel safe with you, though.'

I lean towards him as if drawn by a force far stronger

'Do you think we should leave and find somewhere else?' he asks, ignoring my question. 'This is gonna be ages.'

'No, I think we should wait here, and the food will come when it comes.'

I've gone from enjoying a date with the world's sexiest man to dealing with a five-year-old with a sugar crash.

'Do I need to bring you colouring in crayons to keep you distracted when we go out to eat?' I ask with a little laugh.

'It's not me, it's them.' Tom eyes the waiting staff. 'Look, those people were here after us and they've already got their food.'

I have a flashback to that awful Zingles date with Gareth. I hated how rude he was to Chloe. Is Tom's tantrum a red flag? Or is it just a case of the hangers?

A smiling woman with grey hair pulled atop her head walks towards us, holding two plates of steaming pancakes. Tom's whole demeanour changes. That gorgeous smile spreads across his face and his eyes soften.

'There you go, loves,' says the woman. 'Sorry for the wait. It's busy today.'

'No problem, these look awesome,' says Tom. He holds eye contact with the woman and she giggles and lifts one hand to her neck as if she were a teenage girl with a crush.

'You're like a different person now you're eating.' I tease Tom as he tucks into his pancakes. 'From Hulk to hunk.'

'Oh, come on, that was hardly hulking. I probably have low

blood sugar from you putting me to work last night. No wonder I'm starving.' He has a mischievous glint in his eye, and I wonder if he's remembering our night (and morning) of passion.

'Hmm.' I raise my eyebrows, letting my mind wander back to Tom's kisses. I imagine him feeding me one of the chocolate-covered strawberries that are piled on top of the pancakes.

I can't help comparing this date to my final date with Jeremy. It had been at a little seaside cafe in Hove. Jeremy had ordered a full English including bacon, eggs, and black pudding. When I think of the smell, I feel sick all over again.

'Go on, Chrissy, try some. You'll love it,' he'd said, holding out a forkful of oily animal flesh.

'No thanks. You know I don't eat that. Anyway, my oats are brilliant.'

'God, you're a killjoy.' His face had hardened in an instant. 'We were having a great time, but I should've known you'd do something to ruin the day.'

I watch now as Tom tucks into his pancakes as if he hasn't eaten for days.

'I really appreciate you eating vegan around me,' I say.

'That's okay. I'm practically a carrot muncher like you now.'

'Oi!' I reach out and give his arm a little pinch. 'This isn't exactly a plate of carrots.'

'I'm teasing. I like that you care about animals, and you do something about it. I want to be more like that.'

'You literally save lives as part of your job.'

Tom looks thoughtful as he swallows another forkful of sugary goodness. 'Yeah, I guess.'

'Do you still enjoy it?' I ask.

'I love being back on the beach with the guys. I love the excitement of waiting to see what happens next. And I met a really hot chick.' He winks at me.

I laugh. 'It seems like your dream job. Will you still do it part-time if you open the bar?'

He sighs and shakes his head. 'Running a new business is more than full-time. It's a lifestyle. That's one thing I learned over in the UK.'

'I guess when it's something you love, it's worth it.' I imagine myself running an animal sanctuary like Nahla's Place.

'That's the thing. I'm worried that maybe I won't love it. It was fun in Brighton, kind of like playing pretend with someone else's bar. But things are different now. I want to be by the ocean, doing good, not getting people pissed.'

'There's more to a bar than that. It's a place for people to relax with loved ones, to make new connections and y'know, insult people's tattoos.'

He laughs. 'True, but it doesn't feel quite right.'

'I get it.' I grimace. 'I'm in a bit of a career crisis, too. Right now, I'm living off savings, but they won't last forever.'

'Any school would be mad not to hire you.' He takes another mouthful of pancakes.

'Oh really? And why is that?'

'Well, you're smart, you're funny and, oh yeah, you're hot.'

'And are hot primary school teachers in demand?' I ask with a small smile.

'Of course. Hang on, you've got a little...'

He reaches over the table and uses his thumb to wipe my cheek. He licks the chocolate from his finger. 'Really, though, I bet you're an awesome teacher,' he continues, seemingly unaware that by brushing my cheek, he has charged up every nerve in my body.

'I bet you're a great lifeguard, too. If you love it, you should stick to it.'

'Janine reckons it's a waste of my skills. I studied business at uni, so she thinks I'm throwing my life away. I guess she's right. There's a lot more money in running a Bondi bar.'

'Small businesses are risky though, aren't they?'

'Yeah, but Janine says I'm overthinking it. She reckons this Beaches Bar is a sure thing.'

I clench my back teeth as Janine's name comes up again and again. I'm surprised Tom can't see through this. Clearly, Janine wants to start a business with Tom, so they'll get to spend more time together. It couldn't be more obvious that she wants him back.

Jealousy won't get me anywhere, so I plaster a fake smile on my face and change the subject.

'So, do you have any plans for the weekend?'

'Actually yeah, my mate Zipper – I mean Jamie – is coming down. We used to do nippers together.'

Tom must notice the confused expression on my face, as he explains, 'Surf lifesaving for kids.'

'Aww, you did lifesaving even as a little one. How cute. But why is his nickname Zipper, not Nipper?'

Tom chuckles. 'An incident with a zip a while back.' His hand briefly gestures to his lower abdomen.

My eyes widen. 'Ouch.'

He takes my hand and kisses it. 'Come over on Sunday. I can introduce you. You can stay over if you like.'

I lift my hand from his and stroke his stubble. The crackling energy between us is so powerful I feel like knocking all the plates and cutlery off the table and pouncing on him right now.

'Hey, Tom.' My fingers gently trace a path down his inner arm. 'I'd love to come over on Sunday, but... um... how about heading back to your flat now?'

He tilts his head, a hint of mischief in his eyes. 'You mean—?'

'Yup.' I cut him off, with a grin. My hand now rests on his, a playful challenge in my gaze.

His eyebrows shoot up. 'Again?'

'Yup.' I twirl a curl around my finger and keep my eyes locked on his.

'I'll pay,' he says, his face flushing. He stands up in a rush and almost knocks his chair over.

'I'll text Chloe and let her know I'll be back later.'

As Tom pays, I pat my pockets and rifle in my bag. It hits me that I haven't checked my phone at all over the last twenty-four hours. I must have left it at Chloe's. I guess I've been too... um... distracted to notice.

Tom almost breaks into a jog as he makes his way back to me. I giggle as he takes my hand and leads me out of the cafe and into the bright Bondi sunshine.

33

I'm humming a happy tune to myself as I open the door to Chloe's apartment.

I plan to jump into a warm shower, enjoy a nice cup of tea, and then collapse into bed and catch up on some serious sleep.

Chloe walks out of her bedroom, her usually straight hair styled in loose curls.

'Hey stranger,' she says, a mysterious smile playing on her lips. 'Good surf lesson, I take it?'

I drop my bag on the floor and run a hand through my tangled hair. 'Sorry, Clo, I've been ages, haven't I? I left my phone behind, or I would have let you know.'

'Don't worry about it.' She waves off my apology with a graceful flick of her wrist. 'Someone's here to see you.'

'Is it Brad?' I ask, a stab of guilt twisting in my stomach. It was easy to pretend that whole situation didn't exist when I was tingling under Tom's touch.

'No.' Her eyes dance with amusement. 'But there is someone in your bed.'

I knit my eyebrows together and walk over to my bedroom, tentatively pushing the door open. There, fast asleep under my covers, is Jess.

'Oh my god!' I rush over and throw myself onto the bed, pulling Jess's sleepy form into a hug.

'Chrissy?' she says through a yawn, her eyes blinking open in confusion. 'I called you so many times.'

'Sorry, I forgot my phone. I can't believe you're here. Why didn't you tell me? How is this even possible?'

Jess laughs sleepily. 'Is it a good surprise?' She tries to sit up but finds it hard due to my excessive hugging.

'Amazing, incredible, greatest surprise ever,' I say as I bounce my knees on the bed. 'When did you even plan this? It wasn't that long ago we spoke.'

She yawns and props herself up against the headboard.

'It was Maddie.'

'Mum?'

'Yup, we stayed on the call after you left the other day. When she heard there were issues with Joe, she was on at me to go off on my own adventure. You know what she's like.'

'Um, yes. Yes, I do,' I say, remembering how Mum would try to convince me to skip school and go to the beach every time she deemed the weather 'a scorcher'.

'I wasn't really gonna go on holiday on my own,' she continues. 'But then Joe came home. I wanted to talk to him about Jonah because it was stressing me out how sad that little dog has been. And Joe was like, "I need time to decompress after work. I don't have the emotional bandwidth for this right now."' Jess mimics Joe's voice. 'And so I stormed off in a bit of a huff to the bedroom. And there on the bed was my moonstone.' Her eyes widen and she holds a hand to her chest.

Confused, I try to match her energy by widening my own eyes.

'And remind me what the moonstone is for again?'

'Chrissy... People literally call it the traveller's stone. I didn't put it there, I'm sure of it. So that was a major sign and then I was reading *heat* magazine and the first page it fell open on was horoscopes and it said Leos should spread their wings this month.'

'Ah, and you're a Leo, so—'

'So, I had no choice but to come over. The universe was totally telling me what to do. Well, the universe and your mum.'

'And you got off work just like that?'

Jess shrugs. 'I'm owed a ton of leave. The hospital has been on at me to take it for a while.'

'Well, I'm so happy you're here. So, so happy.' I bounce on the bed again.

She giggles. 'It's surreal. I got an Uber from the airport

and when I stepped out of the car, I just kind of stood there on the pavement looking around me. Palm trees, blue skies, cockatoos, and fit Aussies. I get why you love this place.'

'I can't wait to show you around.' I clasp my hands together, already planning our adventures.

'You don't have a job locked down yet, do you?' Jess asks, her face creased with concern.

'Still a lady of leisure.' I flip my hair with a playful flourish. 'I've got to find something in the next few weeks, but I'm just blowing through my savings for now. You only live once after all.'

'And who needs a house or food, right?' she says, extending her hand for a high five, which I eagerly return.

'Speaking of, do you want me to take you out for something to eat?' I ask. 'I've already stuffed my face, but you know me, I have a separate sweet and savoury stomach.'

'You've already stuffed your face with what, exactly? Chloe said you were with Tom.' She leans towards me with a teasing smirk.

'Jess!' I feign shock putting a hand over my heart. 'I stuffed my face with vegan pancakes.'

'Ignored my advice about Tom, I take it?'

'I didn't ignore your advice. I'll definitely end it with Brad soon. But let's get our priorities straight here. What about food?'

'Chloe made me toast when I got here. She's a sweetheart.'

'I'm not sure "sweetheart" is quite the right word for her, but yeah, she's brilliant. So, what do you wanna do? Do you need more rest? Do you wanna go to the beach? Do you want to get the ferry into Sydney and explore? Give the old selfie stick a workout?'

'How about I freshen up with a quick shower and then hit the beach?' says Jess, pushing back the covers.

'Yay,' I squeal, my own tiredness and aching limbs forgotten.

As Jess swings her legs out of the bed and heads to the shower, my phone vibrates on the bedside table. I lean over and pick it up.

Woah, twenty-three missed calls. Five from Jess, one from Chloe, and sixteen from Brad.

I tap to open the messages, skimming past the excited *I've arrived* texts from Jess and scrolling down to Brad's. I roll my eyes as I read his first message.

BRAD

Missing bootcamp won't help you reach your goals.

Wanna catch up this arvo? We can go for a jog and a HIIT session in the park?

Are you okay?

?

???

Fine. See you tomorrow.

Another missed session. Come on Chrissy, you're never gonna reach the after photo.

He has attached three photos to this message. There's the horrible before photo he took on the beach at the first boot-camp session. There's the one the photographer took at the dance class (yup that's the same one Tom has as his phone's lock screen). And there's another one that Brad must have taken without me realising. In the photo, I'm lying on the beach and propping myself up on my elbows. My fat rolls are on display and the sun is highlighting my cellulite. I am looking down at my phone, creating a less-than-glam multiple chin effect.

I feel a little bit sick.

BRAD

Look, this is your health we're talking about. You're letting yourself down. I'm coming over.

You weren't there. What's going on? Has someone kidnapped you? Haha. Miss you.

But seriously hope you are ok.

?

????

It's those question marks that irritate me the most. I throw my phone at the mattress, realising I'm a coward for not ending things sooner. I think Brad means well, but I've seen this kind of behaviour before.

I remember one time after we'd had dinner with Jess, Jeremy and I were walking hand in hand along Brighton seafront, back to his place.

'What's up?' I asked him as I noticed his handsome face pulled into a grimace.

'I don't want to say.' He looked away from me, out to the grey sea.

'Tell me,' I said as I stopped walking, placed my hands on his shoulders and gently turned him to face me.

He stared at the ground before lifting his gaze up to me and sighing deeply. 'It's Jess.'

'What about her?'

'She's jealous.'

I laughed. 'Jess doesn't have a jealous bone in her body. You know that.'

'She's trying to break us up. Didn't you notice? She kept

speaking over me, disagreeing with everything I said.' His jaw was set, his eyes narrowed.

'She just gets excited when we talk about the animal stuff. She's passionate.'

'And she was flirting with me.'

'She wasn't.' I dropped his hand.

'It was when you were in the bathroom. Didn't you see how she did her make-up like a sex worker?'

'No. Jess likes to experiment with different make-up looks. She did mine too.' I gestured to my face.

'Yeah, I noticed. You look way better without make-up. This' – he waved towards my face – 'just looks cheap. Maybe a model could pull it off, but not someone like you.'

'You've got it wrong,' I said, ignoring his insult. 'Jess only wants what's best for me. She always has.'

'So, you're not going to listen to me?' He pouted and turned abruptly, walking away from me.

'I am listening. But you've got the wrong idea,' I had called after him.

I jogged to catch him up, holding on to his arm to slow him down. 'Jeremy, wait.'

'Leave me alone. If you don't want to be with me, that's fine. You probably won't even care if I swim out to sea and drown.' His voice sounded so desperate, and I could see tears in his eyes.

'Of course, I care,' I said, my voice cracking.

His face softened. 'I love you so much. I can't bear to see

someone take advantage of you like Jess does.'

'I'm sorry, Jeremy. Don't do anything to hurt yourself.' My voice was gentle, but firm.

'So, you believe me about Jess?' His eyes searched mine for affirmation.

'Yeah, yeah, I do. I'll talk to her about it.'

He nodded and pulled me into a hug. 'And don't put all that gunk on your face. Your face shape is all wrong for it.'

Over the following days, Jeremy bombarded me with texts.

JEREMY

Spoken to Jess yet?

I love you so much more than you know.

Send me a pic of your face without make-up. Remember, you can't pull it off. I'm being honest because I love you.

The mix of compliments and insults had me confused and paralysed.

I'm ashamed of how long it took me to end the relationship. By the end, my self-esteem was in tatters, my friendship with Jess had taken a beating and I hadn't had a catch-up with Mum and Dad for ages.

I know Brad isn't Jeremy. But now I see what Jess and Mum meant about him trying to control me, and I can't let myself fall into that situation again. I was hoping Brad might realise that we aren't right together. I thought I could avoid hurting his feelings. But now it's clear I should have acted earlier. I let myself get sucked in by those sparkling blue eyes and the Viking vibe.

Before I can lose my nerve, I click on Brad's last text and press call.

34

'F inally,' says Brad. 'Where have you been?'

He doesn't sound angry; he sounds relieved, and his friendly tone takes me back.

'Sorry I missed your calls,' I say.

'It's okay. I've missed you... I'm keen to get you back on track at bootcamp tomorrow.'

That brief mention of bootcamp gives me the extra momentum I need to take action.

'Brad, I don't want to be on track. I think I'm happy the way I am. Bootcamps and protein shakes just aren't my thing.'

'Don't be silly,' he says.

'I'm not being silly.' I raise my voice in a most un-Chrissy-like way. 'I guess I've discovered that for me, movement is more fun when it's in the form of dance or snorkelling or surfing.'

Brad chuckles. 'No offence, but you'll need to work on your fitness a bit more before you attempt surfing.'

My cheeks heat up as I grip my phone tighter. 'No, I can try anything I like right now.'

'So let me get this straight. First you quit your diet and now you're quitting bootcamp? Do you even care about your body at all? Do you even care about me?'

'What you're doing is working for you, and that's great, but bootcamp isn't for me. Thank you for letting me come along and try it out.' I pause, taking a deep breath and trying to keep my voice steady. 'I love being on the beach and swimming in the sea after, but bootcamp doesn't make me happy.'

'It doesn't make you happy or I don't make you happy?' Brad's voice lowers, his tone serious.

Silence drags between us, as I realise I haven't addressed our relationship at all.

Brad continues, his voice laced with frustration, 'Because there are other bootcamp trainers, like if you want a woman. Or maybe you'd find it easier if you actually eat what I suggest. I don't eat unseasoned chicken breast because I like it, Chrissy. It's for my body. If you eat that too, you might do better at bootcamp.'

'Eating a chicken is not going to magic me into some bodybuilder. In fact, it makes me sick thinking of eating a poor little bi—'

'Don't you dare!' He cuts me off.

'What?'

'Don't you dare tell me that chicken breasts don't build muscle. You can't see this, but I'm flexing right now, and my bicep is huge, Chrissy. HUGE!'

'Well, good for you, but I expect you've done that despite the chicken flesh, not because of it. Look up, Nimai Delgado. He's a vegan bodybuilder.'

Brad scoffs. 'This won't help when you meet my uncle this weekend. We're all big chicken eaters. Uncle Marv is a chook farmer.'

My stomach drops and I shake my head. 'I'm not going to be meeting your family this weekend.'

'What are you talking about?'

'You and me. We aren't a good match. We can't be together.'

'What?' His tone softens. 'Are you serious? But... but... you and me – we're in love. The whole flying from the UK to be with me thing? It's meant to be.'

My anger at Brad simmers and my chest twangs with pity. I imagine little boy Brad desperate to be accepted and loved. I consider faking a crackling line and hanging up, but no, I need to woman up and be honest.

'Brad, you can be so sweet. You're gorgeous and you're a great trainer, but I don't love you. I don't think we are meant to be together. You deserve someone who is into you one hundred per cent. That's not me. You and me, we'd be better off as friends.'

'But I... I bought you your own set of resistance bands. I was going to surprise you.'

'That's kind, but—'

'Is there someone else?' he asks, a hiccup in his voice. I was hoping to avoid this bit. I don't want to lie to him, but I don't want to hurt him even more.

'There is someone I might be interested in.' And the Oscar goes to me for understatement of the year.

'But I've told all my family about you.' Brad's voice breaks, and I can hear the genuine hurt in his tone.

'I'm sorry. I shouldn't have let it get this far.' My voice wavers as I pace around the room.

'And I turned down Melanie.'

'Melanie from bootcamp with the big bum?' I stop pacing and place one hand on my hip.

'That big bum is from a huge amount of training. She's earned those glutes. She asked me out, and I said no, because even though she is massively hot, I was committed to you and the weight loss goals we set for you.'

'Well, I guess you're free to date her now.'

'And this guy.' He spits out the words. 'Is he going to train you?'

'No, no, not at all. He's just a guy, not a trainer or anything.' I force my voice to remain calm.

Brad exhales in a relieved puff. 'At least that's something.

I can still train you. We've already made good progress and we'll be at the after photo before you know it.'

'I don't want to upset you more, but I *am* my after photo. I may get fitter, I may even get slimmer, but that isn't my goal anymore. I've realised I'm fine as I am.'

'Chrissy, you're not making sense. Think about what you're saying, what you're passing up.'

'It makes sense to me.'

'Right, so you're not only ending our relationship, but you're also quitting on your self-improvement? So, this is it? This is all you want to be?'

His tantrum may be designed to make me question my decision, but it's just making me surer of myself.

'I want to enjoy my life as I am.'

'This is unbelievable. Unbelievable!' he says. 'I invited you here to stay with me. I took you on, even when I'm sure millions of guys wouldn't. And now you're too good for me? You are the most selfish person I've ever met. You know how much I need that after photo for my business. My followers are invested in your transformation and now what... you're just going to stay fat?'

'I'm going to go now. This is my decision.'

'You're making a mistake.' His voice cracks as I tap my phone screen to hang up.

I thought this honesty thing was meant to make me feel better, but ugh, this is awful.

'What's wrong?' says Jess as she walks out of the bathroom wrapped in a fluffy white towel with another twisted atop her head.

'I ended it with Brad,' I say. My brow is furrowed, but I don't feel like crying. If emotional weight was weighed in kilos, I would have dropped several dress sizes from breaking it off with Brad.

'Oh, babe.' Jess's eyes soften as she pulls me into a hug. 'It's the right thing to do.'

'Ending it made me feel like another one of his bullies. Like the people he had to put up with at school.'

'You can't be with someone just because you pity them,' she says, pushing a curl away from my face.

'Even if they look like blonde Jason Momoa?'

She laughs. 'Especially then. He should be free to find his perfect partner. Did he take it badly?'

I nod, biting my lip. 'Yeah. Although he was even more upset that I'm not going back to bootcamp. I hope I've made the right decision. I mean being with Tom is amazing, but that's new too.'

'If it doesn't work out with Tom, you can be single in Sydney. There are worse things,' says Jess. 'So, are we hitting the beach or what?'

'Let's go!' I slap my hands on thighs. I need to put Brad and Tom out of my mind for the rest of the day so I can focus on spending time with my amazing friend.

35

I wish I could be more like Jess. I'm drying off on the beach under a shade umbrella whilst Jess is still playing in the ocean. She's jumping over waves with some teenage girls she has befriended in the five minutes since I got out. They are all laughing, but Jess's cackle rings out over the others. She's wearing her new bright red and hot pink bikini and as she jumps, her bum and thighs wobble. I expect her belly is wobbling too, but I know Jess wouldn't even mind me saying this. She just doesn't seem to care. Confidence radiates from her, making her seem even more attractive. I swear her skin is already darkening into a nutty tan, unlike mine, which has an extra pink glow despite a thick layer of factor 50.

Now I've recovered from my conversation with Brad, I feel relieved. I'm free to enjoy my fledgling relationship with

Tom. I'm free to treat my body however I choose, even if that means I lose no weight at all. I close my eyes and lie down on the sand. Is there anything more calming than the sound of the waves?

'You and I need to have a chat.' A shrill voice yanks me out of my relaxed state. My eyes ping open to find Janine's glaring face above me.

'Janine, what's wrong?' I ask as I push myself up onto my elbows.

'I just spoke to Brad.'

'Brad?'

'Yeah, I called him to book into bootcamp.' She brushes a strand of golden hair from her face.

'Right, so is Brad okay?' I push myself further into a seated position and brush the sand from my arms.

'Not really. He's pretty concerned that you're quitting bootcamp,' she says, sitting down in the sand next to me and stretching out her long olive-skinned legs.

'And that I broke up with him?' I ask, my voice catching in my throat.

'He did mention that.' She shrugs. 'I wasn't shocked, considering your obsession with Tom.'

'I'm not—'

'I get it.' She holds up her hand and cuts me off. 'Tom's a good-looking guy. But this is why I want to talk to you. Women need to stick together. And the thing is, he's... well, he's not exactly what he seems. I mean, how would you describe him now?'

She lifts her sunglasses, her bright green eyes fixing on my duller ones.

I want to reply that Tom is a sex god, but since I'm speaking to the ex, I keep that to myself.

'He's lovely; kind, funny, just a great guy.'

'Yup, but when you get to know him, you'll see another side.' She leans closer, her voice dropping to a conspiratorial whisper. 'I've been weighing up whether to say anything, but the truth is... Tom has a temper.'

I suppress a laugh. Is she really warning me off her ex?

'At first it's all good,' she continues, waving her hand in the air as if painting a picture. 'But then he can just lose it. It could be anything from not being able to assemble a flat-pack to not getting his burger on time.'

I remember his little tantrum about the food being late. And there was the aeroplane seat hissy fit. Whilst I want to dismiss everything Janine is saying, perhaps there is a hint of truth to this. I feel a cold knot of uncertainty in my stomach.

'Why are you saying this? I thought you and Tom were friends.'

'Oh yeah, best friends, but I'm still a girl's girl, Chrissy. Guys love me, but I want to hang with my girls, you know?'

'Okay, but Tom hasn't done anything wrong.' I cross my arms, my voice firm, but my mind uneasy.

'Not yet, but keep an eye out. He's not Mr Nice Guy the whole time.'

Is she serious? I mean, could someone as kind and gentle as Tom really be dangerous? Janine may be trying to cause trouble, but what if she's telling the truth? An image of Jeremy flashes into my mind and I blink my eyes rapidly.

I'm grateful to see Jess running towards us, dripping wet.

'That was so fun.' Jess grabs her towel from the sand and wraps it around her body. 'Hi, I'm Jess.' She gives Janine a little wave.

'This is Janine,' I say, my voice monotone, my mind still reeling.

'Oh my god, THE Janine?' Jess bounces up and down in excitement. As she claps her hands together, her towel falls onto the sand.

Janine tilts her head, looking confused.

'The one from the plane who saw Chrissy get naked?' asks Jess, her voice rising in pitch.

I sigh and Janine chuckles.

'Yup that's me. Not exactly what we wanted to see. Your friend is not shy.' Janine raises her thick eyebrows – so on trend, not like my almost transparent ones.

'Think yourself lucky you got to see someone as gorgeous as Chrissy in the buff. She's got nothing to be shy about,' says Jess, placing her hands on her hips. 'She's bloody glorious.'

'I am kind of shy, to be honest,' I say, pulling my knees up to my chest. 'I hated it when my Insta account blew up. The thought of all those people seeing me with my stomach out still makes me sick. Not only did I lose my job, but I got a ton of comments. Jess told me most of them were positive, but still.'

'Ha, I wouldn't say that,' says Janine as she pulls her phone from her pocket and taps on the screen. 'I took some screenshots to use at thinspo... Listen to this: *This came up on my feed and I vomited... literally.* And how about this one? *Could be pretty if she lost weight.*' Janine glances up. 'You could take that as a compliment, especially since you are trying to lose weight.'

My stomach twists as I feel a sharp pang of humiliation. 'Could you not read them, please?'

'Just one more... This person says: *Yikes. My eyes! Have a think about what you are doing. No one wants to see this.*'

'She said to stop,' snaps Jess, her warm voice switching to the matronly tone that she's been bringing out long before she was an actual nurse. I've heard it when boys were giving us unwanted attention. I've heard it when kids were chasing ducklings into the road, and I'm happy to hear it now.

'Okay, okay, it's just harmless fun. But maybe they have a point,' says Janine with a mirthless smile. 'So, you've dumped Brad, but that doesn't mean you have to turn back to the Netflix and nachos lifestyle. The people who commented positive stuff on your socials just want to see you fail. You know how jealous women get.'

I'm not sure what to say. Firstly, how did Janine know

about my love of nachos? Secondly, what gives her the right to comment on my figure, my TV watching habits, or anything else about my life?

Jess points a finger at Janine. 'That's a shitty stereotype about women. And nachos rock, as does a good Netflix session and a tub of vegan Ben and Jerry's.'

'Not another vegan,' says Janine, with an overdramatic roll of her eyes.

'Yup, you've found yourself two fabulous vegan women, so I guess you'll have to like it or lump it,' says Jess with a clap of her hands. 'We don't have time for negativity from you or anyone else. If you want to join us for some fun, go for it, but if you're gonna be a pain in the neck, feel free to sod off.'

'Jess,' I say, wanting to keep the peace. 'Janine isn't trying to be difficult. She just views this stuff differently than we do.'

'No, no, I can take a hint.' Janine stands up and brushes sand from her legs. 'I need to go, anyway. I'm meeting Tom for a drink. But have a think about what I said' – her eyes fix on me – 'about Tom.'

I nod, my throat tight. 'Thanks, but everything will be fine.'

She shrugs and turns away. 'Don't say I didn't warn you.'

'What an utter arse,' Jess mutters as she applies more sun cream on her shoulders.

'Gorgeous though,' I say, my hands fumbling with my sarong as I pull it out of my bag.

'She's okay, but you can tell she's super high maintenance. I bet she wouldn't be much fun to go out to dinner with.'

'Those comments were harsh.' I lay the sarong over my legs.

Jess bends down and rips it away with a dramatic flourish.

'Internet comments are always nonsense,' she says. 'Anyone who left a negative comment is a liar or just plain wrong.'

I smile, wishing every woman could have their own Jess to build them up when others are trying to tear them down.

36

I'm sitting with Jess and Chloe in a restaurant courtyard. The air is balmy, and we're surrounded by trees and fairy lights, making it feel as if our little trio has stepped into a magical forest.

I twirl the umbrella in my strawberry daiquiri as I fill the girls in on the latest with Brad and Tom.

'I don't know what to make of it. My first thought was that Janine was just trying to scare me off. But Tom did have a tantrum on the plane and at the cafe. I saw that with my own eyes. What if there's some truth to it?'

'She's messing with you,' says Chloe definitively. 'From what you've told me, that cafe tantrum was a classic case of the hangers. You should see me when I'm in need of a chocolate fix.'

I chuckle and lean back in my chair. 'Um... I have. The

other night you dragged me out to trek the streets of Bondi in search of a midnight chocolate bar.'

'And I'm saying that is reasonable behaviour,' says Chloe. 'When chocolate calls, I answer.'

I shake my head, my lips curling into a smile, but the worry still tugs at me. 'Maybe I am overreacting.'

There's no need to explain to Chloe why I'm hyper-vigilant about this stuff. It would only dampen the mood. I catch Jess giving me a knowing look. She understands why I'm being cautious.

'So was the food at that cafe worth the wait?' asks Chloe.

'Oh my god, the most amazing pancakes ever.'

'Can we go there?' says Jess, leaning forward with excitement in her eyes. 'Maybe pancakes will cure my jet lag? Will your diet allow for more pancakes, Chrissy?'

'I told you I'm not dieting anymore. I'm just eating more fruit and veggies.' I gesture to my strawberry daiquiri. 'See.'

'I'm glad you've ditched that bootcamp crap,' says Chloe. 'Our schedules weren't synching up with you getting up at the crack of dawn and me working late.'

'It's not for me. Not when I compare it to how much I loved the dance class,' I say.

Jess wiggles on the bench. 'Oh, yes. Please let's do one whilst I'm here. It sounds like so much fun.'

'I still remember when you and Joe were dancing at Mum and Dad's marriage-vow renewal. Joe was so funny.' I splutter on my cocktail at the memory of lanky Joe doing his best to keep up with booty-shaking Jess.

'He tries,' she says with a sigh, gazing into her drink. 'We've actually been going back to salsa since you left.'

'Really?' I ask.

'Yeah, it's been good, but it's also... well, it's not the same,' she says, taking a sip of her drink. 'Things are different... a bit strained since we moved in together, you know?'

'It's a big change in a relationship.' Chloe nods in understanding. 'I never let it get to that stage.'

'I guess with you moving out, Chrissy, I had this idea that Joe and I would have the perfect little love nest. Like, it would be so idyllic, but it's not quite what I imagined.'

'Is he a dud root?' asks Chloe.

'A what?' Jess looks confused.

'She means is he rubbish in bed,' I explain.

Jess's face lights up and she leans back letting out a cackle.

'Oh my god, I love that phrase. I'm gonna use it all the time now. But no, not at all. We've still been at it like rabbits, but something is different. It's not just his disinterest in the rescue centre stuff. He's gone out "running" a couple of times at the weekend, but this is Joe. He wouldn't go running unless it was after a pizza. He comes back hours later and isn't even sweaty. Do you reckon he could be seeing someone else?'

'No way. He's devoted to you,' I say, reaching across the table to squeeze Jess's hand.

'You never know,' says Chloe, tilting her head to the side. 'I'd never have guessed Brad and Ange would split but... well, you know the rest.'

'Or Brad and Jen before that,' says Jess with a frown as she withdraws her hand from mine.

'Or Jen and Justin Theroux after that,' I say, before reminding myself I'm meant to be making Jess feel better, not worse. I change tack. 'Joe's different. He won't be up to anything. He's probably stressed out at work or something. Don't let it get you down.'

Jess's eyes glisten and her voice trembles as she speaks. 'I mean, I do miss him, but for the first time, I'm wondering... is there something wrong with me? Like with my body?'

'Jess, no!' The shock in my voice is real. I don't think I've ever heard Jess express any negative opinions about her body or anyone else's.

'You're hot as,' says Chloe, slamming her drink on the table for emphasis.

Jess wipes a single tear from below her eye and shakes her head.

'Ugh, I'm being silly. It must be the jet lag.'

'Are you gonna be okay?' I ask, wondering if we should switch this to a romcom and popcorn night.

'I'm fine. Nothing a few more drinks and a boogie won't fix. Take me to your cheesiest nightclub and get me some tequila.' Jess plasters a smile over her face. The problem is, I know Jess. She's such a positive person that to express any worry means something must be seriously wrong.

Two hours later, our bellies are full of Chinese food, tequila, and cocktails. Chloe didn't hesitate when it came to choosing the cheesiest nightclub. She said it had to be The Glitterbug in Darling Harbour. Now, as confetti pours from the ceiling, we are trying out some of our best dance moves.

Jess is dominating The Running Man. Chloe is doing her best attempt at The Robot. And I'm trying to replicate some of the Latin moves I learned at Marcel's Boogie Box. We must look like a right pack of wallies, but we're all smiling widely and for once, I don't give a stuff what anyone else thinks.

A stocky guy with bright blonde hair grinds up on Chloe. Jess pulls herself up to her full five-foot-one and takes a step to march forward. She's protective even when sober but give Jess a cocktail and she's ready for a fight. She steps back as Chloe turns and kisses the man right there on the dance floor. Jess's eyes widen, and she beckons for me to follow her to the loos.

'She doesn't waste time, does she?' she says as she leans towards the bathroom mirror. Her eyes narrow with concentration as she carefully reapplies her bright red lipstick, the scarlet colour gleaming under the fluorescent lights. She presses her lips together, then smiles.

'It's kind of her thing,' I say. 'Like, no judgement, but if we had to choose which *Sex and the City* characters we were,

Chloe would be one hundred per cent Samantha.' I chuckle, shaking my head at the thought. 'I've only been here a short time and I've lost count of the number of guys she's been with. But I guess whatever floats her boat.'

'It's not for me. I. Love. Joe,' says Jess, over-enunciating the words and swaying slightly. 'He's lovely, and he's got a perfect donger. Not too big but not too small.'

I hold up my hands. 'Jess, I don't need to know.'

'But why are things weird between us? Why, Chrissy?' Her voice breaks, as she grips the edge of the sink.

I place my hand on her shoulder, giving it a reassuring squeeze. 'I'm sure he's got a good reason. And look at you, even when you're pissed, you declare your love for Joe. You guys will be fine.'

'I'm gonna call him,' she slurs and slumps down into the corner of the bathroom, tapping at her phone.

'Joseph, it's me and I love you. Joe? Joe? Are you there?'

'Hey, Jess,' Joe's voice sounds out on loudspeaker, distant and distracted. 'I'm in the middle of something. Can I call you back?'

'But Joe...'

'Yes?'

'I love you.'

'You too. Sorry, gotta go.'

I feel a twist in my gut. Joe would never usually turn down a chance to chat with Jess. Maybe there is something to worry about. As I stand here in the toilets, the room sways around me. Ah, so it seems I'm a lot more drunk than I realised. I smile into the mirror and give myself a wink. I grab Jess's hands and pull her off the floor.

'He had to go,' she says with her mouth as downturned as a sad emoji. 'Chrissy, I need to go to bed.'

I nod and glance at my phone. There's a message.

TOM

I can't stop thinking about you.

My insides fizz as I read the words. Well, I hope it's from reading the words and not from drunken nausea.

'Okay, Jess, let's go home.'

Jess leans her head on my shoulder, and I lead her back out into the club to find Chloe.

37

J ess is sitting in the front of our Uber, talking the driver's ear off about her swoon-worthy boyfriend. I'm squished in the back with Chloe and the random blonde guy. You'd think they were cast members of Geordie Shore the way they're going at it.

Whilst trying to avoid the groping couple, I rifle in my bag and pull out my Things To Do When I'm Skinny list. I'm under no illusions about my body shape, but whether it's down to the booze or my increased fitness, I feel a surge of confidence. As I scan through the unchecked items, I make my decision. I am going to knock on Tom's door so we can spend the rest of the night together. I am going to tick off number thirty-two: Spur of the moment booty call.

As the Uber pulls up in North Bondi, I practically throw myself out the car door.

I'm hardly able to stand upright myself so I'm amazed I have the wherewithal to help Jess into bed. But living up to my 'best friend' title, I take off her shoes and place pain relief and water on her bedside table before creeping out of the room. I stagger into the bathroom and splash some water over my pits and bits. As I stare into the mirror, I rub my fingers below my eyes to wipe away the mascara smudges.

'You don't look too bad,' I say to my reflection as I give my hair a zhuzh. I guess one thing about having wild curls is that they don't look much different after a night out. I blow a kiss to the mirror before turning and making my way back to the front door, a skip in my step.

As I step into the hallway, I'm confronted with Chloe and the rando who are so caught up in their fumbling, they don't even notice me. I can hear them slurping at each other's faces. Ew. I rush up the stairs, taking two at a time.

I knock lightly on Tom's door and Ned lets out a low growl. He's sniffing and snorting, trying to catch my scent through the tiny gap under the door.

'Hey Ned, it's only me,' I say in a soft voice so as not to disturb the neighbours. God, I'm a considerate drunk.

A ripple of laughter echoes up the stairs. I can hear the murmurs of two male voices. One is Tom's deep, sexy voice and the other must be Zipper. Bugger. I forgot he was spending tonight with his school friend. They must have just arrived back from their night out.

I feel embarrassed and horribly slutty. Tom told me he

was catching up with his old friend this weekend and here I am crashing their time together like some kind of desperado. Oh, tequila, why do you do this to me?

I turn to make my way down the stairs, but the voices are getting closer and there's no way I can make it down to Chloe's floor before they reach me.

Bum! Bum! Bum!

I run back up the stairs and search for somewhere to hide.

Aha, the neighbour has a pot plant, and a huge one at that. I tiptoe over and hide behind the large leaves.

'I can't believe you turned down that hotty. I would have been in there like swimwear,' says the man I'm assuming is Zipper. His voice is a slower Aussie drawl than Tom's and he is slurring his words.

'Yeah, yeah, I'm sure you would have.' That was Tom. 'You know I'm kind of seeing someone.'

I find myself smiling. He's talking about me. I'm the person he's kind of seeing and he must like me if he's turning down hotties in pubs.

'Yeah mate, I know. You've mentioned her heaps. Let's see then.'

'You want to see a photo?'

'Yeah. Let's see if she's good enough for old Tommo.'

There's a brief pause.

'Oh mate, she's reaching.'

'You don't know her. She's way cuter in person,' says Tom.

'I guess she's kind of hot in an unconventional way but come on. You're a ten. You could get anyone.'

'If that's a pick-up line, you'll need to buy me more drinks, Zip.' They laugh, before Tom continues, 'Y'know some people just don't photograph well.'

Their voices are becoming clearer as they make their way slowly up the stairs.

'You mean they're not all like Janine?' says Zipper.

They laugh again.

'Janine may be easy on the eyes, but she's not easy to live with,' says Tom.

They're close to me now and I hold my breath, silently raging at this Zipper man who is so quick to judge me.

'Whatever you say, mate. What about that Spanish girl who was all over you? She didn't make the cut then?'

'I told you, I like Chrissy.' There is a scratching of key against metal as Tom fumbles to unlock the door. Ned lets out an excited bark. 'Maybe she could lose some weight, but looks aren't everything... lucky for you.'

'Oi, you know women find me alluring AF,' says Zipper.

My smile has been replaced by a scowl. I thought Tom found me irresistible. At least, that's what he told me. So why the heck is he talking about my weight?

'Why doesn't she drop some kilos, though?' asks Zipper.

'The mysteries of women, I guess. She's—'

The front door creaks.

'Hey, boy. Hey... where are you off to?' Tom calls.

I peep through the pot plant leaves to see what is going on, but before I see anything, I feel a wet tongue on my leg.

Oh no... Ned.

My stellar hiding place has not fooled his doggy sense of smell. I shuffle further behind the plant, squatting down and leaning against the wall. As I pat Ned, I gently push him away, but this just makes his tail wag even harder.

'Don't tell me he's found something disgusting in the pot plant,' says Tom.

I flick my wrist to mime throwing an imaginary ball for Ned. I hope he will run in the opposite direction to catch it. It doesn't work. He tilts his head at me as if trying to work out exactly when I lost my marbles.

'Come here, Neddy,' says Tom.

I try to press my body even closer to the wall and pull my eyes shut like a child who believes if she can't see the world, then no one can see her.

'What the—?'

I open one eye. Tom is standing above me, his face pulled into a bemused frown.

I don't speak. If I speak, it will make all this real. Ned shoves his nose into my lap, demanding more attention.

'What are you doing?' Tom asks, sounding more concerned than angry.

'Um... I'm...' A moment ago, I wanted to slap Tom, but now I'm so embarrassed I'm not sure whether to laugh or cry. I let out a muffled snort.

'What's going on?' Zipper is at Tom's side.

He's a big guy, twice the width of Tom, but a good few inches shorter. He has golden hair and a rosy face. The two men are staring at me as Ned leans his body against me and licks my hand.

I stand up and stretch my arms above my head, trying to act casual.

'Sorry guys, I was just checking on this plant. Looks like it may have a case of... um... fungal spots.' I hold a leaf in my hand. 'Yup, definitely fungal.'

Why do I keep saying fungal?

'Chrissy, it's two a.m.,' says Tom.

'Oh, is that the time?' I glance at my wrist. There is no Fitbit there. It didn't go with my outfit. 'Okay, better be going.'

I attempt to hold my head up high as I give my hair a little shake.

'That's Chrissy?' says Zipper as I walk by. 'I thought you said she looked better in real life.'

As I take a step away, my embarrassment turns to anger. So what if they think I'm a weirdo for hiding out in a pot plant? They are sexist, gross, sizeist men who judged me for being 'overweight'.

I hold on to the banister for balance.

'Listen here...' I turn back, pointing my free hand at the men for emphasis. 'My body is fine as it is. I don't need to lose weight. Not for you, not for anyone so you can both' – I take a moment to think and wobble on the spot – 'do one.'

I glance down at the dog, who is still wagging his tail. 'Not you, Ned. You're lovely.'

And just as I regain a smidge of dignity, the sting of bile rises in my throat. My head throbs and I know what's coming. I start to run down the steps to Chloe's flat, but just a few steps down, I lose control. I buckle over and vomit loudly, splattering cocktail-pink sick over the floor.

Wiping my mouth with my hand, I glance up to find Tom, Zipper, and Ned looking down at me.

'That's what you get for calling me fat,' I slur.

As I stumble down the stairs, the walls spin, and blur around me.

38

My eyelids feel like rusted hinges as I peel them open. Through blurry vision, I take in the soothing light blue walls and enjoy the sound of ocean waves washing over my parched brain.

But hang on? My room isn't that close to the beach.

My head pounds as I roll over. I glug the water that someone has put beside the bed and oh my, some ibuprofen. Thank you, baby Jesus.

As I swallow the tablets, I scan my surroundings. To my horror, there is a human-shaped lump under the covers next to me. He's facing away from me, but I would recognise that blonde hair anywhere... Brad.

I lift the duvet and peep under. I'm still wearing last night's clothes, well, kind of. My shoes are discarded on the floor and my dress is hoicked up around my chest, but... thank goodness, my knickers are firmly on.

I wince as my brain tries to process mortifying flashbacks from the night before. I remember... ugh, vomiting on the staircase in front of Tom. After that, I'd gone searching for Jess, but she was conked out in bed. I'd stumbled towards Chloe's room, but from the moans and giggles coming from inside, it was clear she was otherwise engaged. What on earth made me think that Brad was the right person to give me the support I needed? I guess mixing tequila and cock-tails wasn't my greatest idea yet.

'Hey, sleepyhead.' Brad rolls over to face me.

'Brad, I have no idea what happened. Did I? Did we?' I stammer, rubbing my eyes.

'Nothing happened. Well, apart from you waking my parents at three a.m. and all three of us carrying you into bed.' A playful grin tugs at the corner of his mouth.

'No, no, no.' I shake my head vigorously, the motion sending a wave of nausea through me.

'Yup, I'm afraid so. You turned up in an Uber, pretty upset. Tom, not the nice guy you thought, I take it?'

It comes back to me in a flash of hurt and embarrass-ment. Tom said I was fat. He was talking to his horrible friend about my weight.

'I won't go into it,' I say with a sigh, pulling the sheet to my chin as if it will shield me from the shame.

'You already told me everything,' he replies, his voice soft, but teasing. 'And you begged me to sleep with you.'

'I didn't.' I sit bolt upright, my head spinning as I do.

'You did, but don't worry, I'm a gentleman. Plus, Mum and Dad were there, so—'

'Oh my god. No!' I groan, clapping a hand to my forehead. 'That's it. I am never, ever drinking again. I'm such a twat. And it's not fair to you after—'

'After you dumped me.'

'Ugh.' My head feels like it might roll right off my neck and bounce away on the floor, so I let it thud back down onto the pillow.

'Yeah, that sucked. I liked you.'

There's an awkward pause that I'm too tired to fill.

Brad continues. 'But it wasn't fair of me to treat you like a project. That wasn't cool. Well, that's what Mum said, at least.'

'She's right,' I groan. 'But I guess I'm not blameless in this.'

'Agreed. We all reckon you're mostly to blame.' He's smiling.

'I know you were trying to help me. I want to be fitter. But I don't think I need to be skinny to be happy, at least I don't think that anymore.' My voice trails off.

'I understand. You deserve to be happy as you are.'

I blink at him, my eyebrows furrowing. 'You're being nice to me,' I say, unable to hide my confusion.

'I was a dick the other day. I don't want to be the guy who insults women who reject him. Anyway, pretty much as soon as I walked away from you, a Brazilian backpacker started flirting with me.' He shrugs, a hint of a smile playing at his lips.

I let out a soft laugh, relieved that the tension in the room has lifted. 'Does this mean we're, like, friends?'

'I guess.' He reaches over and lightly punches my arm, his smile widening. 'At least we can both agree that Tom dude is a massive wanker.'

I'm hit with an uncomfortable pang of protectiveness for Tom, which I mentally bat away. He doesn't deserve me standing up for him.

'I'm gonna have to face your mum and dad,' I say with a groan. I glance at the window and wonder whether I could, perhaps, climb onto the branch of a jacaranda tree, throw myself over to a nearby lamp post and shimmy down. Yes, there would be about a hundred tourists on the street below, but that would be better than facing the people who carried me to bed last night.

'It's not just them,' says Brad. 'You know that uncle I was telling you about?'

'The one with the chicken farm?' I sit up in bed, hugging my knees to my chest.

'Yup.'

'He's not here now?'

Brad nods. 'I heard the car pull up about an hour ago.'

'I can't deal with it. He's gonna say plants feel pain. He's gonna ask what I'd do if I were stuck on a desert island with a pig. I know it.'

'I'll help you get past them if you like,' says Brad. 'Uncle Marv usually asks me a ton of questions about my diet, too. He thinks protein shakes are the devil's work. If he's concentrating on me, you could sneak past and out the front door. No questions asked.'

I must look unconvinced, as Brad continues, 'Marv and Dad will be busy catching up anyway. They won't even notice you.'

After a brief shower in the ensuite, I'm feeling fresher, wearing a pair of Brad's board shorts and one of his singlets. I shuffle behind him as we make our way down the stairs.

'Bradley.' A voice booms from the kitchen and I stand frozen to the spot. Brad trots down the stairs and hugs his uncle, who looks like a very wide and much younger version of Brad's dad.

'Who do we have here? Is this the drunken veggan I've heard all about?'

I cringe. He can't even say the word vegan properly, or maybe he did that on purpose?

'Hi.' I give a little wave and resist the urge to give Brad a good pinch for doing such a poor job of shielding me. 'I'm just heading off.' I jog down the stairs and make for the front door.

'Oh Chrissy, well, isn't it nice to see you standing upright and not quite so covered in vomit,' says Teresa with a laugh in her voice. 'You will join us for breakfast, won't you? If you can stomach it after your... excesses.'

'Chrissy's heading off, Mum. She's got places to be,' says Brad.

'Oh? Brad was telling us how you're a lady of leisure. Got a job, have you?'

'Not yet, although I'm on the lookout. I'm just meeting someone,' I lie as I take a couple of steps towards the door.

'They'll understand,' says Doug as he appears as if from nowhere, blocking my exit. Startled, I glance from Brad to his dad to his mum.

Doug continues, 'Just tell 'em you owe some common courtesy to the people who had to lug your dead weight up the stairs.'

'I'm so sorry about that,' I say, looking down at my feet. 'No more drinking for me.'

'Quite,' says Teresa. She is now standing right in front of me and lowers her voice so only I can hear her. 'We have scones. They're vegan.'

I stifle a laugh. From her tone, you'd think she was offering me crack cocaine rather than baked goods.

Teresa raises her voice to a normal level. 'Eve dropped some scones around this morning. She's a fellow Woman of Waverley; the one who spearheaded that odd little chook charity fundraiser. She loved the photos Brad took. Anyway, you're welcome to a scone and tea.'

I blink, slightly bewildered, but I follow Teresa through to the living room.

I catch Brad's eye to find him giving me a what-do-you-think-you're-doing? look. He gestures to the front door with his head.

'Vegan scones,' I mouth at him.

He shakes his head, grabs his six-pack, and attempts to wobble it, whilst puffing out his cheeks in a fat person imitation. Well, that reminds me why I broke up with him.

'It's quite a shame you made a fool of yourself last night. I was going to ask Brad to contact you,' says Teresa as she gestures for me to sit down at the dining table, which is already laid with plates, cutlery and teacups. She lifts the tea pot, pouring the steaming liquid into delicate cups.

'Oh really? About what?' I ask as I sit down, and the family take their seats around the table.

'Eve is Principal of Ocean Hill Primary and she mentioned there's an opening covering some sick leave for the next few months.' Teresa says as she passes me the oat milk. 'There may even be the possibility of a permanent teaching role.'

I feel a surge of excitement. 'That sounds amazing. Do you think I would be in with a chance?'

Teresa raises her eyebrows and tilts her head at me. 'I'm not sure Ocean Hill is looking for drunken heartbreakers.'

'No offence, love, but I doubt they'd want an extremist

there either. Young minds and all that,' says Uncle Marv as he heaps cream on top of his scones.

'Chrissy isn't an extremist,' Brad cuts in from his seat next to me. 'She just cares about animals.'

I smile at him.

Marv wipes a glob of cream from his mouth onto his sleeve. 'I care about animals more than anyone. But putting family farms like mine out of business isn't the way to go about it.'

'Don't listen to my little brother.' Doug slaps Marv on the back, making him splutter up scone crumbs over the table. 'His "family farm" has how many chooks?'

'Two hundred thousand,' says Marv, looking pleased with himself. 'Each one treated better than my own kid.'

'Ha!' Teresa lets out a guffaw that I would never have expected to come from her mouth. 'If that's the case, I say poor Benjamin. I've seen those chickens, Marvin. I think people should be free to do what they want, but let's not pretend it's an animal rescue now. Each of those birds is for the chop and you know it.'

'Oh, shush you.' Marv gives a good-natured grin as he grabs another scone.

Doug turns to his wife. 'Don't you reckon your friend would give Chrissy a chance?' he asks. 'You could put in a good word. I mean, she and Brad are mates now, eh?'

'Yup,' says Brad, but I notice a flash of hurt behind his eyes.

I lower my gaze to the floor. 'I truly am sorry about last night. I should never have turned up here.'

'We've all been there,' says Doug. 'In fact, that was us last week, wasn't it, Teresa? Too much gin.'

A blush creeps over Teresa's face, but with a swift shake of her head, she dismisses it. 'I don't know what you're talking about.'

'Got any more cream?' asks Uncle Marv as he takes another big bite of his scone.

'Gosh, you got through that quickly,' says Teresa as she bustles out towards the kitchen.

'You say you don't want birds farmed, but you have no problem stuffing these down? You know eggs come from birds, right?' says Uncle Marv, his mouth still full.

'Teresa says these are vegan,' I stammer, glancing at Brad for support.

Brad's face twists into a grimace. Doug waves his hand frantically in front of his neck in a 'stop talking' motion.

'You what? You're not serious, are you?' Marv turns sharply to Teresa, who is coming back into the room with more butter and cream, her face a picture of innocent confusion.

'You pulled a swifty,' he booms. Marv stands up, his chair scraping loudly against the floor, and stomps towards the fridge.

'What's this about?' asks Teresa, her eyes darting between Marv and the rest of us.

Doug rolls his eyes and lets out a long-suffering sigh. 'He knows the scones are vegan.'

'Oh, Marvin, you know we're dedicated to our farmers, but a friend brought these around this morning. And as for the marge and cream, well, I've been trying to eat less dairy for health reasons.' Teresa's voice wavers.

Marvin is standing by the fridge, sticking his tongue in and out as if trying to get a foul taste out of his mouth. He opens the fridge and pulls out... what is that? Yuck, one of those bagged-up cooked chickens. I see the charred body, and I can't help but imagine what the bird went through in the slaughterhouse and how they fought for their life.

Uncle Marv pulls at the flesh with his big fingers, shoving it into his mouth with a satisfied grunt. He closes his eyes as he grabs another handful. 'Thank god for chook, am I right? Get that awful vegan taste out of my mouth.'

Teresa frowns at him, placing her hands on her hips. 'Marv, that was for my lunch!'

Watching him pull off stringy chunks of flesh does nothing to soothe my nausea.

'Next time, don't serve up that veggie nonsense and you can keep your chook. It's bloody deli—' Marv's words are cut off abruptly as he piles another handful of flesh into his mouth.

He freezes, his cheeks turning a shade of red I've never seen before. His blue eyes are bulging. He reaches a shaking hand to his chest and thumps it.

For a second we all sit there, staring, as drool dribbles down Marv's chin and onto the floor.

The spell breaks and Brad and I jump up at the same time, chairs scraping back. My teacher's first-aid training kicks in. I bend Uncle Marv forward and, with the heel of my hand, I bang between his shoulder blades. Thump. Thump. Thump. The first three sharp thumps don't seem to help. Teresa and Doug are standing up now, flapping their arms and fussing around in a circle.

'He's turning purple. He's turning purple,' shrieks Teresa, her eyes wild.

I hit Marv again, as hard as I can. He raises his body and with a giant cough, a glob of chicken flesh propels out of his throat, across the room, and hits Teresa square between her immaculate brows.

Marvin gasps for breath, coughing, and spluttering.

Brad crouches in front of his doubled-over uncle. 'You're okay now,' he says.

Doug is at his brother's side with a glass of water. Teresa places a chair behind Marv and gestures for him to sit down.

After a minute, Marvin can talk again. His face is returning to the usual reddish beige as opposed to the fetching beetroot it was a moment before.

Marvin takes a sip of water, gasps, and fixes his gaze on Teresa.

'Get that... damn veggan... an interview.'

39

I'm making my way across the hall to Chloe's flat, desperate to collapse into bed. The scones did an okay job at soaking up some of the alcohol, but I need sleep. I really need sleep.

I jump as a hand touches my wrist.

It's Tom.

Why do I have to look so terrible? And why should I care that I look terrible? At least I'm showered. I'm barefoot, wearing Brad's tie-dye singlet and board shorts with one of Teresa's canvas shopping bags slung over my shoulder. It contains last night's vomit-covered outfit. My hair hangs in damp curls around my face and that's what lets me down the most – my face. My skin is dry and the dark bags under my eyes would put Pete Davidson to shame.

'I came to find you earlier,' says Tom, who looks fresh, gorgeous, and, well... the complete opposite of me.

'I've been out,' I say, my tone clipped. 'What did you want?'

'We need to talk about last night. I'm not myself when I'm with Zipper – I mean Jamie. Those things I said, that's not how I feel.'

'I need to get some sleep,' I say, ignoring his excuses. Tom runs a hand through his thick, dark hair, his face a picture of exasperation, and that's when he seems to clock my outfit.

'Where have you been?' he asks, his tone darkening.

'It doesn't concern you.'

'Is that Brad's singlet?'

I raise my chin in defiance. 'So what if it is?'

I notice a flash of anger in his dark eyes, and I think back to Janine and her warning.

'Tom, it doesn't matter. The fact is, anything between you and me is over. I've been with a man who gaslit me and put me down and I will never do that again. Never.'

The anger on Tom's face crumbles into hurt and his shoulders slump.

'I'm not like that,' he pleads, taking a step towards me. I take a step back. 'It's not the real me. I should have told Zipper how beautiful you are. I was just agreeing with him because it was easy, but that was wrong.'

'It's over, Tom,' I say, my voice cracking, but resolute.

He reaches out to touch my arm, but I pull away, my eyes stinging with unshed tears.

'You don't mean that.' The sadness in his voice softens my resolve, and I want to throw myself into his arms.

I could push aside the memory of sobbing in Jess's arms after Jeremy made fun of my weight in front of his friends. I could try to forget the night Mum knocked on Jeremy's door and forced him to give back the above-the-knee dresses he was holding hostage until I lost weight.

But I can't risk going through that again.

I fake nonchalance, roll my eyes, and stride across the hall.

'Can we just talk?' he calls as he follows behind me.

I open Chloe's door and close it in Tom's face.

Leaning against the back of the door, I close my eyes and take a deep breath.

'Good night?' asks Chloe from her place on the sofa next to Jess.

I trudge over and plonk myself down.

As I fill the girls in on my night, they say all the right things in all the right places, just as good girlfriends should.

'Sod him,' says Jess. 'One minute pretending to be all body positive, the next shaming you in front of his mate. It's out of order.'

I feel a dig in my stomach and again want to stand up for Tom, but I don't. Instead, I change the subject and Chloe proceeds to tell me all about Oliver, the man who, until an hour ago, had been in her bed.

I wish I had her attitude towards men. She loves 'em and leaves 'em and from where I'm sitting, she has it all figured out.

40

Gosh, I'm nervous. It's been ages since I've had a job interview and a good while since I've had to dress in smart clothes. I've become surprisingly comfy strolling around in my one-piece swimsuit and flowing beach dress.

Yesterday I went shopping with Chloe and Jess. I bought myself a below-the-knee pink dress that screams, 'Of course, I never posted half-naked pics of myself online.'

A cute silver cardi tops off the look. Perhaps this outfit wouldn't be Cheynique-approved, but I reckon I've achieved a certain level of primary-school chic.

I'm sweating as I approach the gates of Ocean Hill House. The school is perched on a headland overlooking the ocean. As I make my way to reception, I take in the scenery around me. The play area is dotted with gum trees and a colourful rainbow lorikeet mural decorates the wall. It's weird to think I could be working here soon. This could be part of my new life; hill walking to work every day, ready to inspire young Aussie minds.

As I push open the door, I'm greeted by a smiley receptionist with her blonde hair up in a swishy ponytail.

'Oh, it's you!' She beams when she sees me.

'Mel... hi.' I almost didn't recognise her in smart, casual clothes. At bootcamp, she always wears those shorts from TikTok with the scrunch in the bum crack. And even though I noted her beauty, the truth is, I was distracted by her phenomenal buttocks. After all, hers is the biggest and perkiest bum I have ever seen in real life. Here, in her receptionist get-up, she's a whole lot less intimidating. 'I didn't know you worked here.'

'Well, I would have told you, but we're both always so puffed at bootcamp, aren't we? Actually...' She takes a deep breath. 'There is something I need to talk to you about.'

'Okay,' I say, feeling a twang of unease. I place my hands on the reception desk and drum my fingernails. Today I have multi-coloured pastel French tips. 'Is it about the teaching position? Has it already been filled?'

'No, no, nothing like that, but it's a bit awkward. It's about Brad.'

'Right?'

'I probably shouldn't be saying this when you're about to go into your interview. But he kind of... sort of... asked me out.' Mel grimaces and shrinks back in her seat as if she fears I may hit her. 'Don't worry, I said no, but I've noticed you haven't been at bootcamp lately, and well, if that's because of me, I promise I'm not trying to steal your man. Has he said anything to you? Because he can bugger off if he thinks—'

'We broke up.' I cut her off and silence the little voice in my head that's stung by Brad's swift rebound.

Mel tilts her head in sympathy.

I continue. 'It's okay, honestly. We're still friends... kind of.'

'I didn't know.' She reaches across her desk, places her hand on mine, and squeezes. 'I'm so sorry.' There's a flash of something behind her eyes. It's like she wants to say more but can't quite summon the courage.

'Mel... if you want to... I wouldn't mind if you went on a date with Brad,' I say, trying really hard to mean it. The rush of hope and excitement I felt when we met at the airport still plays brightly in my mind. But I was the one who chose to break things off and I do want him to be happy.

For a moment she stares at me, still holding my hand.

'Are you serious? You wouldn't be mad?'

'Of course not. You go for it.'

She squeals and throws her whole body across the desk to pull me into a hug. 'Chrissy, I've liked him for ages. I was trying to summon up the courage to ask him out just before he met you.'

I pat her back, smiling at her enthusiasm. 'He obviously likes you, too.'

She squeezes me harder before standing up straight and reverting to professional receptionist mode as if a switch has been flicked.

'So, you might be working here soon?' she asks, not doing a very good job of covering up her grin.

'Fingers crossed.' I nod.

'Fill out this visitor pass, and I'll let Eve know you're here. Do you want water or anything? I've got some of those fancy infusion teabag things.'

'I've got water, thanks,' I say, tapping my bag. One habit that has stuck from my time with Brad is drinking at least two litres of water a day. I always have my water bottle with me these days. And whilst I'd never tell him he was right, it has made my skin glow and put a little pep in my step.

Mel walks away and I clip the visitor pass to my dress.

It's weird how different Mel seems in this environment. I can see why she'd do well working in a school with young kids. She's full of enthusiastic energy. If I hadn't been so intimidated by her perfect booty and supreme fitness, I could have found myself another Aussie friend sooner rather than later.

I hear the clip-clop of heels before I see my potential boss, Eve. As she rounds the corner, I take in her outfit. She's giving off major *The Devil Wears Prada* vibes in her tailored black trousers and white shirt with on-trend puffy sleeves.

And those are the highest, spikiest heels I've ever seen in a primary school. I wonder if I've accidentally wandered into a *Vogue* interview.

My outfit now feels frumpy. But surely I won't be judged on fashion for a primary school teaching interview? I plaster on my best hopeful smile. As my eyes move up the woman's petite body and take in her cropped black hair and elfin features, my hopes plummet into my own flat ballet pumps.

I've met Eve before... twice. She's the Scottish woman from the beach who branded me a honeypants. From the way her face stiffens as she fixes her eyes on me, I can tell that not only does she recognise me, but that there is zero chance I'm getting this job.

41

'And you are' – Eve glances at her clipboard – 'Chrissy Pember?' Her Scottish accent is just as piercing as I remember.

'That's me. It's lovely to meet you.' I hold out my hand and feel like chubby Winnie the Pooh next to little Piglet. I figure I may as well act like I would if the woman didn't think I was a massive slut. I mean, what have I got to lose?

She doesn't shake my hand, so I lift it up and push a curl back over my ear. Smooth move, Chrissy, so natural. I could kick myself for thinking this could be my new workplace.

'And I hear you know Teresa?'

'That's right.' I smile so wide it hurts my cheeks. 'She told me you are the one who nominated Nahla's Place as your fundraising charity this month. I went there to take some photos. Amanda was such an inspiration.'

Eve's face softens, and she takes a deep breath. 'Well, come on then, let's get this over with. What Queen Teresa wants, she gets.' She turns away from me and lowers her voice. 'No matter how inappropriate the candidate may be.'

I trot after Eve and catch Mel's eye. She mouths, 'Good luck' and gives me a double thumbs up.

As I follow Eve into her office, she points to a seat and I sit down, my hands on my lap.

'Lovely dogs,' I say, nodding towards a framed photo of two fluffy, white terriers.

Eve doesn't answer. She stands on the opposite side of the desk, staring at me. Her head is tilted like the dogs in the photo.

After a few seconds of silence, she speaks.

'See, I can't get my head around this. Your resume paints you as an excellent candidate and yet what I've seen of you with my own eyes contradicts that.'

She paces along the desk and turns back to me, placing her hands on the tabletop. I notice a little dirt under her nails. Ha, so she's not one hundred per cent perfect after all.

'I'm sorry,' I lean forward, clasping my hands together to stop them trembling. 'You caught me at a bad moment. A moment that's not reflective of my real self.'

Her eyes narrow. 'So, two separate times I happened upon you, or rather you crashed into me, and both times you were acting in ways that do not reflect the real you?'

'Um, yup.' My voice squeaks and I clear my throat.

'Right.' There's another long pause. This is clearly a lost cause. Why am I even sitting here? Why am I putting myself through this?

'If I could just talk through my resume and my time at Little Elm, I think I can show you why I'm suited for this job.' I reach down to my bag to pull out my folder of references and evidence of projects I've done with the kids.

'Chrissy, you're here because of Teresa. The Women of Waverley stick together. But if it wasn't for her, there is no way you would be anywhere near school property. There are standards to uphold here. We've got a certain reputation in the community, and I'd say from how you were putting it about on the beach, well, you don't exactly fit.' Her eyes flick up and down, scanning my body.

I've been looked at like that one too many times in my life and I won't put up with another person judging me on my body.

'You can't turn me down for a job because of my weight,' I say in a calm voice, immediately wishing I could shove the words back into my mouth.

Eve lets out a sharp hoot of laughter. 'I'm not judging your weight. I'm judging your outfit. Have you been raiding *The Wiggles*' wardrobes?'

My eyes widen in shock. 'This dress is from H&M. It's child appropriate.'

She turns to the window and looks out across the playing field.

'You can see yourself out. Tell Teresa I said hello.'

I lean down and pick up my bag before standing up. As I turn away from the desk, I think of all the times I wish I'd stood up for myself with Jeremy. I think of Amanda and everything she overcame to set up her animal sanctuary, and I think of Chloe and Jess, my cheer squad waiting for me at home.

'I deserve a proper interview.' I turn back to Eve and hold my head up high.

'What?' Her eyebrows attempt to come together in a frown but lose the fight against the Botox.

'I'm a good teacher with excellent references. I'm very keen to work and I deserve an interview. A proper one, where I'm not judged on my clothes, my weight, or what I do in my free time.'

Now, there may be a wobble in my voice, but I know I'm right. I do deserve a chance.

'I don't have time for this nonsense,' snaps Eve. She waves her hand at me in a manner that suggests I should leave the office.

'This isn't nonsense. This is a chance for the children to get the teacher they deserve. Someone who understands the value of excellent education, but also the value of kindness, of compassion. Surely you understand that? That's why you love Nahla's Place. You and I have a lot in common. Teresa told me how much Amanda's work moved you.'

She stares at me for what seems like an eternity. She's certainly not afraid of holding an awkward silence.

'Can you believe all those hens were going to be killed if it wasn't for Amanda?' she says.

I'm caught off guard by the sudden sadness in her eyes.

'I can't get my head around it,' she continues. 'I love animals. I'm vegetarian for god's sake. But I didn't know what happened. Amanda says that all egg-laying hens go to slaughter at eighteen months. Did you know that?'

'I did, but it's well hidden. The industry doesn't want people to find out.'

She slumps down into her chair. Tentatively I sit down opposite her.

'And the cows,' she says, her voice so sad it breaks my heart. 'I'm the principal of one of the best primaries in Sydney. I have two degrees and a masters. How did I not know that a dairy cow has to be pregnant to produce milk? How did that not click?' She clicks her fingers right in front of my face, making me jump. 'I ended up in a YouTube rabbit hole last night. I saw the mother cows being separated from the babies and the babies being killed. It was awful, Chrissy.'

'I get it. It's so much to take in when you start researching it, but now you know, and you can make changes so you're not supporting that.'

She sighs heavily, leaning back in her chair and rubbing her temples. 'I don't know why I'm talking to you about this.' She shakes her head.

I lean forward, my eyes fixed on hers, desperate to make a connection. 'Because not many people understand and it's actually kind of amazing to connect with someone who does?'

Her eyes are wide and thoughtful. 'So, you're vegan, are you?'

I nod.

'I might need to pick your brain about that.'

'Of course.' I pause and take a deep breath before taking my chance. 'And maybe you could give me a proper interview? I would love to show you that I am a good fit for this school.'

For a moment, I'm distracted by the sound of a baby crying. I glance out of Eve's window. Below is the playing field and the street beyond. A mother is pushing a pram. She stops to soothe her crying baby, and the wailing stops.

'I have another meeting to prepare for,' says Eve, shuffling papers on her desk, her movements quick and agitated.

What can I do? I can't exactly force Eve to give me a chance. I'm about to leave when I notice wet patches spread across her white shirt.

'Goodbye, Chrissy.'

'Um, before I go. You have a... um.' I gesture to my chest, feeling my cheeks heat.

She looks down and slams a hand on the table. 'Damn it! This wasn't meant to happen on my first day back.'

'Do you have a jacket or anything?' I ask, glancing around the room.

'It's summer. Why on earth would I bring a jacket?' she snaps.

'I just meant, well, never mind. You can borrow my cardigan. It'll be a bit big, but it'll do the job.' I pull off my silver cardi and hold it out to Eve.

She hesitates for a moment and then, with a roll of her eyes, she takes it and puts it on, covering up the wet patches. The cardigan dwarfs her petite frame.

'You're breastfeeding?' I ask gently.

'Obviously. It's that damn baby crying.' She shakes her head and I notice her reddening cheeks.

'It's okay,' I soothe. I place my bag on the table. Digging inside it, I pull out a fresh pack of tissues and pass them to her. 'Oh, and are you a chocolate fan? Give this a try.' I pull out a salted caramel Nomo bar that was going to be my after-interview treat.

'If I take this, it doesn't mean you have the job.' She sniffs but takes the chocolate, breaking it and giving half back to me. 'How do women do this, Chrissy? How do they have babies and work and not burst out crying due to a wardrobe malfunction?'

'They do it just like you're doing it. No one is perfect. You're here, aren't you? You're trying? Your hormones are probably all over the place. But look at you.' I gesture to her office. 'You're running a school. You're doing a great job.'

She drops her eyes, her voice catching. 'This isn't the real me. I'm tough. I'm known for it. Just because I spawned a small human a few weeks ago, doesn't mean I should be breaking down in floods of tears and stressing out over baby cows. This is my third baby. I should be over it by now. Here's me saying you won't fit in here. I'm not even Ocean Hill House material anymore.'

I offer her a bottle of water from my bag.

'Who are you? Mary Poppins?' she says with a small laugh.

It's true: I do fit a lot in my Matt and Nat backpack.

'We all have moments like this, Eve. Just because you're upset now doesn't mean you aren't a strong, effective principal. As for the cow stuff, the fact you're researching means you're tough enough to make informed decisions. But are you serious that you had a baby a few weeks ago? What are you doing at work?'

'Failing. And being a mess. I didn't even want another baby and now look at me.' She wipes her fingers under her eyes to remove any mascara.

I lean in closer, speaking softly. 'You need to be kinder to yourself. If you give me a chance, you could get one thing ticked off your to-do list. I could be the teacher you're looking for.'

She growls and throws her hands up in the air. 'Fine, fine. Let's start again. You'll get your interview, but any of that honeypants behaviour from the beach, I mean any, then you're out. Deported... back to the UK.'

'I don't think you have that power.' I grin. After seeing the human side of Eve, I feel a whole lot more comfortable around her.

'Just try me, missy,' she says with a half-smile.

I place my bag back on the floor, a buzz of excitement within me.

'I guess I may have been wrong about you, Chrissy. You may have some good points. And I suppose your nails are rather fabulous despite being Wiggles-esque.'

She blows her nose into the tissue I gave her.

I lay my fingers out so she can see the full range of colours on my nails. She takes my hand, flips it over, and places her used tissue in my palm before closing my hand and patting it.

She adjusts the cardigan and gazes at me with that penetrating stare as if the whole meltdown had never happened.

'So, Chrissy, tell me why you would be the perfect fit for Ocean Hill House.'

Thirty minutes later, as I walk out of the school, I can't keep the smile off my face. I could be in with a chance here. I could be working at one of the most esteemed primary schools in Sydney.

This whole new Chrissy thing really is coming together.

42

I'm sitting on Bondi Beach in the warm shade of an umbrella. I flick through my phone and smile at the photos of our girls' volunteering day at Nahla's Place.

There's one of Nahla the hen pecking at Jess's hair and there's one of Annie the piglet lying on Chloe's stomach. And amongst all the photos, there is not a single photo of a man having a tantrum... bliss.

It's been a week since my Ocean Hill House interview, and I haven't heard back. I've been driving myself a little bit mad thinking about it. Maybe Eve still sees me as a maneater with no redeemable qualities. Thank goodness I've had Chloe and Jess to distract me.

I stretch my arms above my head, noticing an ache in my triceps. It's from dancing at Marcel's Boogie Box. It's a whole other level of fun with Jess here. She shakes her booty like no other. We ended up going dancing four times in the last week, not to mention all the swimming, hiking, and mostly failed attempts at surfing. I glance down at my body. I haven't weighed myself since I ditched Brad, but I feel different... more confident. I prod my stomach. Yup, the rolls are still here. Jess has always said they're cute. I never believed her, but now I wonder if perhaps she's right.

'What are you thinking about?' asks Jess in a sleepy voice from her beach towel next to me as she props herself up on her elbows.

'Just that I'm more comfortable in my skin than I used to be.'

She sits up, her surprise giving way to a warm smile. 'That's so good. You have every reason to be confident. Look at you.'

I laugh and nudge her playfully. 'You're not biased, of course.'

She feigns shock, placing a hand over her heart. 'Not at all.'

'And what have you been thinking about?' I ask with raised eyebrows.

I already know the answer and I say it with her.

'Joe.'

Jess groans, hiding her head in her hands.

'Are you still feeling weird about things?' I ask.

'I guess,' she says as she lowers her hands. Her eyes are

filled with confusion. 'You know I'm madly in love with him, right?'

'Right.' I nod.

Jess drops her gaze to the sand, and her finger absently traces patterns. 'But despite that, there's something weird. It's like he's hiding something. Like he's holding back on me. He's never done that before. I don't get it. I don't get what could have changed for him.'

'Have you asked him?'

'I asked if he was okay. He said he's been busy at work, and he's had some stuff on his mind, but then he changed the subject.'

I shake my head. 'Bloody ambiguous men.'

We fall silent and I gaze out at the ocean. A smile spreads over my face as I take it in. This is another one of those moments where I can't quite believe I'm here.

'This place suits you,' says Jess. 'It's making you happy, isn't it? Being here, I mean.'

I turn to her, my smile widening. 'I love it, Jess.'

'Well, that bloody sucks, because I want you to come home.' She pouts, flopping back on her towel with a dramatic flair. 'I understand why you love it though, especially now you've given those rotten men the flick.'

Pain twists in my gut as Tom's face pops into my mind. He's messaged me a couple of times over the last week and tried to call, but I didn't respond. I wanted to, but Jess and Chloe are right. I can't be with a man who doesn't accept me for who I am, no matter how strongly I feel pulled towards him.

'Chloe rips through them, doesn't she?' says Jess, pulling me out of my Tom daydream.

'She's sex positive, I guess?' I reply with a shrug.

'I couldn't do it; one man is more than enough hassle. She seems happy, though.'

'I just wish the walls were thicker.' I grimace.

Jess honks with laughter, her body shaking with the force of it. 'A bit vocal, is she?'

'Not her, her latest booty call. Didn't you hear? He moaned, grunted, and groaned all night. I don't know how she put up with it. It would give me the ick. I mean, sure, a bit of vocalising is all well and good, but this was constant.'

'How did I not hear?'

'Just be grateful you sleep like the dead.' I watch as waves roll onto the golden sand. 'Fancy a dip?'

'Go on then.'

The sand is hot on my feet as we run on our tiptoes down to the water's edge. I pull my sarong off just before I reach the water to save the beachgoers from getting an eyeful of my cellulite. In front of the bathroom mirror, my legs looked a bit dimpled, but I'm well aware that in full sunlight, they appear to have suffered severe hail damage. I run into the ocean and throw myself under a wave letting the white-water rush over my head. As I pop up, I turn to watch Jess. She's taking small steps, cupping water and trickling it over her arms. I wade over and flick water at her.

'No! I'm easing in!' she shrieks, splashing me back.

As I splash her again, she plunges under the surface. She grabs my leg and yanks it, causing me to tumble into the water. I'm almost in hysterics as she pulls me up again. As we hold hands, jumping over the waves and giggling, we could just as easily be back in our primary school days.

'Hey, ladies, pull your knees up and you'll be doing a nice little tuck jump,' calls Brad as he wades over to us, shirtless. His muscles are bronzed and wet.

'Jess and I are fans of a new fitness regime called wave jumping,' I say, deadpan. 'We jump as high as we can over the wave like this...' I demonstrate, jumping over an incoming wave. 'And then, of course, to build the booty, we squat right down like this.' In giggles, we both squat and promptly get knocked over by the next little wave.

Brad's brow furrows. 'Jess, is it? I'm Brad, and your form is off.'

I remember that, bless his heart, Brad just doesn't get sarcasm.

Jess grins, wiping water from her eyes. 'Oh, you're the famous Brad!'

'How are you, anyway?' I ask him.

He shrugs, still looking a bit confused. 'Good, yeah. You know Mel from bootcamp?'

'Ah yes, the one who put me to shame with her ability to

do about a thousand burpees without breaking a sweat.' And my future colleague, all being well.

'Right. Well, we're kind of on a date. She's up there.' He points up the sand and although Mel is lying on her stomach, I recognise her bright yellow thong and sculpted bubble butt from a distance. 'We had a picnic,' he says. 'She brought loads of high protein options.'

I smile as I catch his slight blush. 'That's great. Mel's lovely.'

It's so weird to think of Brad with someone else and I wouldn't say it feels comfortable, but at least one of us should be happy.

He looks embarrassed. 'I thought I should come over and tell you face to face. I didn't want you to be heartbroken.'

I nod, 'It's fine, Brad.'

'It's good to see you. You're looking well.'

'Thanks.' I feel genuine warmth for this man.

He opens his arms and I go in for a hug. His wet skin presses against my skimpiest one-piece yet. I breathe in his salty smell. There's no denying he's gorgeous, but he's not... Tom.

As if my mind has conjured him, I hear Tom's voice as I pull away from my hug with Brad.

'Come on, don't be a dick,' says Tom. I glance up to see him crouched down on the sand. Two other lifeguards stand near him.

'Excuse me, guys,' I say to Brad and Jess as I wade

towards the sand, leaving them to chat. I grab my sarong and wrap it around my waist as I walk out of the water.

'Keep doing those squats and even you could get a bum like Melanie's,' calls Brad from behind me. I ignore him and jog up the sand towards Tom.

'It's vermin, mate, just leave it,' says the older lifeguard before heading off back to the tower, followed by his colleague.

As I get closer, I notice a small, grey pigeon on the sand.

Tom edges towards the bird, who flaps away a metre or so. The bird is hobbled by fishing wire around his legs. His wings are unhindered, which makes catching him that bit harder.

I walk over quietly so as not to scare the bird and tap Tom on the shoulder, making him jump.

'Chrissy.' The relief in his voice fills me with happiness. It's good to see his face – the stubbled jawline, dark eyebrows, and serious deep brown eyes.

'Do you need a hand?' I ask in a quiet voice, gesturing to the pigeon.

Tom's eyes flash with frustration. 'Some bastards left fishing gear, and he got tangled,' he says. 'I called a wildlife rescue, but they said if they collect him, they'll put him down since pigeons are "feral". Could you go around the other side and maybe we can catch him and see if we can help him ourselves?'

I slowly walk to the other side of the little pigeon before taking off my sarong and holding it out like a sheet.

As Tom edges closer, I notice the terror in the bird's eyes. He flounders, flapping away from Tom and towards me. In a flash, I throw the sarong over him and Tom rushes to hold the material down, capturing the bird.

Relief floods through me as Tom gently pulls the bird from the sarong.

'Okay, little one, let's get you sorted,' he says cradling the pigeon in both hands.

So, it's official, I'm in love. Hearing Tom speak so sweetly to this vulnerable little bird has the same effect on me as women under twenty-five have on Leonardo DiCaprio.

The grey bird looked plain from a distance, but now I notice the rainbow colours on his neck, glistening in the morning sun.

As we walk to the lifeguard tower, I hold the sarong, letting it swing beside me.

I follow Tom up the steps, feeling like a VIP.

'You got the little bugger,' says a skinny but muscular young man with a mess of black hair.

'Yup. No thanks to you.' Tom eyes the young lifeguard with mock severity.

'I wanted to help. It was just Jono. You know what he's like.'

Tom gives him a look that is half amused, half disapproving before gesturing to me.

'This is Chrissy, rescuer of pigeons, Chrissy, this is Kyle, who'd rather watch from afar.' Tom's tone is teasing.

Kyle rolls his eyes, but he's grinning. He opens a drawer and rifles through an array of clutter before finding a pair of scissors and bringing them over to me.

'I don't want to see it suffering,' says Kyle, 'but I don't want to touch it. You can do this bit.'

He goes back to staring out at the ocean, scanning for anyone in trouble. Tom sits on a chair, and I kneel in front of him. Gosh, in another scenario, we could be about to do something quite different.

My body fizzes as I glance up at Tom, catching his eye. Those deep brown eyes are filled with concern. He really does care.

With extreme care I snip the fishing line from around the pigeon's feet, trying not to nick his skin.

'Yes!' I celebrate in a quiet voice as I snip the final bit of the line. Carefully I unwrap the wire from the pigeon's legs, wincing at the dented and reddened flesh. As I inspect him more closely, I'm relieved to see no signs of lasting injury.

'Should we take him to the vet?' asks Tom.

I shake my head slowly, weighing up our options. 'With another animal, I would, but I'm worried they'll put him down.'

'Well, he seems okay. His legs aren't injured, just a bit bruised.' He chuckles as the pigeon kicks out, as if to prove a point. 'See? Kicking like a little ninja. We can probably let him go.'

'May have been a while without being able to get to drinking water, poor guy,' I say.

I stand up and walk over to the tap, where there is a water bottle next to the sink. I pour some water into the bottle cap and move back to the pigeon. As I hold out the makeshift bowl, he takes a sip.

After the pigeon has drunk his water, Tom looks up at me. 'Time for the big release?'

We walk up from the beach to the grassy area where parents, nannies and children are gathered having a chat and a coffee. There are a fair few pigeons here. Tom crouches down and places the little bird on the grass.

As he lifts his hands away, the pigeon flies straight over to the flock, taking big steps when he lands, as if he can't quite believe his legs are free.

Tom's eyes crinkle at the corners and a grin spreads across his face. 'What a team!' In a sudden, joyous motion, he reaches out and pulls me into a hug, lifting me off the ground.

'We should name him,' I say as Tom sets me back on the grass. His hands linger on my waist, and my fingers rest on his broad shoulders. We watch the bird strutting about, probably telling the ladies about his survival against the odds.

'He looks like a Rogelio,' Tom suggests, his voice filled with amusement.

I laugh. 'Rogelio it is. Rogelio the womaniser.'

I find myself gazing back into Tom's eyes and a charge seems to pass between us as the seconds stretch out.

'It's so good to see you,' he says, his voice dropping to a soft, intimate tone. His hands shift on my waist. Even through my swimsuit the feel of his fingers causes a shiver to run through me.

'It's good to see you too.' I reply, my voice barely above a whisper.

His gaze drifts down. 'And you look amazing. I noticed even Billy Bob is peeping out.'

I am very aware that I'm standing here, on the grass, in just my one-piece with the low cut-out back. But despite showing way more flesh than I usually would, I don't really care. What does it matter what other people think? As Tom's fingers trace my waist, he leans towards me. I want to kiss him. I really want to kiss him.

Jeremy's angry face flashes into my mind. It's the face where the Y-shaped vein throbbed in his forehead. It was the face he pulled after he'd tracked my car to the pub I was at with Jess. I'd looked up from chatting to some boys Jess and I knew from school and there he was, looming above me, vein throbbing. He asked to speak to me outside. His voice was slow and steady, but something was off. As soon as we were outside, he yanked me around the corner of the pub by the neck of my jumper. He leaned in so his face was almost touching mine, spitting as he spoke.

'You are disgusting. Do you get it?' he'd yelled. 'You think you're so hot, off flirting with all these other men. They're just laughing at you. They think you're a joke. Everyone thinks you're a slut. A fat, disgusting slut.'

'Chrissy, is everything okay?' Jess is calling me now, just as she had done then.

I turn from Tom towards her.

'Yup, yup, I'm coming. See you, Tom,' I say without looking at him.

'Chrissy... wait,' he calls after me, but I don't turn back.

43

'Tell me again why this was a good idea?' I puff.

'Because, Chrissy, when else will you and I get a chance to watch the Aussie sunrise?' says Jess. 'And if we don't power walk, you'll never get a "bonza butt" like Melanie from bootcamp?' She laughs at her own attempt at Brad's accent.

Jess has way too much energy considering we dragged ourselves out of bed before light. I mean, are we actual masochists?

'It's not fair that you're going home soon,' I whine as we trudge along the Ben Buckler headland towards North Bondi lookout. 'It won't be the same without you.'

'I know. I wouldn't go home if it wasn't for work.'

I stop to tie my shoelace and look up at her. 'And Joe too, right?'

'Yeah.' She sighs. 'He didn't seem all that excited when I reminded him I'm back soon. It's making me feel a bit shit, to be honest.'

Grimacing, I straighten up and reach for her hand. 'It's gonna be okay, Jess. He loves you.' Although it's taking all my willpower not to call Joe up right now and give him a piece of my mind.

We reach the lookout spot and sit side by side on a flat rock.

'Where's this sun at then?' I ask, flicking off my headlamp and squinting out into the dim light.

Jess shrugs off her backpack to rummage for her water bottle. 'Good things come to those who wait. Speaking of, have you heard anything from Ocean Hill House yet?'

I scoff. 'Don't you think I'd have told you?'

Jess takes a sip from her bottle and grins. 'If you don't get it, you'll just have to come home and be my personal assistant.'

I laugh and turn to face her. 'And what would I assist you with, exactly?'

'Well, for starters, you could find out what's up with Joe.'

I roll my eyes, kicking at a small stone. 'Oh shush, he adores you. Look at my lame excuse for a love life. That should make you feel better by comparison. I had one guy who treated me like a *Biggest Loser* contestant and one guy who has anger issues.'

Jess pauses, squinting her eyes as she looks at me. 'Do

you really think Tom is like Jeremy? I mean, I know I kind of warned you off him, but he was being such a sweetie with that pigeon. I wonder if I got him wrong.'

I shake my head, picking at a tuft of grass that is growing through the rock. 'Jeremy had his sweet moments too, though. It was only an hour after you saw him yell at me outside The Dolphin that he was texting me love poems.'

'But not all men are like Jeremy.'

I frown. 'You're not seriously rolling out the "not all men" card?'

'No, but you seemed so excited about Tom and then so down when it didn't work out. It's like you've lost a little sparkle.'

I puff out my cheeks, exhaling loudly. 'Um... Rude. I'm as sparkly as ever.' I pull out my phone and, my thumb almost on autopilot, scrolls my emails again. Since my job interview, I've developed a habit of doing this about fifty times a day.

Jess squeezes my thigh. 'Look up, will you?'

I glance up from my phone to be greeted by the first pink swirls of dawn.

'Wow. Okay, so maybe the early morning was worth it.'

'Told you.' Jess smirks, triumphant.

I drag my eyes from the awesome sight for a second. I have a new email. It's from Ms Rogers back at Little Elm.

Subject: Your position at Little Elm.

Hello Chrissy,

I hope you are well and have been enjoying some reflection and downtime.

After much discussion with both the school board and the teacher's union, I am delighted to inform you that you have been cleared to return to work.

The board noted your statement acknowledging that your behaviour was not suitable for a Little Elm teacher. They also noted your decision to delete your social media accounts.

In addition, several parents came forward to highlight the positive impact you had on their children. Taking everything into account, I recommended your immediate reinstatement.

I would also like to inform you that Miss Maggie Connor has delayed her return from maternity leave, and I would like to offer you her previous position on a full-time basis.

Please call me at your earliest convenience to discuss this further. I'm excited to welcome you back to Little Elm next Monday.

Kind regards

Ms Rogers

My eyes refocus on the melting pot of colours in the sky above me and I take some deep breaths. Little Elm want me back. They really want me back. I can't believe it. I wipe a tear from below my eye. Since uni, my dream has been to secure a permanent role at Little Elm. If I'd been asked a month ago, I wouldn't have just said yes, I would have hosted a party to celebrate. So why, instead of immense relief, do I feel a heavy weight in my stomach?

'What's wrong?' asks Jess a couple of minutes later, her eyebrows knitted together.

I clear my throat before answering. 'I got an email.' There is a wobble in my voice. 'About my job.'

Jess's face clouds with sympathy. 'Oh... you didn't get it? You're too good for that snobby Ocean Hill House anyway.'

I shake my head. 'No, from Little Elm. They want me back on Monday. And they want me to be a permanent teacher there.'

'Oh my god!' Jess leaps up, grabbing both my arms to drag me up from my seat on the rock. 'Chrissy! This is your dream. This is amazing.'

Her enthusiasm lifts my spirits and I find myself jumping and laughing with her.

'You can stay with us while you look for a place to live,' she says, a huge smile plastered over her face. 'I'm so excited you're coming home.'

'Me too.' I don't tell her that going back to the UK doesn't feel so much like going home. It feels like I've failed at my new Aussie life.

44

'But you've only been there a few weeks,' says Mum, her voice drenched in disappointment.

I shift in my seat, clenching my fist to control my irritation. 'I thought you'd be happy for me. You know I've wanted a permanent teaching role for ages.'

She exhales, her eyes softening. 'I am happy for you. Of course I am. It's just that you're having such a great time over there. It doesn't make sense to end it so early. What about all the Aussie hunks?'

I roll my eyes skyward. My mum must be the only one in the world who would try to convince their daughter to turn down a stable job. She'd probably be happier if I got myself a reputation as the Bondi bike.

'I wasn't planning on leaving early, but I don't see how I can turn the job offer down. Ms Rogers stuck her neck out for me, and I can't throw that in her face.' Rubbing the bridge of my nose, I continue. 'Look, Brighton is home. It's great living near you, Dad and Jess. And the rescue dogs will be happy to see me. I mean, I love it here, but coming home is the best thing, isn't it?'

Mum tilts her head, giving me that oh so familiar, sceptical look. 'Are you trying to convince me or yourself? Can't you tell Little Elm that you need a couple more months?'

My fingers tighten around my phone as I shake my head. 'It doesn't work like that. I'm lucky to be getting another chance. How can I pass it up?'

'I suppose I can't force you, but I love the idea of you down under having a cowabunga time,' Mum says with a dreadful Australian accent.

I suppress a snicker before correcting her. 'Cowabunga isn't an Australian word, Mum. Isn't it just teenage mutant hero turtles who say that?'

She waves her hand dismissively. 'Open your mind. You can still have a cowabunga time even if you're not a turtle. Anyway, what are your men gonna do without you?'

I blink, taken aback. 'My men?'

'Yes, that hunky Brad and the dark and mysterious Tom.'

'I broke it off with Brad, but we're still friends... kind of.'

'And Tom? The one you're in love with.'

I stiffen. 'What makes you think that?'

'I'm not senile yet, daughter. I saw the look on your face when you told me about him.'

'He's okay, I guess... He rescued a pigeon the other day.'

'Oooh.' Mum shrieks as if I'd just told her Tom had performed an erotic striptease. 'I bet your ovaries almost burst.'

'Yuck! I hate when people say that. It was quite sweet, though. He is... well, he's gorgeous and he's funny and he's smart. But I can't go there.'

'From what you've told me, *I'm* about ready to go there.'

'Mum! It's not that simple. His ex told me something worrying about him.'

She leans forward, her jovial expression fading. 'Yes?'

I swallow hard before I speak. 'She said he has another side to him. That he could be abusive.'

Mum draws in a sharp intake of breath. 'And you believe her?'

'I don't know. I feel safer and more comfortable around Tom than anyone. Being with him is the only time that I don't feel like a great big blob of lard.'

'Don't say that, Chris.'

'Yeah, yeah, but you get what I mean.'

She leans in closer to her camera, as if trying to cross the digital divide between us. 'So maybe you need to work out whether this ex is telling the truth.'

'Or maybe I need to steer clear. I'm coming back to the UK, anyway, so I guess this thing with Tom isn't meant to be.'

Mum lets out an audible huff. 'So much for a whole new Chrissy.'

'That's not fair. I've changed a lot here. But how can I turn down this job? My savings won't last forever.'

Her face softens and her shoulders drop. 'I just want you to be happy.'

'I know and—' I'm interrupted by my phone buzzing. 'Oh, I'm getting another call.'

'Okay, love. You'd better get it. Maybe it's one of your admirers. I'll call you soon. Miss you lots.' Mum's words tumble out in a rush.

'Miss you,' I say, clicking over to the other call.

'Well, I'm glad I made an impression,' a loud Scottish voice snips down the phone line. 'This is Eve from Ocean Hill House.'

'Oh hi, hiya, hello, so good to hear from you. How are you?' I slap a hand over my mouth to stop any more anxious words from bubbling up.

Eve's voice is crisp. 'Look, Chrissy, I'm ringing because we'd like to offer you the role with us at Ocean Hill House. It starts with two-months sick leave cover, but a longer contract may follow. Mel has made a start on the bridging visa paperwork. You just need to come in and finish it off so she can submit everything.'

'I got the job?'

'You got the job,' she says with a rare smile in her voice.

'Oh wow. I thought... well... it'd been a while since the interview. This is brilliant,' I say, beaming. But it takes just a moment for reality to set in and for my smile to morph into a grimace. It would be totally irresponsible to turn down a full-time teaching job for a two-month contract.

'Eve, thank you. I mean, what an opportunity. But I've had an offer from back home, from Little Elm. There's a full-time position for me. I don't think I can say no.'

'Oh,' says Eve, her voice instantly cold. 'So, you wasted my time for nothing?'

'I'm so sorry. I only got the offer earlier today. I haven't accepted yet. It's just—'

'Full-time positions are scarce.' She finishes my sentence for me.

Guilt washes over me. 'I'm sorry,' I say again, staring down at my lilac toenails.

'You should be. You won't find a better school than Ocean Hill House.'

'Thanks for the oppor—' I say, but before I finish the sentence, Eve has hung up.

I collapse onto my bed and push my face into the pillow. A lump forms in my throat as hot tears burn at the back of my eyes. Why am I so sad when I'm getting everything I wanted?

'Ready for the airport, hon?' calls Jess, cracking open the door.

'Yup,' I call back.

'Thanks for coming with me. It's like a practice run for when you come back later this week. Woohoo!' she shrieks.

A few minutes later I'm rolling Jess's suitcase out of the

apartment. It feels so weird that Jess is leaving. It feels even weirder that I'll be leaving soon.

'Woah!' I almost trip over Ned as he barrels out of the door behind me and wiggles his body into my legs.

'Sorry, I would have waited. I didn't realise you were out here,' says Tom, his eyes meeting mine.

'Have you been avoiding me?' I ask, sounding hurt, even though I have definitely been avoiding him.

He looks down at Ned. 'No, it's just a bit awkward after... well, you and Brad.'

'What do you mean?'

'After you...' He exhales sharply, as if bracing himself. 'You know. I thought we were together and then you spent the night—'

I cut him off, shaking my head vigorously. 'No, I didn't. Well, not like that. I stayed at his place, but he slept on the floor.'

Tom's jaw is tense. 'Why were you wearing his clothes, then?'

For a moment I consider explaining, but then I remember, I have nothing to apologise for.

'Tom, you told your friend that I should lose weight. You made me feel fat and disgusting. I don't want to get into this here, but I can't be in a relationship again with someone like you.'

His eyes widen. 'Someone like me?'

I lean in closer, lowering my voice. 'Someone with anger and control issues.'

I scruff Ned's ears and turn to walk towards Jess and Chloe who are waiting next to the car.

'Chrissy, I don't know what you mean. Can we talk about this? I'm sorry about that Zipper stuff. There's no excuse for it, but I promise you, I didn't mean it.'

Pausing, I turn back around, locking eyes. 'Don't worry, Tom, I'm going back to the UK in a few days, so it'll be very easy to avoid me.'

'What?' Disbelief clouds his features.

'Yeah, I got offered my old job back.'

'But I thought you loved it here? I thought—'

'Bye, Tom.' I turn and stride towards the car, throwing the baggage into the boot before slamming it shut. As I take my seat in the car, I wipe away a stray tear.

'You alright?' asks Chloe, who is sitting in the driver's seat. 'Was he being a dick again?'

'I'm fine.' I take a deep breath. 'Let's concentrate on giving Jess the send-off she deserves.'

45

Chloe flops down next to me on the sofa, her eyes zeroing in on my tub of Ben and Jerry's. 'Maybe it's time to stop wallowing?' she suggests, a teasing lilt in her voice.

'I'm not wallowing.' I roll my eyes and load up another spoonful of ice cream.

'Well, you cancelled the dance class and now you're moping.'

I pause, the spoon halfway to my mouth and exhale sharply. 'What? I'm relaxing. I'm on my period. I feel like shit, and I miss Jess. No big deal.'

Chloe leans in closer, scrutinising my face. 'You've been crying. You've got mascara down your cheeks. If you feel so bad about your decision to go back to the UK, why don't you stay here?'

'It's not even about that. It's this show.' I gesture at the TV with my spoon, but I'm quite clearly watching *Broad City*, which is not sad at all. In fact, it's hilarious.

'I just don't get it.' Chloe leans over and grabs the TV controls from next to me, turning down the volume. 'You were loving life here and now I've got this grump hanging around the apartment. What gives?'

I take a deep breath and lock eyes with Chloe. 'I know I'm being a pain. I guess I'm worried that I'm making bad decisions when it comes to where I work, where I live, and who I date. But I'll make it up to you. We'll go dancing tomorrow, I promise.'

'Tomorrow I'm going on a date.' Chloe says with a smug smile.

'Is this with Mr Gym Bod from the other day?'

'Nah, this is a new guy.' She grins as she shifts in her seat and pulls her phone from her pocket. 'We matched on Zingles.'

'So go on then, spill the tea. Tall, dark, and handsome, is he?' I ask, placing my empty ice cream tub on the coffee table.

She swipes on her phone a few times and then chuckles. 'I can't even remember what he looks like. I think he's blonde with blue eyes and tattoos. Pretty hot if we believe the pics.'

'Give me a look then.' I reach out.

Chloe taps on her phone and hands it to me, the screen illuminated with the guy's profile picture.

'Very handsome,' I say, just as a message notification pops up on the screen.

TOM UPSTAIRS

Thanks for the pics. Very hot.

I stare at the screen, a nauseating wave of confusion washing over me. Why is Tom texting Chloe? Why is she texting him hot pics? As my stomach flip-flops, the text disappears from the screen.

I watch as Chloe stretches her arms above her head, exposing her taut stomach. I mean, look at her compared to me. No wonder Tom is texting her.

I pass her phone back to her. 'So, what's this guy's personality like?' I ask, making a herculean effort to act like I haven't just discovered Chloe's dirty little secret.

She shrugs as she leans back into the couch. 'I don't know. It doesn't matter, does it?'

I shake my head, fighting back the rising irritation. 'I thought I was the one with relationship issues.'

Chloe cocks her head to the side. 'What's that supposed to mean?'

'I'm just saying, perhaps if you cared more about the guy's personality than his looks, you'd find more meaning in these relationships.'

'Don't lecture me on relationships,' she snaps, getting up from the sofa. 'At least I'm getting some.'

I keep my tone casual, even though I'm feeling anything but. 'Sex is just sex though, isn't it? You can moan and scream all night, but at the end of the day, you're still alone.'

'Wow. Judgy much?'

'I'm not judging,' I say, totally judging her. 'But do you really think you'll find happiness that way?'

Chloe huffs and crosses her arms over her chest. 'What about you? You act like your life is so bloody tough, but what it boils down to is you have two great jobs to choose from and two great men to choose from. Don't be such a drama queen.'

'I'm not being a drama queen.' I push myself up from the sofa with quite the dramatic flourish. 'This job decision will affect my whole life. And if you think Tom is so great, why don't you go ahead and shag him.'

Her forehead creases in confusion before she spins around and stomps back to her bedroom. 'I can't talk to you when you're like this.'

I throw my hands up in the air. 'Fine.'

Her door slams and her voice sounds from the other side. 'Fine.'

I turn off the TV and stomp to my bedroom. I need to talk to the one person who will understand. The one person who knows why things feel so complicated with Tom.

I lie on my bed, propping myself up on my pillows, and swipe through my contacts, before tapping the video call icon for Jess. As the phone rings, I shake my head, trying to shake off my bad mood.

'Hey! How much are you missing me?' Jess's face pops up on the screen, her eyes bright.

'Like you wouldn't believe,' I say, forcing a smile. 'How was your flight? Is it brilliant being home with Joe?'

She yawns before speaking. 'Well, I'm super jet-lagged, but it's been way better than I thought. Joe has—'

I cut her off, my words tumbling out in a rush, my voice slightly lowered to make sure Chloe doesn't hear. 'It's not been the same since you've gone. Chloe's been giving me a hard time. She's got a revolving door of men coming in and out and it's like, keep it in your knickers. Plus, I saw this dodgy text from Tom on her phone. Something is going on between them. And get this, she has the nerve to be all judgy because I can't decide about coming back to the UK.'

Jess raises her eyebrows. 'What? Are you serious? I thought you were set on coming home.'

Her face falls as I fill her in on the Ocean Hill House job, but she quickly plasters on a supportive smile.

'Chrissy, that's what you wanted. That's brilliant. I mean, it will suck for me if you don't come back, but if it's the right move for you, I would understand.'

I pinch the bridge of my nose as if that will help me think clearly. 'I don't know what I want. Part of me would love to be back with you, but another part wants to continue my new life here. I guess I am wallowing a little bit about Tom too.'

'A little bit?' Jess leans closer to the camera, 'Chrissy,

mate, I can see the panda eyes. Is this like when Jeremy dumped you that first time?'

'No, not like that,' I snap. 'And after what Jeremy did, how could I risk dating Tom? What if I end up in that situation again?'

Jess's eyes soften. 'But what if you don't?'

A knot of anxiety tightens in my stomach. 'You're not seriously telling me to pursue a relationship with an abuser, are you? You saw what I went through.'

'Okay, take a breath. I'm not telling you to do anything, but from what Chloe told me, Tom isn't an abusive guy. She reckons you should give him a chance, but she says she can't get through to you about it. And I'm sure you don't need to worry about her hooking up with Tom. It's not like that between them.'

I grip my phone tighter, my knuckles turning white as Jess's words sink in. 'Hang on. You and Chloe have been talking behind my back? And you reckon I'm lying about what I saw on her phone?'

Jess's eyes dart to the side for a moment as if searching for the right words. 'I'm not saying you're lying, but you don't know anything about the context. And of course we haven't been talking about you. It's just we got on and she reached out when I got home because you've been in one of your moods lately. She just wanted some advice... a bit of a pep talk.'

I rake my hand through my hair, agitated. 'And you

decided to dissect my love life, too? Talk about all my past mistakes?' Frustrated tears burn behind my eyes.

Jess hesitates, her face flushed. 'Okay, we're getting off track here. Maybe we should chat about this when you've had a chance to take a breath. I've got something to tell—'

I cut her off. 'No, no, it doesn't surprise me that Little Miss Boring Relationship and Little Miss Slut get on. I guess you balance each other out. I bet you've told her all about what happened with Jeremy, too?'

There's a pause and Jess takes a deep breath.

'You have? You've told her.' I press.

'I had to help her understand. I had to let her know why what Janine said was so difficult for you. Other people would just date the guy they were interested in, see for themselves, and not bring everyone around them down. And you know what, Chrissy?' the rise in Jess's volume takes me aback and I notice she's now pacing the room. 'I may be Little Miss Boring Relationship to you, but me and Joe are happy. We have fun together. We're in love. If you stay closed off, you'll never have that, and it's not about your weight or anything else you think people are so bothered about. It's these stupid walls you build up around yourself.'

I slam my free hand down on the bed. 'You really don't get it, do you, Jess?'

'I get you were hurt.' Jess is speaking in her matronly tone, which is hardly ever used against me. 'I get it was awful, but not everyone is Jeremy, and you can't let that bastard rule your life. You can't make him rule mine either. And you can't use it to control Chloe. Pull yourself together.'

Fuming, I swipe away a rebellious tear that has trickled down my cheek.

'Thanks for that, Jess,' I manage to spit the words out through a sob. 'I guess you can go and discuss your big, fat loser of a friend with Chloe now.'

Jess shakes her head in disbelief. 'This is so silly. Why are we even fighting? I was excited to talk to you. I had something to share. Not everything is about you.'

I let out a shaky breath. 'But some things *are* about me.'

Frustrated I tap the end call button and hurl my phone across the bed. Storming to the closet, I yank it open and pull on my running shoes.

46

I push my hair back over my ears as I take powerful strides down the stairs, out the front door and towards the beach. The darkening sky is thick with grey clouds. Light rain is frizzing up my hair. With weather like this, I may as well be back in Brighton.

I mean, okay, so Chloe is new in my life. She doesn't know everything I've been through. But isn't it universal girl code not to crack on to a friend's love interest?

But Jess! Jess was there through it all. Anger bubbles up inside me again and as I reach the beach, I break into a jog, the wind whipping ocean spray across my face.

I pump my arms back and forth and plunge my trainers in and out of the wet sand. My legs ache, but I want it to hurt. The beach is empty. I can hear the odd cackle of laughter carried on the wind from the twinkling bars. The sound of people enjoying themselves. The sound of people getting on with life.

I push my legs harder as an image flashes into my mind of Jeremy leaning over me, pressing his red face into mine, the vein bulging on his forehead. I had looked away then and pulled my head into my knees, scrunching into a foetal position on the sofa. His words hardly registered over my own yells for him to stop. But he was jealous. He was always jealous. And he wanted to hurt me. Not physically, but with words.

I wish I could say that was the day I left, but it wasn't. Another image flashes into my mind: Jeremy pulling me into his arms, cradling my head and stroking my hair, saying how sorry he was, how much he loved me.

Ugh, just the thought of it makes me want to scream. I reach the end of the beach and my legs burn as I slow to a walk and make my way up the steps and the steep slope towards Bondi Road.

My T-shirt is plastered to my skin now. A fat drop of rain plops off my nose. I hear yells from the hostel across the road. I keep going and as the road flattens, I run. Bright car lights pass me, and I wonder what the drivers make of this big mess hurtling through the rain.

I stand waiting to cross the road, leaning my hands on my thighs, taking in deep gulps of air. As I lift my gaze, I see the lights of Beaches Bar, Janine's new place. It looks warm, inviting, and dry. I plod across the road, realising that the rage and stress have dissipated somewhat. I stand in the doorway, gazing into the yellow light. Groups of people sit around drinking and laughing. And there she is, Janine. She seems at home behind the bar as she makes a drink for a tall, red-headed man. I open the door and walk in. I expect everyone to turn around and look at me as they would in a village pub, but they don't. They're all too busy enjoying themselves.

I stand on the doormat and a young woman greets me.

'G'day. Are you eating or just grabbing a drink? You're soaked, poor thing. Shall I see if we have a towel somewhere for you?'

'Could I speak to Janine for a moment?' I ask.

'Uh, sure.' The waiter stands aside, and my wet shoes squeak against the polished floor as I take slow steps towards the bar.

'Oh, it's you,' says Janine as she spots me. 'You're finally following my advice and checking this place out? I see you dressed to impress.'

Casting a glance down at my rain-soaked attire, I shrug. 'The place looks great.' I mutter, still unsure of what I'm doing here, or what I'm going to say.

She gestures to a bar stool. 'Take a seat, I'll make you something.'

'Sounds lovely, but I'll pass on the alcohol. I've got to run back.' I lean against the bar, my elbows leaving damp spots against the surface.

'You ran here?' Janine arches an eyebrow, clearly amused.

'Yeah, I think I overdid it.'

She chuckles. 'Nah, you must be pretty fit by now, even if you are too good for Brad's Bootcamp.'

My eyes meet hers as I start to protest. 'I don't think I'm too good, I—'

'I'm kidding,' she says with a dismissive wave of her hand. 'Chloe filled me in and told me you two are setting the town on fire with your dancing or whatever.'

I manage an uneasy, 'Oh right.'

'I've taken your spot at Brad's Bootcamp, anyway. I better keep up my hot bod if I'm gonna lure in the punters.'

She places a bright red drink in front of me. 'Don't worry it's a mocktail. On the house.' She winks.

I smile my thanks, tapping my fingers nervously against the glass. 'So, do you own this place now?'

She nods, her expression becoming serious. 'Yup, and it's pretty good so far. It feels surreal. Me and Tom have been dreaming about this for so long and now it's happening.'

I take a sip of the sweet, strawberry-flavoured drink. 'I was hoping to talk to you about that. About Tom, I mean.'

Her eyes meet mine, narrowing slightly. 'What about him?'

I pause. 'I... um, well, it was what you said the other day... about what he did to you. The other side to him you were talking about.'

A momentary flicker of surprise passes across her face. 'Oh, that.'

My heart pounds a little faster as I shift in my seat. 'Yeah... you don't have to share with me or anything. It's just, I've been through something similar to what I'm guessing you went through.'

'Your boyfriend ditched plans to start a business with you, too?'

'No, no, not that,' I stammer. 'Has he?'

Janine lets out a dry laugh. 'He's so into his precious life-guarding. Too damn heroic for his own good. He's been a massive help though... really involved. He's using any excuse to pop by and give me a hand.'

'So, does he seem happy now? Now he's made that decision?'

She smirks. 'He'd honestly be so much happier if we got back together, but men can be too stupid to know what's good for them.' She swishes her sleek ponytail. 'I mean, no offence, Chrissy, but the fact you turned his head just shows what a messed-up place he's in right now.'

Taking a long glug of my mocktail, I let the sweet taste soothe the sting of the insult.

Setting the glass down, I muster up the courage to go on. 'I know you and Tom had good times in your relationship. But I guess I'm kind of surprised that you want to be with him again, after what you said about his temper. Was he... abusive, towards you?'

Janine locks eyes with me, as if trying to read my thoughts. 'Have you seen that side to him?' Her voice is hushed, and she leans in towards me so I can smell her minty breath.

I shake my head, cautiously. 'No, I don't think so. Unless... well, I guess when we went out for food, he was very impatient. It would seem like nothing to someone else, but I've been through a tough time with an ex who was really controlling.'

She inches even closer. 'Did your ex hit you?'

'No, never, but —'

She cuts me off with a curt nod. 'Right.'

'But I've learned since that it is still abuse, even if it is gaslighting and verbal insults.'

Janine, cocks her head, assessing me. 'You and Tom wouldn't suit then.'

'What do you mean?'

She hesitates. Her eyes darting around as if searching for an escape. 'Look, Tom and my lives are so tied up that we kind of have to get together again. We're like Ross and Rachel, Mindy and Danny. But there is something...'

I reach out, placing my hand on her forearm. 'Tell me.'

She takes a deep, shuddery breath, her eyes glistening with unshed tears.

'I can't lie to you. Not after what you've been through. Yes, Tom can be abusive... sometimes even physically.'

I reel back as if she has slapped me.

'What?' A deep voice sounds from the hallway beside the bar.

'Tom.' Janine blinks rapidly. 'You aren't meant to be here yet.' With hurried steps she closes the distance between them and plants a kiss on his cheek.

'What were you saying?' he asks, his voice steady and deep.

'Oh, nothing, babe. I was just chatting with Chrissy here. She was whingeing about her ex. You know how she is.' She moves her hands in a yap, yap, yap motion.

I move from my spot and walk behind the bar and stand next to Janine.

'What are you doing? Get back behind there,' she snaps at me.

I square my shoulders. 'No, you're not facing him alone.'

Janine speaks in a lowered voice. 'Don't worry about it, Chrissy. Seriously. I'm used to dealing with him.'

Tom's eyes dart between us, agitated. 'Dealing with me? What are you talking about?'

I step forward, standing in front of Janine, positioning myself between her and Tom.

'Leave her alone,' I growl.

'This is nothing to do with you,' says Janine, pushing me out of the way with more force than I expected. 'I'm fine.'

'I've been where you are,' I say. 'I know it feels like you have to go it alone... but you don't. There are people who can support you.'

'It's nothing,' Janine dismisses me, her voice strained.

'Tom, just ignore her. She's taken something I said out of context.'

I recognise the way she is standing up for him. It's just like I used to do with Jeremy.

'I heard what you said,' says Tom, his gaze still locked on Janine. The colour has drained from his face.

Janine exhales sharply. 'Okay, so I guess it sounded bad, but I had to say that. She didn't leave me any choice. When I first said you had another side to you, I just meant that you get moody when you're hungry. It's not my fault she took it like you are some kind of monster, is it? She's not right for you. Look at her.' Janine flings my hands in my direction.

'So, you told her I'm an abuser?'

'Well, you do get grumpy when your food is late,' she snaps back.

Stunned, I turn to look at Janine. 'Hang on, so Tom hasn't been abusive to you?'

Janine huffs, crossing her arms defensively. 'He made us leave a restaurant once when we'd been waiting thirty minutes, and the food would've come really soon, so I was starving hungry.'

'Annoying sure, but not abuse!' I take a step away from her.

'Tell her, Janine,' says Tom, his jaw tense. 'Tell Chrissy the truth.'

Janine turns towards me but looks at the floor, a pout on her perfect face.

'Fine. Tom isn't abusive, but neither was your ex since he never actually hit you, so how about you stop whining about it and grow up? And maybe look for a man in your own league.'

Adrenaline surges through my body, leaving me cold as I realise what she's done. She's made it all up. The room rolls around me as I spin on my heels and turn to leave the restaurant.

The rain is pouring down outside, and I lean against the wall, unsure of what to do.

'Chrissy, wait.' Tom reaches me.

Staring at him, I fumble for words. 'Tom... I thought... Janine told me on the beach that you were—'

'I know,' Tom cuts me off, his voice tinged with regret. 'I'm so sorry.'

I let out a shaky laugh. 'This whole time, I thought I was an idiot for being wildly attracted to another controlling arsehole. I'm so glad that isn't true. Instead, I'm just attracted to a womanising arsehole.'

Tom's eyes widen and his mouth falls open as silence stretches between us.

Nervously twisting the hem of my soaked shirt, I break the silence. 'I saw your message to Chloe. I know you've been texting her. I guess it's a good thing I found out now.'

His eyes dart to mine, panic giving way to something more pleading. 'I promise you I can explain that text. There's nothing to it... nothing. I would never – could never, hurt you.' He pauses and pushes a wet strand of hair from my face. He's so close now, I can feel his breath on my skin. His lips lift at the corners. 'You really find me wildly attractive?'

As I take in that smile it is as if all my concerns about Tom evaporate into the rain-soaked air. I try to remember what they were, but how can I focus on that when every nerve in my body is tingling? I let him draw me close and his lips are on mine, wet from the rain. A wave of warmth spreads within me.

When we finally part, he cradles my face in his hands and we both seem to realise we are standing here, soaked to the bone.

His fingers interlock with mine and without a word, we break into a run towards home. Our laughter melds with the patter of the rain.

Outside the apartment, Tom holds me in his arms and dots my face with little, quick kisses.

'Are you sure you can't come up now?' he asks, his voice a low murmur against my cheek. 'Ned would love to see you.'

My eyes meet his, conflicted. 'I want to. I really want to. But I need to make things right with Chloe and Jess. I acted like a massive dick. Can we meet tomorrow?'

'Yes, please.' He leans in capturing my lips in a soft, lingering kiss. I feel like I might collapse from a lust over-dose. 'Keep the whole of next week free,' he says.

A smile tugs at my lips as I raise my eyebrows at him.

'I had the week off to help Janine in the bar, but screw that. Let's spend it together, making up for lost time.'

'I would love that,' I say, and he enfolds me in his arms, for another kiss.

Then I remember, and my stomach plummets as if I am in a dream where I've fallen off a kerb.

'Oh no. I can't,' I say, taking a step back, feeling winded by the realisation. 'My flight back to the UK is booked for Friday.'

'This Friday?'

I nod, biting my lip. 'Yeah, remember? I got my old job back. A full-time teaching job is what I've wanted ever since I finished uni.'

'Oh... Oh yeah, I thought maybe... Never mind. It doesn't matter.' A flash of disappointment crosses his face. 'You'll be amazing,' he says. 'You are amazing.'

'I guess we don't have much time left together,' I say with a hitch in my voice.

His lips press into a thin line. 'I guess not.'

As we stand here, looking into each other's eyes, all I want is for him to ask me to stay.

47

Maybe I should behave like a twat more often. It seemed to fuel my run like nothing else. After Tom went inside to feed Ned, I sat under the awning of the apartment building watching the rain pour down and I realised I don't want to leave.

I'm not ready to leave this place. And it's not about Tom or the job. It's about me.

Now I'm outside Chloe's apartment, covered in an attractive mix of sweat and rainwater. I'm desperate to be soothed by a warm shower, but first I need to make things right with Chloe.

I open the door to the apartment hesitating as I see Chloe sitting on the sofa.

'I'm so sorry,' I blurt out.

'What happened to you?' she asks as she takes in my sodden form.

'I've been out running and had some time to think. I need to apologise for acting like such a giant plonker.'

Chloe purses her lips, considering this. 'Yeah, you were a dick.' There's an awkward pause. She leans forward and picks up her wine glass, taking a slow sip. Her eyes search my face as if considering my sincerity. 'Jess called and I guess I didn't fully understand what was going on for you. I'm sorry if I've made you feel uncomfortable here.'

A stab of unease twists in my gut at the thought of Jess ranting about me to Chloe straight after our argument, but I push it down.

'If you asked me if I would ever slut-shame someone, I would have said no,' I say as I hover by the sofa, not wanting to sit down and wet the fabric.

A flash of indignation crosses her face. 'Who are you calling a slut?'

'Oh god, I'm sorry.'

She shakes her head, her lips curling into a half smile. 'I'm joking. I guess there's the teeniest chance you could be right about the way I'm handling relationships at the moment. Sometimes I wonder what it would be like to get to know someone properly. It's been ages since I had a long-term relationship – and by long-term, I mean a month. I don't know, maybe I'm messed up.'

I take a step closer to her, waving my hands for emphasis

as I speak. 'You're not messed up. You're the most amazing person – my own fairy godmother. You mean so much to me. I'm sorry if I made you doubt that. And just because you've been texting Tom, that doesn't matter. I mean, he is gorgeous, and you are only human.'

Chloe rises from the sofa abruptly. 'I'm not texting Tom.'

I tilt my head. I want things to be good between us, but I won't put up with being lied to.

'Well, I am, but not in the way you think,' she continues.

'What's going on, then?'

She hesitates, her lips parting as if to speak, but she shakes her head. 'I can't say.'

I'm desperate to ask more questions, but I fight the urge. The truth is, whether or not she was cracking onto Tom, Chloe's friendship is too important to throw away.

'So, do you forgive me?' I open my arms for a hug.

'All is forgiven.' Chloe opens her arms too, but as she notices the full extent of my rain-soaked body, she backs away.

'Come on, give us a hug,' I growl as I lunge after her with my arms open.

Giggling, she runs around the sofa.

I turn to walk to the bathroom.

'Chrissy?' Chloe calls after me.

'Yeah.' I pause and turn back to her.

Her eyes search mine. 'What happened? You seem so much more relaxed... happier.'

'I'm not sure if it was the exercise or Tom or that I've come to a decision.'

'About going home?'

A smile creeps onto my face. 'Yeah. I'm wondering if you'd be willing to put up with me for a bit longer. Like in a proper, rent paying, room-matey kind of situation?'

Her face breaks into a beaming smile. 'Oh my god, yes! That would be awesome. So, you're not going home?'

'I think I'm already there.' For a beat, the silence hangs around us, thick and loaded. But then I shatter it. 'This definitely calls for a hug.' I giggle and run at Chloe again. Letting out a shriek of laughter, she picks up a blue cushion from the sofa and lobs it in my direction.

I SIT on the edge of the bed, my hair wrapped in a towel, feeling so much better after my shower. Jess doesn't answer the first two times I call, but on the third try, her face pops onto the screen. She has puffy eyes and trails down her cheeks. I could slap myself for being the one responsible for that.

'What?' she snaps.

I take a shaky breath. 'Jess, I'm so sorry.'

Her eyes flash, brimming with emotion. 'You can't just do and say whatever you like and then apologise for it. Words hurt.'

'I know they do, and I totally overreacted. It's a good thing you hit it off with Chloe. Now you have someone to rant to when I'm being a total arse.'

Her features soften slightly, and she sniffles, wiping away a tear that trickles down her cheek. 'We weren't ranting about you. I guess I was feeling left out what with you two getting close. I was hoping you wouldn't forget me if I became friends with Chloe too.'

I bring the screen closer to my face. 'As if I would ever forget you. I don't think it matters where I go or who I meet, I miss you every day.'

Jess nods. 'I miss you too. But I still can't believe you think... I'm boring.' The last word comes out in a wail.

'No, no, no. Forget I said that. I was talking nonsense.' I wave my free hand vehemently as if trying to swat away my previous words. 'You are the most vibrant ball of energy I have ever met. If anything, you're too exciting.'

'Steady on,' she says through a smile mixed with a hiccup.

'I'm serious, Jess. You are everything I want to be. You're gorgeous, confident, beautiful. In fact, come back to Sydney, and let's get married.' We both giggle.

Just then a soft blur of fur sneaks into the side of the screen. I recognise that fluffy little head. My breath catches as the dog pushes himself fully into the frame and licks away Jess's tears.

Jess grins. 'So, you remember I was trying to tell you

something?'

'Yes?'

She giggles, obviously relishing the moment. 'It turns out Joe was jumping through all the hoops to adopt Jonah.'

'No way.' My mouth falls open.

'Yes way,' she beams. 'That's why he was being so secretive. Joe is useless at keeping secrets, so he just avoided the phone.'

'But the building doesn't allow pets,' I say remembering the building rules when we tried to adopt a bunny.

Jess waves her hand dismissively. 'Joe sorted it all with the building manager.'

'And the shelter let him adopt Jonah for you, just like that?'

Jess shakes her head. 'No, no. They don't adopt animals out as surprises. When I got home, Joe had this whole romantic setup ready; a candlelit dinner and everything. Then he gave me this envelope and in it was a photo of Jonah and the words *Please adopt me*. I couldn't believe it. The next day, we went to the shelter, and we officially adopted Jonah then. All the shelter staff were thrilled.'

I look from Jess to sweet Jonah beside her. 'Oh my gosh. This is... well... this is everything, Jess.'

Happy tears are streaming down my face as I ask about a million questions.

Jonah paws at Jess's jumper, trying to get attention, and I realise that perhaps boring Joe isn't so boring after all.

48

I gaze out to sea, imagining I'm one of the lifeguards. There are so many people on the beach that I'm not sure how they keep track of everyone. Tom asked me to meet him below the lifeguard tower at two p.m. I glance at my Fitbit again. It's ten past.

'There he is,' I yelp to no one as I catch a glimpse of Tom approaching through the crowds. The fizzing inside me starts as soon as I see him in his lifeguard uniform. I want to run across the beach, bowl him over, and rip his clothes off right there on the sand. As he walks up to the tower, I channel my energy into fidgeting with my blue ombre sarong, which is pulled into a halter dress over my bikini.

'Tom.' I'm grinning as I cover the final few steps to meet him.

'Sorry I'm a bit late,' he says, as his eyes meet mine.

'It's okay. I need to tell you something.' I'm so excited I want to jump up and down.

He cocks his head to the side. 'Me too.'

I grab his hands, unable to contain myself any longer. 'Okay, me first. I spoke to Little Elm this morning. I've turned down the job. I'm going for the short contract at Ocean Hill House. I'm staying here in Sydney.'

Tom's eyes widen and then, to my relief, that gorgeous smile spreads over his face.

'You chose to stay? For me?'

'For both of us. This place feels like home already.' My words fall out in a rush. 'But I do want to be with you, Tom. At least I want to give us a real try. It's like when I'm around you, I can be the real me.'

My words hang in the air for a moment, before he draws me into his arms. Warmth washes over me, as I run my hands down his strong back, noticing the ripple of his muscles.

'Ouch' He jumps back as my hands skim the top of his blue board shorts.

'What?'

'Um... so I didn't know you had decided to stay. And the thing is, I really don't want you to leave. I thought maybe you needed a grand gesture.'

'A grand gesture?'

Tom turns around and points to his lower back, where a

small piece of gauze peeps out from beneath his board shorts.

'Did you hurt yourself?' I ask, running a finger above the gauze and feeling the heat of his skin beneath my fingertip.

'Yeah, I did. Well, Hugo at Kaleidoscope Tattoos did actually... with the help of Chloe.'

'You got a tattoo?'

He feigns a mansplaining tone. 'I think you'll find it's a tramp stamp.'

'You didn't?'

'Take a look.'

Mindful of the tender skin, I lower his board shorts and carefully peel back the surgical tape before lifting the gauze. There, at the top of Tom's buttocks, is a little green Hulk in full raging mode, holding a carrot.

'It's you,' I say, trying to stifle a giggle. 'A hungry hulk.'

'Not just a hungry hulk, but a carrot-munching hulk.'

'Are you saying...?'

'Yup, I'm gonna be a carrot muncher like you. This masterpiece is all for you, Chrissy. Our first chat was about your tramp stamp, and if it's good enough for you, then it's good enough for me.'

He turns towards me, looks into my eyes and his sincere face cracks into a grin. I fall forward into his arms, laughing with him.

'You did that for me?' My words come out in a splutter as I attempt to speak through giggles.

'Yup, I got a tacky tramp stamp for you, and I don't even care who knows it.'

'You know, you might be the only person who makes a tramp stamp look hot,' I tease, placing my hands on his broad shoulders.

'Not the only person.'

My whole body tingles as his fingers softly cradle my face and he pulls me towards him.

As his lips meet mine, I have no doubt I've made the right decision.

'Have you got time for a walk before work?' I ask as we pull apart. I don't want to let him go.

A smile tugs at his lips. 'I'm all yours until two thirty.'

He takes my hand and leads me away from the tower and towards the edge of the ocean.

I glance up at him as we walk hand in hand. 'You know, you could date any person on this beach. I'm so glad you've chosen me, even if I don't quite understand why.'

He stops walking and turns to me. 'When will you believe you are beautiful?'

A warm courage rises within me as I untie my sarong at the neck and let it fall to the sand, revealing my new turquoise bikini.

I honestly can't remember the last time I wore a bikini. I've always been self-conscious in swimwear. And yet, standing here with Tom as his eyes scan down my body, I do feel beautiful.

'You know my list?' I ask Tom as we walk along the water's edge.

He grins, 'Ah yes, the skinny list?'

I nod. 'I've been thinking that I don't want to wait anymore. I want to do everything on my list. I want to do it whether I lose more weight, gain weight or stay the same. And I was thinking maybe I can do some of it with you.'

He smiles and there is a mischievous glint in his eyes. 'Isn't booty call on the list? I can definitely help with that.'

I slap him on the bum, and he leans in and kisses me again.

As he pulls away, I reach into my bikini top and pull out the list. I unfold it and gaze at the scrawled handwriting. Many of the items are already checked off.

1. Spend six months in Australia

I can't check it off yet, but I've fallen in love with this place and don't see myself leaving anytime soon.

2. Wear a bikini in public

Check. And I'm rocking it, if I do say so myself.

3. Go to a group dance class

Check. I've been multiple times and had a ball. It seems I

have quite the talent for booty shaking. Cheynique would be proud!

4. Learn to surf

Um, well, I'm giving it a try. Let's call this a work in progress.

5. Do something spontaneous

This whole trip has been kind of spontaneous, so check, check, check.

15. Wear a body-con dress

So I can't exactly check this off, but I gave it a red hot try. I know I could buy one in a bigger size, and it would probably look awesome, but I'm not sure it's me. I don't want my flesh to be all squidged up like a vegan sausage. I'm getting comfy with who I am and that includes not stuffing myself into clothes that make me feel claustrophobic.

32. Spur of the moment booty call

Hmm, I may be checking this one off sooner than expected.

I scrunch up the list and throw it into the sea.

'Bugger off, skinny list,' I yell, a surge of happiness jolting through me as it whizzes through the air.

Tom erupts into laughter and twirls me around.

I wriggle out of his arms. 'Hang on, that was symbolic, but I'm not a litter bug.' I stumble to grab the wet paper. 'I typed it all up on the computer anyway.'

'Of course you did,' he says, an affectionate glimmer in his eyes. 'So, what do you think of the little Hulk?'

'I love him.' My face splits into a grin.

'You can thank Chloe. She designed it.'

I remember the message on Chloe's phone. 'Did she text you the designs?'

'Yeah, just the other night.'

'The message that popped up on her phone.' I point in the air as if Chloe's phone is right there. 'It said *Very hot*. Was it about the tattoo?'

Tom chuckles. 'Obviously. I mean, how hot is the little guy?'

My head spins. I have been worrying about nothing.

'Do you still want to spend the next week with me?' I ask, unable to keep the giddy smile off my face.

'Next week, next month, next year?' he shrugs, his grin widening. 'Let's see what happens.'

EPILOGUE

'Didn't Amanda say lunch would be at 12.30?' asks Tom, as he sits on the grass, glancing at his phone.

'It's only 12.35,' I reply, laughing as Nahla the hen hops onto his outstretched legs.

'I bet we'll be waiting for ages,' he huffs.

I snap a photo of him and Nahla and then a close-up of his face.

'What are you doing?' he asks.

'I'm documenting the hanger. Your inner Hulk is trying to get out.'

He rolls his eyes in an over-the-top manner, and I take another photo.

'Do you like your spic-and-span new bed?' I ask the little

hen as she hops off Tom's long legs and scratches the fresh straw.

'Lunch is up,' Amanda calls from outside the enclosure.

Tom is up like a shot, but before he stands, I snap another photo, showing how his face has morphed into an ecstatic grin. I can't help giggling at how much food affects his mood. I know when I show him the photos later, he'll find it just as funny as I do.

I follow Tom out of the enclosure. Keith, the sanctuary dog, and Ned take a break from their playing and bolt up to greet us as we shut the gate.

'Thanks for all your help. This guy is about a million times more useful than the last one you brought here,' says Amanda with a cheeky grin. I laugh as I remember Brad being so precious about avoiding the mud.

'Brad's alright,' I say. 'But yeah, I'm pretty happy with this one.'

In front of us is a variety of vegan food brought by the other volunteers. I kind of want to dive straight into the chocolate cupcakes, but first I pile on a helping of potato gratin, mac n cheese, and sweet potato salad. The last time I came here with Brad, I wouldn't have even considered eating like this. I was so worried that people were judging me. But now I'm enjoying as much as I like, and I know I can stop when I'm full. I'm not sure what's changed. Maybe I'm just happy?

Tom's hand rests around my waist and I glance up at him.

It's hard to believe we've only been dating for a month. I feel so comfortable with this man and my life in Sydney. Chloe is a brilliant roommate and I've got used to her constant parade of men. Well, kind of. I did bang on her door the other night when she had a very shouty man in her bed. She yelled back at me to 'suck it up, princess,' so that was me told. We're still going to Marcel's Boogie Box a couple of times a week. Marcel has even commissioned Chloe to create a mural for the back wall of the dance studio. So, when Chloe's not shagging her way around Bondi or dancing with me, she's got her head stuck in a sketchbook. I can't wait to see what she comes up with.

I'm in a pretty solid routine now with Ocean Hill House. Thank god, they hadn't filled the position by the time I made up my mind. Eve still has her scary moments, but at least she's dropped the whole honeypants thing. When she's not channelling Meryl Streep's character from *The Devil Wears Prada*, she's busy picking my brain about going vegan. Mel and I have gotten closer too. We spend our lunch breaks together when we can. For such a fit woman with such a phenomenal arse, I've been pleasantly surprised that Mel always has delicious biscuits to share. And of course, my year-one class is super cute. Even when someone's having a tantrum it's a little more tolerable coming from a kid with an Aussie accent.

In our spare time, Tom and I have been having loads of fun: exploring Sydney, walking Ned, and sometimes just watching Netflix and, um... chilling. Plenty of red-hot chilling. In fact, the best chilling I have ever had.

Tom was the one who suggested we help at Nahla's Place. I was surprised. I mean, it's one thing to go vegan, but another to be willing to shovel the poop of rescued animals. I guess I should have known he'd love the sanctuary, given how he is with Ned.

After we've eaten, we walk back over to the chicken enclosure with a big box of greens to distribute to the chickens. They scrabble excitedly at our feet as we open the double gates.

We place the box down and the girls dive in. As we watch them enjoy the treats, I catch Tom staring at me.

'What?' I ask, reaching a hand to my face. Knowing my luck, there's probably a big blob of potato gratin on my chin.

'You're beautiful,' he says, brushing a red curl off my cheek. I feel a fizz inside me.

He leans in to kiss me, but at that moment a hen named Little Red makes a bold leap, flapping her wings and landing on Tom's shoulder.

We both dissolve into laughter. Tom is giggling but trying to keep his shoulders as still as possible so as not to throw Little Red off balance.

'I love you,' I say through my laughter.

There's a pause, which gives me enough time to be filled with regret at letting that slip out. The truth is I've been thinking it for weeks. But what if it's too soon? What if he doesn't say it back? I will have ruined everything.

Little Red jumps off Tom's shoulder and lands with a bump next to my feet, where she proceeds to preen my shoelace. I keep my head down to watch her. This gives me the perfect opportunity to let my hair hang down and cover my face. It makes it easier to pretend that the last thirty seconds never happened.

'Chrissy?' says Tom, his voice serious.

I look up, my face creased with worry. There are a few seconds of silence that seem to stretch out for minutes.

He takes a deep breath. 'I love you too.'

I exhale. My whole body relaxes at those words.

He pulls me to his chest. 'Did you think I wouldn't say it back?'

'I don't know,' I say with a shrug.

'Well, I do. I love you. I love you. I love you.' He covers my face with kisses and then his lips are on mine, kissing me deeply.

He pulls away and a smile stretches wide across my face. I stand by Tom's side and lean my head against his shoulder. I feel like I am home.

I may be in a whole new country, with a whole new man and a whole new job, but it turns out that I don't need to be a whole new Chrissy. I have found happiness just by being me.

BONUS EPILOGUE

Hi Reader!

Thank you from the bottom of my heart for joining Chrissy on her travels.

Feeling a bit of Chrissy withdrawal? I have the perfect treat for you – Love on the Run – Chrissy's Hilarious 5k Adventure. Come with me as we jump forward a month and find out what Chrissy and the gang have been up to.

Follow Chrissy's uproarious adventure as she takes on her first ever 5k through scenic Sydney.

With charming Tom and reluctant Chloe by her side, it's a bonus epilogue where fitness meets fun, and every step is a giggle!

Simply go to CatherineKelaher.com/ChrissyBonus and sign up for my free newsletter and you'll get instant access to the story.

Don't worry, I won't bug you all the time. I'm not Brad! I'll just update you about once a month on what I've been up to and what exciting new writing projects I'm working on.

With all my love and gratitude,

Catherine x

P.S If you enjoyed this book, I'd be really grateful if you would leave a positive review on Amazon or your favourite bookseller.

ACKNOWLEDGMENTS

To David, my own rom com hero. 19 years after we had our own meet cute, I am still so in love with you. You are the funniest person I know, and you still make me giggle non-stop with your stream of nonsense. You were the first reader of this book, and I am so grateful that you took the time to make the funny bits even funnier. I appreciate everything about you.

To Isy, I know I wouldn't have finished this without our 5.30am writing club. I may have secretly been cursing you when that alarm went off, but I am so grateful. You are endlessly supportive, creative and motivating. It's great to have someone to chat about writing and animal rights with, without feeling like I'm boring the pants off them. Thank you for being my sidekick and it's a pleasure being yours.

Dad, you kept me motivated with our early morning phone calls in the first draft stage of this book. I miss you a lot being so far away, but I know you are always there for me.

Adam, not only are you the best little brother a girl could wish for, you and Audrey are also proof that it is possible to find true love on a dating app. You really are the bee's knees, but... "bee's knees are hard to live with 24/7."

Mel, you are such an inspiration to me in the joyous way you live your life. I remember thinking clearly, I would like to be friends with that one, and asking he who shall not be named, to connect us. I remember the immediate click as we sat side by side in the Indian restaurant before a rescue, showing off our high school French. Oui! Merci!

Sarah, when you came to volunteer at the hen rescue, I feel like I captured you immediately as a friend and I am not at all sorry about that. I love throwing story ideas around with you. After all this is done, I would love to have a sleep-over, eat plates of yellow food and watch Love Island together.

Melissa, I miss you so much. I loved growing up with you and possibly being not very nice children. Let's not forget my writing career started by being your co-author of Bungus the Gnome.

Sharron, thank you for being my VFF, being endlessly supportive and being by my side through the beginnings of the hen rescue and to this day.

To all the girls in Not the Fat Club, thank you for your support.

Thank you to Manda Waller for editing this book. You really are a gem to work with.

Thank you to Bailey McGinn for designing the cover. You

capture Chrissy perfectly. Why the heck is she even worried about her weight? She's flippin' gorgeous!

Thank you to Federica Leonardis for your expert proof reading skills.

Thank you to Mum and Amanda, who I miss every day.

Thank you to the animals. You are my life's purpose and I hope so much that the world will be a different place for you by the time I leave this planet.

To the person I have definitely forgotten—you are the one I'm most grateful for.

ABOUT THE AUTHOR

Catherine Kelaher was born in the UK in a town called Crowborough where she had brilliant adventures on the Ashdown Forest with her dog, Poppy, and childhood bestie, Melissa.

She studied Creative Writing and English Literature at Kingston Upon Thames University.

Catherine is the founder of NSW Hen Rescue

(henrescue.org), a charity that rescues and rehabilitates ex-battery hens and other factory farmed animals.

Catherine has written two other books, Amanda the Teen Activist (if you liked when Amanda met Chrissy you have to read this) and Saving Animals: A Future Activist's Guide (non-fiction). Catherine really wants the world to be kinder, but until then rom coms provide her with the perfect escapism and belly laughs at the end of a day of animal rescue.

At 21 Catherine met her own Aussie barman in the UK and moved to Australia. She now lives in the Northern Rivers of NSW where she is 'going troppo' as we speak.